The Strange Girl, the previous Sam Dyke thriller, was described as 'diverting' by industry bible The Bookseller, with Sam Dyke being 'Crewe's answer to Philip Marlowe'. *The Secret Sharers* is the latest instalment in this series.

Also by Keith Dixon

The Sam Dyke Series

Altered Life
The Private Lie
The Hard Swim
The Bleak
The Strange Girl
The Secret Sharers
The Innocent Dead
The Second Guess (short story)

The Paul Storey Thriller Series

Storey
One Punch
The Song of Geneva Chance

Standalone Novels

A French Darcy – a Romance
Actress – a Contemporary novel

Essays on Writing

The Idle Writer
Crime Writing Confidential

Blog

www.cwconfidential.blogspot.com

Webpage

http://www.keithdixonnovels.com

THE SECRET SHARERS

KEITH DIXON

A Sam Dyke Investigation

Semiologic Ltd

THE SECRET SHARERS

A Sam Dyke Investigation

For Holly

Visit the Website at www.keithdixonnovels.com or the Blog at
www.cwconfidential.blogspot.com

THE SECRET SHARERS

A secret agent who throws his secrecy to the winds from desire of vengeance, and flaunts his achievements before the public eye, becomes the mark for desperate and bloodthirsty indignations.

Joseph Conrad, *The Secret Agent*

CHAPTER ONE

THERE WAS A MAN sitting in my office at nine o'clock that morning, and there were two things wrong with this picture.

First, he was sitting in my chair. And second, I'd locked the office door the previous night.

He added a third wrong thing by lying about it: 'Hope you don't mind, the door was open.'

He was a respectable-looking geezer somewhere in his sixties with a long, serious face and wearing a country gentleman's outfit—a green Barbour jacket, a grey flat cap, and, poking out from under my desk, a pair of solid brown shoes, probably by Church. There was a thin walnut cane leaning against the desk. My desk. His eyes were steady and there was a slightly challenging air about the way he reclined in the seat and waited for my response.

I came into the room and closed the door and considered putting my hands on my hips to show how offended I was.

I said, 'If you're selling subscriptions to Country Life, I have to tell you I sold my horse and hounds pack last year. Couldn't afford all that raw meat.'

He grinned. 'I knew you were a witty man. When I read that interview with you in the Manchester Evening News I could tell you had a sense of humour.'

A few months ago I'd been involved in preventing a frustrated ideologue carry out a plan to gas commuters in Piccadilly Station in Manchester. My punishment had been a certain amount of notoriety for a week, including the kind of media exposure that you think is going to be good for business but never is. The public have such short memories.

The man went on, 'I hope you're not upset by my being here. When I found the door open I thought it much more sensible to come inside and wait rather than clutter up the corridor.'

'You and I both know the door wasn't open. There isn't a mark on it, so it wasn't forced. And I know I locked it last night.'

'Are you certain? How can you be certain about anything?'

'Can I have my chair back, please?'

'Oh, certainly.'

He stood up and made great play of pulling the chair out and presenting it for me. Then he walked around to the other side of the desk and sat down in one of the upright client chairs. I took my seat, noticing that he'd left his walking stick on my side. I handed it to him and he accepted it with a gracious bow of his head.

He said, 'So, Mr Dyke, I suppose we should get down to business now.'

'I'm not looking for any more clients at the moment. My case load is full.'

He seemed taken aback at this and pursed his lips, which were white and thin.

'That's unfortunate. I suppose all the publicity you received as a result of your recent cases means that adulterers and fraudsters are beating a path to your door.'

'Describing my work like that isn't likely to dispose me towards taking on your case, is it?'

He raised his hands palm up in apology.

'I'm sorry, I'm lapsing into stereotype.'

'Look, what exactly is it that you want, Mr … ?'

He lowered his hands and looked at the back of them, as though surprised to find the liver spots and raised veins that confronted him. Then he lifted his eyes towards me and there was an urgency behind them that was new.

He said, 'My name is Frank Wallace. And I want you to watch me.'

AFTER MY LAST couple of big cases I didn't want anything complicated or even mildly dangerous. I'd basked a little in the respect I'd been shown in my local pub and at the garage when I'd bought petrol for my new car … but work-wise, I'd wanted tranquillity. For one thing, I'd had to organise the rebuilding of my house, which had been burned to the ground by some oriental thugs, taking my clothes, furniture and—not least—my CD collection with it.

So I'd gone back to the mundane jobs that had been meat-and-drink for me in the last few years—benefit fraudsters, rent-skippers, identity checks and so on.

On the rare occasions I thought about it, I realised I'd been bunkering-down, like a tortoise who'd had too much of the outside world and preferred his own shell to the glamorous temptation of the next lettuce leaf. I hadn't been speaking much to my son, Dan, though he continued to look after my Bitcoin portfolio and do research for me; nor had I been in contact with my some-time partner, Belinda McFee. I was becoming that rare beast, the Reclusive Detective, seen only in the glare of a camera flash or in a back-alley talking to someone you'd normally cross the street to avoid.

Frank Wallace had been watching me think and must have thought I was considering taking him on as a client. He said, 'What do you need to know? How do we do this?'

'I'm sorry, Mr Wallace, but I wasn't flapping my lips for the sake of it. I'm too busy to take the case. And besides, why do you want me to watch you?'

He smiled slowly. 'See, I knew you'd be interested.'

'Call it a mild curiosity.'

He'd taken hold of his walking cane and now rapped it once against the edge of my desk, as if he were firing a starter's gun.

'I used to work as a project manager at the Toyota factory in Derby. Well, outside Derby, actually. You've probably been past it on your travels.'

'I've seen the road signs.'

'Exactly. Big place. Anyway, that's all besides the point. Except insofar as to say that towards the end of my working life there I had a … well, I suppose you'd call it an affair.' He looked at me, grinning, as though it was rather devilish for someone of an advanced age to have such an adventure. 'You must understand that my wife died years ago, but the woman I was seeing was well and truly married. The affair carried on for a couple of years and then I retired and for one reason or another we never saw each other again.'

'So what's the problem?'

'Someone's watching me. Even following me.'

'Are you certain? You're sure you're not just imagining it?'

He looked cross. 'Don't patronise me, Mr Dyke. I'm not going senile and I'm not making this up. I've seen the man in the street, in his car, down at the café. He's been there for a couple of weeks.'

'Who do you think he is?'

'Don't you see? Wendy's husband must have found out and is observing me.'

'For what reason?'

'How should I know? Perhaps he wants to bump me off.'

He put inverted commas around this phrase with his voice and his eyes danced with the perversity of the idea.

I said, 'This is all a bit far-fetched, if you don't mind me saying. How do you know this man is really watching you and not just going about his own business? You've become aware of him once or twice and now you're seeing him everywhere.'

He leaned back in the chair and glanced out of my window on to the streets of Crewe. The morning was gaining some heat and the pavements were beginning to whiten in the glare of the early sun.

He said, 'You know when the back of your neck bristles? And you turn around because you think someone's just said your name, or has come into a room when you thought you were alone? It's that feeling. Sometimes I see him and sometimes I don't but I know he's there even when I *can't* see him.'

He said all this in a melancholy tone, but he suddenly brightened and reached inside his green jacket, pulling out a thick wallet. He opened it and extracted a fistful of notes. He rested his elbow on my desk and held the notes in the air like a prize. Thankfully he didn't wave them or I might have snatched them from his hand.

'There's three thousand, five hundred pounds here. We'll call it a down payment. Seven days at five hundred pounds a day, which I guess is about your going rate. When can you start?'

I stared at him with exasperation. I wasn't as busy as I'd led him to believe, but I couldn't see this working. He was acting like a paranoid pensioner looking for a spot of adventure to brighten his drab days.

In the end, I said, 'I don't need all that as a retainer.'

'Nonsense. And there's more where that came from.' He placed the cash on the desktop then took out a business card from the wallet and laid it next to the money. 'These are my numbers and my address. Do we have to sign a contract of some kind and identify milestones and goals and so forth?'

He really was a project manager.

Wearily, I said, 'I'll get one in the post to you.'

'If you have it in pdf format you can email it and I'll sign it electronically, if that would suffice.'

'Fine.'

I was actually thinking it might not get that far.

He said, 'Let's be clear: there are two things that I want to come out of this. First, I want to be sure I'm being followed. Secondly, I want to know by whom. Do we understand each other?'

I assured him I knew what he wanted, but even as I was telling him this I wondered when I'd actually agreed to take the job. Then I asked myself how hard it could be … watch his place for a while, follow him to his local café or bank, persuade him he's been imagining the whole thing. Perhaps it would be good for me to work for a private individual again, rather than the local government types who'd made up the majority of my clients for the last couple of months.

I didn't realise the irony of that thought for several weeks.

Wallace began to gather himself together, putting away his wallet and picking up his cane. He said, 'When will you start?'

'It's probably better if you don't know. And I have a question for you.'

'Oh, good.'

'If you believe you're being followed by this man, how do you know he didn't follow you here?'

His reply should have made me think twice about taking on the case right there.

He said, 'Because I made sure he didn't.'

CHAPTER TWO

IT WAS A WHILE since I'd been to Buxton. I'd forgotten how bleak the drive through the wilds of the Peak District could be, especially as night was falling. You climbed narrow winding roads up the sides of difficult wooded hills, engine straining, for half the distance, then descended with brakes on full bore for the other half.

Finally I entered the town and my GPS directed me towards a long, straight avenue bordered by cherry trees just coming into blossom. It was the day after Wallace's visit to my office, and I'd decided to come over and have a look around. If he was right and there was somebody watching him I was sure I'd be able to spot the surveillance. It was something I'd done a lot of myself.

Now I was here I was even more certain. For one thing, there was nowhere to hide. Wallace lived on a street that was simply two rows of semi-detached houses fronted by small gardens, with a cherry tree planted on the edge of the wide pavement every thirty yards or so. There were cars parked on the street in front of every house—no garages were built for residents in the days when few people had cars—but there were no other buildings behind which a bad guy could hide.

Although I'd started out in daylight it was dark now. I drove to the end of the street, noting Wallace's house as I passed, then turned around at the T-junction and drove back.

I parked fifty yards this side of Wallace's house and waited.

After five minutes I was bored, so I climbed out of my new Mondeo and leaned with my back against it. The air was cooling but still pleasant, and warm enough to carry sounds from further away.

I looked in both directions up the street—nothing to see except the slight blue glare of television sets in front rooms. No youths hanging about, smoking. Or ingesting even worse kinds of chemical. No motorcycle gangs tearing up the tarmac. No street-corner lovelies with come-hither eyes and pale faces.

It was all very suburban and middle-class, exactly where I would have imagined someone like Frank Wallace to live.

I took my phone out of my pocket and pretended to be looking at it and texting as I walked past Wallace's house. It was double-fronted with stone-framed bay windows in a twenties style. There was a short flight of stone steps from his gate to his front door, a chunky affair with a brass lion's head for a knocker. His curtains were drawn closed downstairs but through an upstairs window I could see a dim light as if from a stairwell. I passed by, still engrossed in my phone's screen.

At the end of the street I turned and looked back, then crossed to the other side and began walking towards my car once more. This time I checked the parked vehicles, looking for drivers or passengers who seemed to be doing nothing but could have been observing Wallace's house. There was nobody.

Which made it all the more surprising when I felt the unmistakable point of a sharp knife sticking into the small of my back, accompanied by a hand on my left shoulder. He was good: I hadn't heard a thing.

'Don't turn and don't move,' a man's voice said, muffled as if by a scarf or balaclava. I could tell he was tall from the direction of the voice and strong by the grip he had on my shoulder.

Despite what people might think, in my line of work you don't often come across people willing to stick knives into your back. It calls for a certain amount of psychopathology to do it in the middle of a suburban street, too, so I thought it best to follow orders and do nothing.

The voice said, 'What are you doing here? Why are you looking at that house?'

'Isn't it for sale? I thought I might make an offer.'

The knife dug a little further into the fleshy part below my ribs.

'Answer the question.'

'I don't think I will. You're not going to knife me in the middle of the street and get away with it. You know it and I know it.'

'Clever man. Count this as a warning. Stay away from the house or it might be bad for your health.'

'Who writes your lines—Tony Soprano?'

The hand on my shoulder had gone, and a moment later the point of the knife released its insistent pressure on my spine. I heard a car approach and as I turned saw a tall man wearing a black tee-shirt and a knitted balaclava climbing into the back seat of a long car, perhaps an Audi. It pulled away and the yellow light from the street lamps was too dim to reveal its license plate.

I rolled my shoulders, looked back at Frank Wallace's house, then returned to my car. I could have knocked on his door and told him what had happened, but I didn't want to frighten him.

I was frightened enough for myself.

SO INSTEAD I drove around the corner, parked on a quiet street, and thought about what had just taken place. It seemed that Wallace wasn't as paranoid as I'd believed. Someone was watching his house and didn't like the fact that I was watching it too. But that person wasn't acting alone: someone had driven the car my bad guy had climbed into. It had been dark and the driver was on the far side, with his head turned away, looking for traffic coming from behind before he pulled out.

So I had no means of identifying who had stuck a knife in my back and nothing to go on except that he'd been tall, strong and had a generic middle-class accent, probably from somewhere south.

I pulled out my phone and called Frank Wallace's home number. He answered on the fourth ring.

'Who is this?'

'Sam Dyke. Are you okay?'

'Yes, why shouldn't I be? Oh, have you seen something?'

'I'm just checking in. Can we meet tomorrow?'

'Of course. Do you know Buxton?'

'A little.'

He gave me directions to a pub I knew was around the corner from his house because I was staring at it.

I said, 'You know that story you told me about an angry husband?'

He was wary. 'Yes …'

'It's not true, is it?'

'Why do you say that?'

'Call it a hunch.'

He surprised me by laughing.

'The great detective follows a hunch. Never mind clues or evidence, gut feeling is what counts. Is that what I'm paying you for? Intuition?'

I said nothing. I was suddenly angry.

He went on, 'Meet me tomorrow lunchtime and I'll explain everything. I guarantee you'll be interested.'

He hung up a second before I did.

IT WAS AFTER eleven o'clock by the time I got home — too late for a drink, too early to go to bed.

I phoned Dan, knowing he'd be awake and about to start his online stint trading Bitcoins. He answered at the first ring.

'Dad, hurry it up. Craig is coming round.'

Craig was his new boyfriend. I hadn't met him yet, though I'd seen his fancy Porsche pulling away from Dan's house a couple of weeks ago.

I gave Dan Frank Wallace's details and asked him to find out what he could from his usual nefarious sources. He was a wiz at discovering stuff not only through Google but with his own ability to gain entrance to databases closed to the general public. So far I'd managed to put the illegality of these searches to the back of my mind, but lately I'd begun to realise that I was suborning him to break the law. I'd have to do something about that.

He said, 'A project manager at Toyota? Not your usual high-profile client, then.'

'There's more to him than meets the eye.'

'What should I be looking for?'

'Anything unusual.'

'Oh, give me a break. How do I know what's unusual for a project manager at Toyota?'

'Use your imagination.'

'Okay.'

I paused. 'How's it going with Craig?'

'I think he's going to split up with me. That's why he's coming round so late.'

'You don't sound too upset. I thought it was going well.'

'So did I. But hey, things change.'

'When did you get so casual?'

'When my mum was murdered and my dad had his house and car burned to a cinder.'

I took a beat. I'd never really thought about the impact of what I did on his developing personality. He hadn't known his mother because she'd given him up for fostering, without telling me, but I supposed the fact she'd been murdered was likely to have some say in the way he viewed the world.

I said, 'Take care. Plenty more fish in the sea.'

'You're a great comfort.'

We hung up and I suddenly felt as miserable as a three-legged greyhound.

Then I thought back to my phone call with Frank Wallace. For a man who'd said his life was in danger, he sounded awful jaunty.

CHAPTER THREE

I WAS SITTING in the lounge of the Duke of Hereford ten minutes before I'd agreed to meet Frank Wallace when my phone bleeped to say I'd had a text message.

It was ostensibly from an Unknown Caller, but it was signed by Wallace. It said there'd been a change of venue and I was to come out of the pub, turn left and walk two hundred and fifty yards, where I'd find a café-bar 'with a sporting theme'.

I sighed, finished my drink, and followed his instructions.

As far as I could tell, The Players' Bar had in fact no connection to sportsmen—or to travelling theatre troupes, for that matter. There were no photographs of visiting football teams, no wooden, heart-shaped trophies propped behind the bar and no timetables of upcoming fixtures. Perhaps the owners were liable under the Trades Description Act for false advertising, but I doubt they were too worried. The place had a high ceiling and black-and-white floor tiles and the tables were square and modern. There were no cosy alcoves for secret trysts or client meetings. A party of young mothers with babies and their associated strollers took up a third of the space at the back, some of the kids wailing while the others watched in goggling bemusement.

Wallace had found a seat facing the door and I sat opposite him with my back to it. He was wearing a tweed jacket with elbow patches and large spectacles that lent him a faintly startled expression. His hair was white and thick and bushed over the top of his ears. A girl in a black outfit took my order for coffee and I gave Wallace my hardest stare.

I said, 'It's not a distraught husband, is it?'

'Why do you say that?'

'I was approached by a man last night outside your house. He was young and fit. And you'll excuse me for saying so, but if you really had an affair at Toyota I suspect it would have been with someone a little closer to your own age, not someone married to a man in his thirties.'

'Are you casting doubt on my sex appeal to the younger female?'

'When he spoke to me he never mentioned you or asked who I was. He was just trying to throw a scare into me. And he had a colleague.'

His expression turned more serious. 'Did you see either of these men?'

'Not directly, no. They were good. Almost professional.'

I left that statement hanging in the air to see what he'd make of it. He leaned back in his chair and folded his arms but seemed to want me to continue. He had a guarded alertness that I'd seen mainly in police officers with many years' experience, an unwillingness to take anything at face value.

I said, 'So who are they?'

He took a sip from his milky coffee and leaned forward

in his chair.

'Have you heard of Shoemaker Systems?'

'A little.'

'What do you know?'

'What I've read in the papers. They're a large security company. International.'

'And what exactly does that mean to you?'

'Is this part of the conversation actually relevant?'

'Please, just go with it.'

I thought back to what I'd read of Shoemaker Systems over the last couple of years. They were habitually linked to large organisations involved in overseas operations. They'd provide security for consultants working in difficult African or ex-Soviet Bloc nations; they supplied protection against cyber-crime; they had a litigation department that helped companies defend themselves against legal challenges. In general these types of companies classified what they did as 'risk management'—whatever kind of risk was involved.

I said, 'They're the big fish in the pond and I'm the algae.'

'Would it surprise you to learn that I used to work for them?'

'Their Toyota branch?'

He smiled and tipped his head apologetically, his glasses flashing in the overhead light.

'A cover story to get you interested. You wouldn't have believed me if I said one of the largest security companies in the world was watching me. You'd have put me in the box marked Paranoid Nutter.'

'What makes you think you're not still in it?'

'You saw the men. They were real, weren't they?'

'One of them nearly punctured my leather jacket with his knife. There'd have been hell to pay if he had.'

This time he didn't smile. He turned serious again. It

seemed he could change his emotional temperature at a moment's notice.

He said, 'Can I tell you a story?'

I nodded.

'You may have believed that Britain's intelligence services only recruited upper class people from Oxford or Cambridge. But that's not true—or at least it wasn't by the time I left university. Yes, I went to Oxford, to study mathematics as it happens, but my background is very humble. So I suppose you could say I was flattered to be asked.'

I stared at him, reconfiguring my knowledge of who he was.

I said, 'And you accepted the offer?'

'I did. Who didn't see themselves as James Bond at one time or another? But I was employed as an analyst—the most boring spy work you could hope to engage in. Reading through lots of transcripts of dull conversations between Soviet functionaries. But I did see the world, or at least eastern Europe. I suppose it was quite an exciting time for us in the seventies and eighties, though I didn't participate in much of the excitement.'

'Is that why you left?'

He leaned back in his seat and cast a glance sideways as if about to impart a great secret.

'I had a very good friend in the service, Kelvin Shoemaker. Yes, that Shoemaker. He left to set up his own organisation in the mid-nineties and asked me to join him. I had a child by then and the prospect of earning more money was too good to pass up.'

I wondered briefly why he mentioned his child without having mentioned getting married. And what had happened to his wife?

He continued, telling me that Shoemaker had built up his business almost from scratch, using contacts made during both his own career in government service and Wallace's. They had focused on corporate due diligence—checking, for example, that when company A was about to take over or merge with company B, the latter's financial situation and place in the market was exactly as company B's representatives said it was.

He said, 'The nineties were a boom time for mergers and acquisitions, so we did very well with that line of work. We also dabbled in a bit of cyber-security, which was just starting up as a commercial necessity then, and we provided physical security services from time to time as well.'

'Iraq?'

He waved that notion away with a hand. 'We couldn't compete with Blackwater so we didn't try.'

I told him to carry on but he paused. His face had been animated and his eyes lively while he described his past. Now his focus turned inward and his cheeks seemed to hollow out. He looked older for the first time since I'd met him.

He said quietly, 'Kelvin had never married. We'd been going six or seven years when he met Jocasta. Greek-born girl with an English father. A beauty, spoke five languages. Twenty five years younger than him and he fell like a stone off a cliff. They married quickly and before you know it, she was chief analyst. I didn't mind that so much because I didn't want that role any more ... but in short order she was guiding policy and strategy at Shoemaker Systems.'

'In what way?'

'We started doing less of the corporate work and more work for the government. And not just our government—all sorts of foreign governments. In some cases, the very people

I'd been working against twenty years earlier. Life's a bastard sometimes, isn't it?'

'Did you talk to Kelvin about the situation?'

He frowned. 'Of course I did. Do you think I'm an idiot? I warned him it could be dangerous—not in a personal sense, but for the business as a whole. You take on rogue countries as clients and you can soon find yourself shunned in the international marketplace.'

'I'm betting he didn't listen.'

'I never really got to find out. He died shortly after we had the discussion. He was hospitalised with a minor complaint of some kind but died soon afterwards. He was just fifty nine. He left the controlling interest in the company to Jocasta and all I got was a bit of money. She became chairman and assumed power as if she'd been waiting for it all her life, not six years. I hung on as long as I could for my retirement pot and came out last year. Moved out of London and bought that place round the corner.'

He blew out his cheeks and placed his hands palm down on the table, either side of his drink. I think telling his story had depleted him in some way.

Then he looked up at me from hooded eyelids.

'Despite appearances, I'm not a sad old man. You ever have regrets, Dyke? Wish you could go back and do things differently?'

'Every day.'

'Well I don't, as it happens. I learned very early in my career that you can't change the past and you can't undo mistakes. But the corollary is that I can't abide for the things I've built to be cast aside. And Shoemaker Systems is in part my legacy. Jocasta Shoemaker is throwing her husband's work—and mine—under a train.'

'Are you suggesting those men last night were working

for her? What are they trying to do by following you or watching your house?'

In reply, he reached inside his tweed jacket's pocket and pulled out a small newspaper. It was black-and-white, about A4 in size, held together by two staples on the spine, and folded once down the middle so that it would fit in his pocket. There were maybe a dozen pages in it, judging by its thickness. He laid it on the table. Reading it upside down, I saw it was called 'Intelligence Today'.

He said, 'Page five.'

I picked up the photocopied paper and leafed through until I found the right page. The articles seemed to be summaries of various news reports from *The Guardian* and other slightly left-of-centre publications. At the top of page five there was a headline titled: 'Shoemaker Systems and the end of Accountability.' The by-line was Frank Wallace.

He said, 'You don't have to read it now. It's number three in a series of six I'm writing.'

I held up the paper. 'Who reads this?'

'Interested parties. After Snowden there was an upsurge in concern about intelligence matters in this country. I've written for a couple of other magazines, too. I'm in a privileged position to expose what's going on in this country, and I'm going to take advantage of that position so long as Jocasta is dismantling the name and reputation of the company I helped to build.'

'And you think they're out to silence you, one way or another?'

'I worked there. I know how they think. I wouldn't put it past them.'

CHAPTER FOUR

I FINISHED MY coffee and looked around. The café had grown busier and louder as lunch had progressed but I hadn't been aware of it. My head had been buried in this strange, secret environment that Frank Wallace had been part of for most of his life and now carried around with him. It was as if through gestures and asides and knowing looks he could bring you inside that world so you became as secretive and cautious as he was.

I said, 'Are you sure you weren't followed here?'

'They were out front. They don't know I've got a door in the fence out back into my neighbour's property. He doesn't mind me using it because it's a short-cut to the shops.'

'If you're so dangerous to them, why are they only watching? Why don't they do something?'

He shook his finger at me like a dog owner correcting bad behaviour.

'You're too obvious. Intelligence agencies don't act like that, on the whole. They're probably setting me up for something—an accident, or a staged disappearance.'

'Are you that important?'

'You'd be surprised. I've known cases where whole

families have been disappeared. In the country's interest.' He drew a deep breath. 'You haven't asked what I want from you. What do you think about what you've heard?'

'I'm thinking I want nothing to do with this.'

'Understandable. But let me tell you what I want before you dump me as a client. First, my apologies for misleading you with the story about the cuckolded husband. I thought it was the kind of "case" you'd be willing to be engaged on, and I needed to get you on my side before I took it further. So, to business. I intend to expose what Jocasta Shoemaker is doing. In my view, she's distorting the relationship between public and private security. I know she's not the first or even the biggest culprit. But she's the one I know about. Firms like Shoemaker should not be contracting with governments. And governments should not be contracting with firms like Shoemaker. The company is swimming in ex-Intelligence Service officers parlaying their former friendships with government agencies into commercial contracts. Likewise, the Intelligence Services are full of bureaucrats just waiting to have served time so they can leave government and join a high-paying private agency.'

'Like you did.'

'Yes, and I did it for the money, too. But I left MI6 behind when I quit. I used my expertise, learned on the job, to get the work done. I didn't go back to my old employers and finesse them into working for me.'

'Looks to me like you're splitting a very fine hair there, Frank.'

His expression became exasperated.

'You don't have to agree with my motives. I realise I'm going out on a limb here and I don't want to endanger anyone else.'

'So what exactly is it you want?'

He looked down at the table and I saw the neat part in his hair. When he looked up this time there was a hint of desperation in his eyes.

He said, 'It may not seem like it, but I'm scared. I don't know what Jocasta Shoemaker is capable of. She has no real history in Intelligence and as far as I can tell hasn't developed a workable set of values. So I want you to hide me and, if necessary, protect me.'

Because of the kind of work I do you often have to size people up quickly. Some people come into my office nervous because they think they might be on the verge of exposing themselves to ridicule. Some act tough because they think it's how I'm going to behave and they don't want to be brow-beaten. Mostly they're afraid—afraid of the consequences of what they're going to ask me to do.

Frank Wallace wasn't afraid. There was no fear of what might happen in his eyes, just a calculating appraisal of what I might say.

I said, 'I'll put you somewhere safe until we decide what to do next. Do you need to pack a bag, at least for tonight?'

'No, I don't.' He reached behind him and pulled forward two heavy objects: a green roll-bag and a wooden box about eighteen inches in length and height and a foot deep.

He grinned at me. 'I knew you'd say yes.'

HE LET ME carry the roll-bag out of the café but he held on tightly to the wooden box, which was shiny with wear and a little battered around the edges. The name 'Edison' was stencilled on the side in faint letters. He held it by a wooden handle attached by two brass fixtures to its top surface. It looked to be about the size and weight of a sewing machine.

As we walked to my car I nodded to the box and said, 'What's that?'

'Heirloom. Not important. Where are we going?'

'Friend of mine. I'll have to call her first.'

At the car I put his belongings in the boot and got him into the passenger seat, then stepped away and called Belinda. The air was fresh, spring moving into a warmer spell after a short winter. My hands were barely cold at all.

There was no reply from her home phone so I tried her mobile. She answered sounding slightly out of breath.

'Sammy, how the devil are you?'

'Better for hearing your voice.'

She laughed. 'Ah, so what do you want, you smooth talker? I don't hear from you for weeks and then you call when you want something. Typical.'

Belinda McFee was a private investigator based in south Manchester. We'd worked on a couple of things together in the last year. She was tough and resourceful but was still learning the ropes of investigation. I was about two weeks ahead of her but she seemed to see me as a mentor nonetheless.

I said, 'Can you be home in half an hour?'

'I'm just finishing up, so yes.'

'What are you doing?'

'Training. Has to be done if you're gonna fight the bad guys.'

Despite the fact that she was trained in Krav Maga, an Israeli special forces fighting technique, a man had broken two of her fingers the last time we worked together. I knew this had made her even more determined to stay fit and sharp. The fractures would have made most people more cautious; they simply made Belinda more aggressive.

I asked if her spare bedroom was still empty and would she mind baby-sitting someone for a couple of days.

'Male or female?'

'Male. An older guy.'

'What's he been up to?'

'To be decided.'

She laughed again. 'Bring him over. I'll be there in ten.'

MY GPS ROUTED us north to Fallowfield via the A6, a secondary road that was always busy but nonetheless pleasant on a sunny day. Wallace sat upright in the passenger seat and seemed interested in everything, his head following road signs as they flashed past and smiling at kids shouting and running in their playgrounds.

He offered nothing in conversation and I didn't much feel like it myself. I didn't know what I was getting myself and Belinda into, but I had three and a half thousand pounds of his money in my locked desk drawer so I felt I owed him something.

Belinda's pink Volvo was parked directly outside her house and she came to the door before I knocked, taking Wallace's bag from me and leading the way inside.

'I've got the kettle on. I bet you'll drink tea.'

She was medium-height and slim and had a bounce in her step that was probably a holdover from the exercise she'd just put herself through. Unless she was just pleased to see me.

Wallace had come in behind me and I stood aside to let him enter. He glanced down at the tiled hall and up the staircase, then saw the door to the front room on the left.

He said, 'I'll put this in here, shall I?' and went into the room without waiting for a reply. From the kitchen at the back, Belinda poured water into a teapot then turned to me and raised her eyebrows playfully. I shrugged and followed Wallace into the room.

He'd placed his box in a corner and was peering at

Belinda's photos, especially those which showed her posing with tanks in Germany, where she'd served for a while. He stood upright when she came in with the tea-tray, then bent solicitously to move some books on her coffee table to make room.

With everything settled, he held out his hand: 'Frank Wallace. Thank you for being my new landlady. I really appreciate it. I suppose Mr Dyke has explained why I'm going to be enjoying your hospitality for a short while?'

Belinda shook the hand and glanced at me. 'Sam tells me nothing. He thinks I'm safer if I'm ignorant.'

'Well, I'm certainly not going to argue with the professional. He can tell you when it's appropriate.'

Belinda poured tea and we sat like a Sunday afternoon church committee dunking biscuits and smiling at each other.

Wallace said to me, 'How long do you think I should try Miss McFee's patience as a lodger? What's our plan?'

'I haven't formulated a plan yet. The first step was to get you out from under the people watching you.'

'If you don't mind, I've been thinking about what I'd like you to do.'

I stared at him. I supposed if he'd worked in Intelligence for many years he was always thinking one step ahead. I couldn't blame him.

I said, 'Go on. Say what you think and then we'll discuss it.'

He gave me his conspiratorial grin and placed the palms of his hands together.

'I'd like you to visit Jocasta Shoemaker and tell her to back off. To chain her dogs. Use whatever language you see fit.'

'Do you think that will work? The way you talked about

her made her sound very determined.'

'You should tell her she won't be able to shut me up and her tactics have now been exposed because you, Sam Dyke, also know what's going on.'

'That'll really throw a scare into her.'

'You don't understand. She doesn't want publicity. She hates it. The security industry as a whole hates it. They trade in secrets so they don't want the general public, and especially the press, to know anything about what they do. My little scribblings in these tiny magazines are as nothing compared to an exposé in *The Guardian* or *Private Eye*. But if she carries on pursuing me it could all blow up in her face.'

I sipped my tea. I might even have raised my little finger, to show I was concentrating.

I couldn't see where this was going or what he hoped to achieve by challenging Shoemaker in this way. I glanced at Belinda but she knew nothing about the situation and couldn't help. She sat back in her chair and glanced alertly from Wallace to me and back again as though watching a slow-motion tennis match.

Finally I said, 'I'll call her. I guess if I use your name she'll take the call?'

Wallace made a shape with his lips. 'Calling's no good. You'll have to see her in person. I know from experience that she doesn't take many calls—she prefers face-to-face meetings.'

'London's a long way to go on the chance she'll see me.'

'You can make an appointment. I've got her secretary's direct line. Say you've got a message from Frank Wallace that she'll be interested in hearing.'

'Will she, though, really?'

'You're going to tell her something she won't believe, and that will make her angry.'

'How will that help?'

'Angry people make mistakes.'

I LEFT BELINDA'S house at seven o'clock and was climbing into my car when my phone rang. It was Dan.

He said, 'So, who's the mystery man?'

'Frank Wallace?'

'If that's his real name. I can't find anything for anyone with the description you gave me—either in Toyota or anywhere else.'

'He didn't work for Toyota.'

'You're telling me. I searched high and low and couldn't find anyone over the age of fifty by that name, or anything close. So I went wider … no Social Security number, no passport, no bank accounts. Well, of course there are Frank Wallaces, but none fitting the facts you had. There was one up in Edinburgh, but he's thirty-three and has worked in banking since he left college. And there are a couple in London, but again too young.'

Given Wallace's background as I now understood it, I wasn't surprised there was no public record. If he'd worked clandestinely for MI6 it was likely his details were either hidden or masked. Maybe when he joined Shoemaker Systems he'd kept the privacy button pressed.

I said, 'Don't worry about it. Change of plan. He's admitted to not telling the whole truth.'

'So he's not Frank Wallace?'

That was a good question. A lot of what he'd told me turned out to be fiction or at least an elaboration on the truth. Perhaps even his name was an invention intended to keep me in the dark. I'd know soon enough when I tried to use it to gain access to Jocasta Shoemaker: if it was an alias, she might not recognise it and therefore refuse to see me.

But what would be the point of that?

I realised I'd been thinking and not talking, and then I remembered my conversation with Dan the previous night.

I said, 'How did it go with Craig? Are you all right?'

Dan generally had a serious demeanour, despite his light-hearted approach to conversations with me. Now he surprised me by letting out a laugh that was almost a giggle, as though he couldn't believe what he was about to say.

'I thought he was going to dump me, didn't I?'

'That's what you said.'

'Well, my radar is way out. He asked if I wanted to move in with him.'

'What did you tell him?'

'I was too dumb-struck to say anything, you know?'

'Where does he live?'

'A fancy apartment in Alderley Edge.'

I remembered the Porsche—Craig wasn't short of cash with that car and that postcode. Dan had spent his childhood in foster homes in and around London. I wondered how he'd fit into the footballers' wives crowd in Alderley Edge and Wilmslow.

I was also a little sad to think that he might move out of Crewe and be further away from my occasional visits.

'So what are you going to do?'

'I said I'd think on it.'

'Do you think you'll do it? Nice place, that. Close to Manchester.'

'Dad, you're so obvious.'

'What?'

'I know what you're thinking … close to Manchester means close to Canal Street and all that gay activity. You're worried I might lose my head.'

'Nothing could be further from my mind.'

'Well nothing's decided yet.'

'Keep me up to speed.'

'Will do.'

We hung up and I stared through the windscreen for a few minutes before starting the engine. I didn't care that he was gay, but he was still young and essentially inexperienced in relationships. And there was nothing I could do about that.

I DROVE BACK to my newly-restored house in Crewe and locked the doors and turned on all the lights. Although the house had been reconstructed as an almost-exact replica of the one that had burned down, it still didn't seem 'lived in': it was like a collection of those make-believe rooms in Ikea stores, everything in the right place but no animation. I hadn't chipped the furniture or stained the carpets or spilled wine on the walls yet. I told myself that's what happens when you try to recreate a nineteenth century property with twenty-first century materials.

Perhaps the house was a mirror of me, I thought: something created in modern times but constructed and operating according to long-forgotten values.

To get past these sombre and self-flattering thoughts I turned on the television and watched Question Time until I got bored.

It was past eleven o'clock so I turned off all the lights again and was about to go to bed when my phone rang.

It was a man's voice, and one that I didn't recognise. It was light in tone and almost matter-of-fact, like a mid-level bureaucrat telling you that your income tax return is late and that you should submit it at once.

He said, 'Mr Dyke, you don't know me and I'm not about

to tell you my name, but I think you should know that Frank Wallace isn't what he seems and you should distance yourself from him as soon as you can.'

'This is a novel way of selling insurance.'

'I was told you'd be flippant, but this is no joke. Frank Wallace is dangerous.'

'As only a sixty-five-year old man can be.'

'You're just proving to me that you have no idea who you're dealing with.'

'Who are you, anyway? Are you from Shoemaker? MI5? Citizens' Advice Bureau?'

'You can describe this as a courtesy call. Because of your relatively high profile at the moment and our belief that you're involved in this through ignorance, not malice.'

'Involved in what?'

'Goodnight, Mr Dyke. Sleep well. Don't forget to turn off the light in the second bedroom.'

He hung up and I followed suit. I went upstairs and looked into the second bedroom. The bedside light was on.

Somewhat disgruntled, I switched it off.

CHAPTER FIVE

THE FOLLOWING MORNING I found the number Wallace had given me for Jocasta Shoemaker's Personal Assistant. At first she insisted that Mrs Shoemaker was fully booked for the next three weeks, but I played the 'Frank Wallace' card and the line went silent; I assumed she was checking with her boss. Eventually she came back and said Mrs Shoemaker could fit me in between two and two-thirty the following day, Friday. I said that would be peachy and asked for directions to their office and she said she'd email them to me.

I hung up feeling as though I'd been put through a test of some kind and wondering whether it was wise to give them my email. God knows what kind of search they could do on me now.

Next I rang Belinda to check up on Wallace. She took the phone into another room and said quietly that he was okay. He didn't seem worried. He'd asked her to buy a newspaper when she went out for groceries, but he'd actually spent most of his time watching daytime TV.

I said, 'He must be losing his mind.'

'*Au contraire*, he's loving it. He laughs at the talk show guests and gets engrossed in the American TV movies. He's the perfect viewer. He's like David Bowie in *The Man Who Fell to Earth*. If I could fit in a wall of TV screens I think he'd be my friend for life.'

'Don't let him talk you into doing anything you don't want to do.'

'He's fine, I'm fine. Just do your job and let me do mine, Sam.'

I hung up with a vague sense of unease in my stomach. The man who'd called the night before said Wallace wasn't who he seemed, and this happy-go-lucky, television-watching pensioner behaviour didn't fit with the character of someone who'd worked in Intelligence for most of his adult life.

But maybe I was being too harsh. After all, he'd told me he was afraid and I'd done something to make him more secure. Perhaps what Belinda was seeing was just a natural release of tension, an easing back into 'normal' life after the stress of the last few days. I didn't know Wallace well enough yet to be able to track his emotional transitions. At times he seemed canny, at others he was like an old dog looking for a new owner, an air of desperation playing in the corner of his eyes. I decided that it would be best if I kept my cards close to my chest with him, while at the same time running a slide rule over everything he said.

My last act of the morning was to book my ticket from Crewe to Euston Station. The online booking system was straightforward and I chose to pick up the ticket from one of the machines in the station entrance hall.

Then I spent the afternoon paying bills and making out invoices and posting them, as though I knew I wouldn't have time in the coming days and weeks for such trivia.

I can be very insightful when I put my mind to it.

CHAPTER SIX

THE JOURNEY DOWN was the usual dull ninety minutes, during which I started reading Gordon Thomas' *Inside British Intelligence*, which I'd bought online that morning and downloaded to my tablet. Dan had insisted I buy one because it was easier for me to carry around than a laptop if he needed to send me information.

At Euston I bought a slice of pizza in the food hall and killed an hour until it was time for me to take a cab to Shoemaker's offices.

The cabbie took me east through Shoreditch and Limehouse, then ran parallel to the river for a while before heading into the Isle of Dogs. He finally deposited me outside a tall steel and glass complex with a wide entrance that led to a bank of three Reception desks.

As the carousel door swung closed behind me I moved from the glare of natural sunlight and the clatter and crash of the street into a hushed, controlled environment where sound seemed to travel through a thicker atmosphere and at a slower pace.

One of the three identikit receptionists found my appointment on the computer and issued me with a badge that she printed beneath the counter and placed inside a plastic holder. She said I should take the second lift on the right and go to the twentieth floor, where I'd be met by Mrs Shoemaker's assistant.

I did as I was told, crossed the inch-thick corporate carpet and entered the lift. I hadn't seen anyone yet except the three receptionists, who I imagined powering down now until the next guest arrived.

The doors opened to the smiling face and blonde bobbed hair of Jocasta Shoemaker's assistant, who introduced herself as Ann and asked me to follow her, which I did. There's something about this routine which, if you're not careful, positions you as a supplicant, as if you're a serf about to petition the king to lighten up on the grain tax this year. You find yourself accommodating to the behaviour and expectations of the people you're going to meet, disempowering yourself and handing a stacked deck of cards to the other person.

I thought by now I'd got past this feeling but habits of mind die hard.

Ann deposited me in a comfortable leather chair in a foyer as wide and plush as an ante-room in Buckingham Palace and disappeared. I thought I could hear a muffled voice behind a door but I wasn't certain—it could have been the rumble of air conditioning or someone playing a video on YouTube.

I stared out of the window, mesmerised by the view of Canary Wharf a few hundred yards down the river. I'd never seen it from this height before and it was even more impressive than from the ground. I knew how high I was, but the cluster of other buildings was higher, the people inside them like the small creatures you find in tree bark, hustling away to no apparent benefit.

A voice broke my reverie—a woman's voice but deep and warm, the kind of warm a woman uses when she wants you to like her.

She said, 'I'm sorry to have kept you waiting, Mr Dyke. I'm Jocasta Shoemaker.'

I turned from the window and Frank Wallace was right: she was a beauty. Slender and slightly above average height, with a heavy head of rich black hair that fell to her shoulders. She was around forty, perhaps a bit younger, but her make-up was flawless and emphasised her large eyes and full lips. She wore a nicely-tailored suit and skirt over a white blouse.

By now I'd stood up and we shook hands, then she smiled a wide and generous smile that I wasn't expecting and made me want to smile back at her. So I did.

She said, 'Let's go to my office and talk about this poor sad man.'

She led the way down a corridor, past a number of doors with people's names on them. I half-expected them to be titled 'Special Agent Smithers' or something similar, but first and last names seemed to suffice.

Her office was noticeably warmer than the foyer and was already occupied by a tall, thick-set man in his late-thirties with short black hair and a tense, frowning expression. He wore a black high-necked jacket and dark trousers and by his stance seemed conscious of wearing them as a uniform. Perhaps it was the house style, I thought.

Jocasta Shoemaker introduced him.

'Mr Dyke, this is John Gale, my head of security at these offices.'

He nodded at me and I nodded back. We all sat down on soft leather seats around a low coffee table. The view from her windows was as breathtaking as the view up-river and there was a faint musk in the air, as though the odour from the Thames had been purified and scrubbed before being filtered into the office's atmosphere.

I said to Jocasta, 'You have your own security even though you're a security business?'

'I'm not actually prepared to discuss our office arrangements, Mr Dyke. I'm seeing you only as a courtesy and because Frank Wallace served this company and my husband for many years.'

Gale said, 'What does the old man want? More money? Some consultancy work?'

I thought there was no point beating around any bushes so I repeated what Wallace had instructed me to say.

'He's asked me to tell you that if you don't stop harassing him, he'll publish information that'll embarrass Shoemaker Systems and endanger all of your client relations.'

Jocasta Shoemaker raised her eyebrows.

'In what way have we been harassing him?'

'He believes you've been following him and watching his house. I don't think he's entirely wrong.'

Gale let out a grunt. 'We looked you up, Dyke. Low level snooper who had a couple of big scores lately. That doesn't give you the right to accuse us of harassing ordinary citizens. Get your facts straight before you go throwing accusations around.'

Jocasta raised an arm towards him.

'All right, John. Mr Dyke, I'm interested in why he thinks we'd be doing anything of the sort. What possible reason would we have for harassing him?'

'He thinks the articles he's been writing are getting to you. Revealing information you'd rather have kept to yourself.'

She looked at Gale and then around the room, as if searching for guidance amongst the bookshelves and expensive corporate artwork. I admired the regularity of her nose and chin and the nicely aesthetic relationship they had with her cheekbones and eyes.

Finally her gaze came back to me and her voice was even warmer and more honeyed than before. If she was irritated she wasn't going to show it to the likes of me.

'Of course we're aware of what Frank's been writing, but I have to say we're very relaxed about the articles. What's the total circulation? Fifteen hundred copies, on a good day? You can tell him that we've had nothing to do with any surveillance, and if we had, as he well knows, he wouldn't have seen it. Neither, Mr Dyke, would you.'

This worried me because it was exactly what I'd been thinking. Shoemaker Systems didn't reel in the money they did by being obvious on suburban streets and by holding knives against people's ribs.

Gale said, 'Frank Wallace has had his time. He's a bit pathetic, actually, living on past glories and memories of when intelligence work was a big game, for both sides. The world's changed and he should move on. Tell him he's fantasising and he should just carry on writing his little articles that no one reads.'

Jocasta Shoemaker stood up. 'What exactly has he asked you to do, Mr Dyke? Deliver the message? Is that all?'

'He wanted me to meet you face-to-face and make my own judgement. Whether you've had him under observation or not, there was someone on his street the other night.'

'You saw them?'

'I felt his knife-point in my back.'

'That sounds very … crude. I hope you understand we wouldn't do anything of that kind, especially not to an ex-employee with Frank's reputation.'

She had moved slightly and I realised she was

manoeuvring me towards the door. Gale had stood up but was posing again, staring at me with his hands in his pockets and a look of disdain on his face.

I stopped before she ejected me completely from the room.

'I don't understand anything of what you do, Mrs Shoemaker. I know you and Captain Bligh here are very smooth, but I'm no more likely to believe anything you tell me than Frank Wallace.'

She paused with what appeared to be a genuine smile on her face.

'Aren't you the flatterer? I'm sorry if we've given the impression that we don't take you or Frank seriously. But you should know this is a very busy time for us—you were lucky I could fit you in this afternoon—and we just can't sit around worrying about a few idle words spread in the ether by an ex-colleague. We'd never get anything done. I hope you see that.'

'I see lots of things, Mrs Shoemaker. I see a couple of professional bullshitters trying to pull rank on a hick from the sticks. And I see a fancy office founded on the insecurities of companies whose fears you create in the first place. If that's what Frank Wallace is trying to combat, then I think I'm probably side by side in the trenches with him.'

Now her face had turned dark and when she spoke her voice had lost its softness.

'When you leave this office and travel north to your box-room in Crewe, and when you talk to Frank about this meeting, remind him that we have as much tittle-tattle on him as he thinks he has on us. That's the nature of intelligence work: just when you think you have the upper hand, someone comes along and sells you out. Gale, make sure Mr Dyke leaves the office safely.'

Gale was grinning as he came around the chairs towards me. I opened the door and left before he arrived. Otherwise I might have kicked that grin down his throat.

I DON'T THINK the trio of receptionists were laughing at me as I was escorted across the carpet to the exit carousel, but I couldn't be sure. I held my head up and made a point of turning to Gale when he stopped just before the glass.

I stuck out my hand. 'Thanks for everything. It's been real.'

He stared at the hand as if he didn't recognise what it was, then reached up and plucked the security badge from my jacket lapel. He took out the printed ID from its plastic holder and screwed it up in his hand. Having made a point of some kind, he turned and strode back into the darkness without saying a word.

There was something nagging in the back of my mind about Gale but I couldn't place it. Perhaps he reminded me of other ex-forces mercenaries I'd come across—the same self-possession, the aura of belonging to a secret club that you could never understand, the compact strength that showed in the tendons of the neck and the knots of muscle in the shoulders. I was disposed to recognise the type and bristle immediately, which wasn't exactly his fault.

Out on the street I felt as though everyone was aware of my humiliation and was ignoring me out of embarrassment. Then I realised this was just London's way of being friendly, so I thought I'd find somewhere to sit while I drank coffee and reported back.

Fifty yards down the road was a Starbucks, and when I switched on my phone I saw a missed call from Belinda. Doubtless she was dying to know how the meeting had gone—in many ways she was as solitary as me and probably didn't relish having an unwanted lodger. I called her back.

She answered with, 'Don't say a word, Sam. Just listen. He's gone. Packed his bag—which I don't think he actually unpacked—and went. I was down the shops getting him another newspaper. By the time I came back the house was empty.'

I stared through the Starbucks window at the pedestrians and the traffic beyond. This had felt like a waste of time from the beginning. He'd paid me for a week in advance and I'd spent some of it on the train fare, and given some to Belinda, but there was nothing to show for his money. What was he up to? Where would he go now?

Belinda was speaking again.

'I know I told you not to say anything, but if you wanted to speak, now would be the time.'

'I'm thinking. Something I've not been very good at lately.'

'What do you want me to do? Try the train stations? He could have called a taxi and gone anywhere from here.'

'No, forget him. The meeting was weird and I don't think there's any mileage in carrying on with this.'

'You say so, boss man.'

'He's an old man wanting attention. We've given him as much as he deserves.'

'He left a thank-you note, if that's any consolation.'

I wondered what he was thanking us for.

CHAPTER SEVEN

THAT WAS FRIDAY. Monday morning I was back in my office with a spring in my step and a future to contemplate.

My first act was to take the cash that Frank Wallace had given me from my desk drawer, put fifteen hundred of it back in the drawer and go to the bank to deposit the remaining two thousand in my account. Life was good.

When I returned to the office there was a young woman waiting outside the door. She was wearing neatly-pressed green pants and a white padded parka, as though she were expecting snow. She had straight blonde hair that came down to her shoulders and was kept from her forehead by a barrette above her left ear. I guessed she was in her early thirties. I knew she was very attractive, in a business-like way, with efficient make-up and a pert demeanour.

She smiled as I reached the top of the stairs and found the door key.

'Mr Dyke?'

'Twenty-four seven. Would you like to see the inside of the office?'

She smiled again, but this time it wasn't on full beam. I regretted my levity and held out my arm to usher her inside.

When we were seated and she'd unzipped her parka and crossed her legs and refused a cup of coffee, she burst into tears.

At times like these I tend not to get involved. I don't offer handkerchiefs or sympathy, first because I'm not sure it helps, but mainly because I'm not very good at it.

In the end she found her own tissues and tore one angrily from its wrapping, dabbing it against her eyes and concluding by blowing her nose. The fit of tears subsided and she smiled weakly at me.

She said, 'Damnit, I was determined not to do that.'

'It's okay, I often have that effect on women. I can't tell whether it's a good or a bad thing.'

She laughed. 'You must see a lot of tears in this chair. Sorry, I don't mean from women who … oh, damnit, you know what I mean … '

'I think so. Are you okay to talk now? Do you want to tell me what this is all about?'

She took her time and gathered herself, looking out of the window as if seeing her thoughts lining up in a shopping list.

Then she turned back to me and gave me the full-beam smile.

'My name's Emily Wallace, and I want you to help me find my father.'

THE WORDS WERE out of my mouth before I could stop them.

'You've got to be kidding me.'

I thought she'd be upset but she took it well. She sighed and shrugged her shoulders as though expecting my response.

'I know, strange, isn't it? I understand you've been

working for him this last week and he's run away. I know all that.'

'How do you know?'

'He phoned me yesterday. He told me he'd hired an investigator to go and see Jocasta Shoemaker. It's an obsession with him, what she's doing to his company. Well, not his company but I daresay you know what I mean.'

I nodded. 'He's very persuasive on that.'

'Isn't he just?'

'What makes you think he needs finding?'

'I heard it in his voice. He has periods like this when he gets manic about something. Usually about Jocasta Shoemaker. He should never have retired, damnit. As soon as he did, all this bitterness and anger started coming out. At least while he was working he had something to do. I suppose when you've worked all your life in interesting places and "made a contribution", whatever that means, you can feel a bit used up when there's nothing urgent for you to do.'

I looked at her and wasn't sure what I felt. I understood her feelings for her father, but at that moment I had no real urge to want to help him. I had a sense I'd been duped by him for some obscure reason of his own. I couldn't believe delivering a message to Jocasta Shoemaker was all he wanted.

I said, 'So he told you about me?'

'Yes. He'd read a lot about you and thought you'd get the job done. He said he admired your guts.'

'He gave me a lot of money. That buys a lot of guts.'

'I don't want it back, if that's what you're worried about.'

'I wouldn't give it back.'

She lowered her eyes. 'No, of course not, that was between you and him. But I'm willing to pay you more to find him.'

'To be honest, I don't think I want to. He seems to be playing games.'

'This is my father you're talking about.'

'I'm sorry.'

'He got under your skin, didn't he? The hangdog look and poor-me behaviour. I know, I've been there.'

There was a screech of brakes outside and we both glanced through the window. The pedestrians were unperturbed and the traffic seemed to be carrying on as though nothing had happened.

I thought about Frank Wallace and his obsession with Jocasta Shoemaker. I wondered what was driving him to behave like one of those doom-sayers you used to see in a sandwich-board on the street, forecasting death and destruction. While Jocasta Shoemaker and her organisation were slick and smooth-tongued, I couldn't see what she personally had done to warrant this amount of personal spite. She was running a business in a very high-powered and competitive environment. Neither Wallace nor I had to like it, but it was her business.

I made a decision.

I said, 'What exactly do you want me to do? If I find him I can hardly wrap him in a carpet and lock him in his house.'

'Does this mean you'll look for him?'

'I'll give it a couple of days. I owe him one for sending me on several wild goose chases.'

She brightened. 'Thank you. As for what you should do, I hadn't thought that far ahead. What do you suggest?'

'I suggest you go to the police and report him missing.'

'Doesn't he have to be gone for a certain amount of time before they show any interest? I spoke to him yesterday so I don't suppose they'd be bothered. Besides, it's not as though he's got Alzheimer's or anything. He's just a bit … obsessed.'

A thought occurred to me.

'When you spoke to him did he happen to mention where he was?'

'Don't you think I'd have told you that?'

'Just asking. What about the phone call—was it from a fixed line or a mobile?'

In response, she bent down and rummaged in her handbag. She came up with her own mobile phone and started flipping her finger up and down the screen.

'As it happens he called me on my mobile so the number will be on it … here it is.'

She read out the number and I wrote it down. It was a fixed line number and what we in the trade call a Clue. I asked her for her own numbers and wrote them down, too. I noted that her home phone was a London number.

I said, 'So you were in the area when he phoned? I mean, hereabouts?'

She frowned slightly. 'If you must know I was driving to Buxton to see him. I had to pull over to take his call. I hadn't spoken to him in a couple of weeks and he wasn't answering his phone or returning messages, so I was worried. By the time I spoke to him yesterday he'd already been in your care and run off. I went to the house anyway last night and drove here early this morning. Does that answer your question?'

She'd become tense very quickly and I backed off. Asking loaded questions becomes a habit and you can forget how irritating they can be.

I said, 'I'm sorry. I'm just trying to establish a time-line. Did it seem to you that he knew where you were?'

'No, how could he?'

'Did you tell him?'

'Of course. And he told me I should carry on to the house

rather than drive back. I have a key. He worries about me being alone on the road.'

'So he knew where you were this morning.'

'Yes. What are you getting at?'

'Only that if he knew where you were this morning, he might well know where you are now.'

Instinctively, we both looked out of the window again, as though we might catch him in the square outside Marks & Spencer watching us through field glasses.

She turned back to me, a sceptical look on her face.

'I don't understand why he would follow me here if he's already run away from you once. What would he be trying to prove?'

I sighed and folded the piece of paper on which I'd written the telephone numbers.

'I have no idea why he should do any such thing. I was just floating a notion. It strikes me if your father is as experienced in Intelligence work as he claims, he could be playing all of us.'

'Why on earth would he do that?'

'I'm afraid it's another one of those things about which I have no idea. But it doesn't mean I'm wrong.'

She had no reply to that, so then we discussed my rates and she agreed to them and signed a pro-forma contract. Then I saw her to the door and she shook my hand. Her blue eyes were clear again after her tears and she'd rediscovered the professional poise she'd had when I first saw her outside my office.

I said, 'I'll be in touch when I know something. Are you going back to London now?'

'I have to work, too, you know. We can't all sit around in our offices watching the traffic on the street.'

At least she said this with a smile in her eyes. I'd thought for a terrible moment that she had my number.

And as she went down the stairs, treading daintily on each wooden riser, I thought back to the moment when she shook my hand. Had her fingers stayed in my palm just a little longer than was expected? Or was I being fanciful?

WHEN I HEARD the downstairs exit swing shut I closed the office door and walked back to my window. I could see Emily Wallace walking across the square, heading towards the car park behind the Benefit offices.

I wondered what I was getting myself into. It struck me that the Wallaces had both used a kind of emotional blackmail to get me onside with them—one using his age and fearfulness, the other … well, just tears and an appeal to filial responsibility. Was this a family trait? The ability to turn on the metaphorical—and physical—waterworks when needed? If so, it had worked both times and I'd fallen for it. They were shaping up to be a handful.

I called Dan, hoping he'd still be up after a night online. His voice was bleary but at least he picked up.

'You've got no sense of timing, Dad. Here I am working my arse off to make you money and you keep interrupting my beauty sleep.'

'Did we do well?'

'Could have been better. People are running a bit scared at the moment. But you don't want to hear that. Don't worry, your portfolio is safe with me. Now, what do you want?'

I told him about Emily Wallace's visit and that she wanted me to find her father.

'You mean the one who ran away? Mr Invisible?'

'He's not completely invisible. He used a land-line to make a phone call yesterday. Can you back-trace it?'

'Number one on my list of skills. Hold on while I get a

pen.'

When he came back I gave him the information and told him it would be good if we could get the address quickly: there was no guarantee that Wallace would stay there for any length of time.

Dan said, 'It might be a pub or a train station. Do pubs have pay phones any more? I never look.'

'There used to be things called phone boxes on street corners, where you could put money in a slot and talk to people a long way away.'

'You're kidding, right? And people used to pay for phone calls? That's prehistoric. You'll be telling me next people went to big rooms called cinemas and paid money to watch films. Thank God the Internet invented downloading.'

'I didn't hear that.'

'Hear what?'

CHAPTER EIGHT

I PICKED UP Belinda on the way into Manchester and we talked about Frank Wallace's disappearance. There'd been no sign or forewarning that he was about to run. He'd got up early Friday morning and sat watching breakfast television, then asked if Belinda was going out. She hadn't planned to but she sensed that he wanted something so said she might pop out for some sugar. He'd asked for a copy of *The Guardian,* if she wouldn't mind, then settled back in his seat again.

'Swear to God, Sam, I thought he was in for the duration. I was only fifteen minutes. He must have already been packed and just waited for me to turn the corner before he legged it. He'd have been able to get a taxi on the Wilmslow Road straight into town and after that go wherever he liked. Sorry, but the old coot fooled me.'

'He's fooled a lot of people.'

'What's his daughter like?'

'A bit fragile. She veered between being upset about her dad and hard-headed about me.'

'The whole thing sounds screwy.'

'Why?'

'If she talked to him on Sunday why was she so worried that she felt obliged to track you down on Monday? I know you're a babe-magnet and all, but she drove from Buxton to Crewe to hire you when she could have gone back to London and hired one of the big guns.'

'Thanks for the vote of confidence.'

'You know what I mean. If he told her you hadn't been able to get a satisfactory reply from Jocasta, why would his daughter turn to you for help in finding him? What have you done to gain her confidence? The whole thing is bizarre.'

I'd turned on to the Mancunian Way to avoid the centre of Manchester. We crossed the canal and I headed north, thinking about what Belinda had said. At the time it had seemed perfectly reasonable for Emily Wallace to come visit me if she thought her father was going off the rails. She was genuinely upset in my office and perhaps she wasn't thinking straight. Perhaps she thought that as I was the last person to see him—except for Belinda, who she probably didn't know about—I'd have information about his state of mind or intentions.

I said, 'Let's see what we get out of this place before we start making any judgements.'

Belinda lifted her chin to acknowledge I'd spoken though I felt she wasn't convinced. But one of my skills, I like to think, is that I have a pretty good grasp of character and Emily Wallace had seemed genuinely upset by her father's disappearance. So in my view it was perfectly understandable that she'd want me to find him.

The address Dan had uncovered from the telephone number given to me by Emily was in a row of red-brick terraced houses in north Manchester. The area was slightly run down, with an abandoned car stuck on bricks at one end of the road and an empty house with a broken fence sprouting weeds at the other. I'd parked thirty yards from the house and we sat for ten minutes watching it. No one walked past in that time, and only one car drove by.

Belinda said, 'Think he's in?'

'I doubt it but we ought to find out.'

I climbed from the car and Belinda followed. I walked up the short path to the door and knocked.

The door swung open, its catch broken.

We glanced at each other and I saw Belinda tighten her fists and rise to the balls of her feet.

I said, 'He's sixty-five years old. Think you can take him?'

She relaxed the tension from her body and gave me a lopsided grin.

'If you help out.'

I went inside. It was a standard layout—carpeted stairs going up to the left, a short corridor straight ahead leading to a kitchen at the back of the house. Two rooms off the corridor: front parlour and back room. There were probably three small bedrooms and a bathroom upstairs. The place smelled fusty with damp and there were cobwebs hanging from the door into the kitchen. It felt as if it hadn't been lived in for months.

I tried the front parlour door and saw there was a lock on it.

I said, 'It's flats. Two down here and probably a couple upstairs. Shared bathroom and kitchen.'

'It smells empty.'

'Still, if we're breaking and entering we should at least make sure we have the right one.'

'How do we know which is his?'

I waggled my eyebrows at her and took out my phone. I dialled the number Emily Wallace had given me and we heard a telephone ring upstairs.

We climbed the stairs slowly, listening for any sign of human habitation. The phone was still ringing and was coming from what would be the front bedroom. Like the room downstairs it was locked.

Belinda said, 'Do you want me to kick it in? He's not there or he would have answered the phone. And please don't waggle your eyebrows at me again—it's creepy.'

So I winked at her instead and took my lock-pick set from my jacket pocket. A minute later the simple lock clicked and I pushed the door open.

I'd guessed it would resemble bed-sits all over the country, so I wasn't surprised when it did. There was a bed—the bedclothes neatly made up—a table in front of the window, a thin wooden chair and an old telephone: a black Bakelite job that had been fitted with a modern connector. On the wall there was a dusty oil painting after Constable— a long way after—and next to the table a grey wire waste bin of the kind you can buy from office supply stores. Heating was provided by an actual open fireplace; no radiator.

And, after having a good look around, there was no sign of Frank Wallace having been there … except for one item: a charred piece of paper in the waste bin. I reached down and plucked it out with two fingers, then laid it flat on the table.

Belinda peered over my shoulder.

'Looks like something from a chemistry textbook. Formulae and so on.'

The paper was burnt around the edges but otherwise white. It was large enough to have been a sheet of A4, so probably not torn from a textbook but printed out. Perhaps downloaded from the Net.

Belinda said, 'Any idea? Do you do chemistry?'

'Only when cooking. I'll get Dan on it. Anything else

strike you about the room?'

She turned and looked around, taking in the floral-patterned wallpaper, the slender wooden wardrobe, the metal-framed bed. She went up to the oil painting and stared at it for a moment, then turned away.

She said, 'I don't think he stayed here, if that's what you mean. It smells mouldy.' She put her hand under the bed cover and felt the sheets. 'Feels damp. If he slept here on Sunday night I doubt it would be this damp again by Tuesday morning.'

'Good. Anything else?'

'What is this, Twenty Questions?'

'Look at the fireplace.'

She turned and went up to it. It was a traditional Victorian fireplace made for small spaces like bedrooms, with a black mantelpiece about four feet high and a bow-fronted grate. The grate itself was pitted and stained and the fire-surround was bordered with cream tiles with a floral pattern that were cracked and discoloured.

She looked at me and shrugged.

In reply I held up the paper from the waste bin.

'This is charred but there are no ashes in the fireplace or in the bin. And there's no ash tray for cigarettes. So what did he do, half-burn it somewhere else and then bring it here to drop it, still legible, in the bin where we couldn't fail to see it?'

'You think he's playing more games?'

'Whatever he's doing, he's doing it with a full deck of cards. He's not stupid enough to have left a 'clue' like this without any surrounding circumstantial evidence. He knows what he's doing, which is laying a trail of bread-crumbs. He wants me to keep coming after him. If he accidentally left a chemical formula for a high-explosive still smoking in the fire grate it would be one thing. But this amateurishness is deliberate.'

'So what's that about?'

'He's trying to intrigue me.'

'It's working, isn't it?'

I said nothing and walked out of the bedroom.

OUTSIDE IT HAD turned cool and we sat in the car for a while with the engine running and the heating on.

I said, 'I'm going to make a call. Are you okay for a while?'

'By your command, boss man.'

I switched off the engine and took out my phone and dialled Shoemaker Systems. I got straight through to Ann with the blonde bobbed hair and she started the resistance, telling me that Mrs Shoemaker wasn't available, she was in a meeting, she couldn't possibly interrupt, she doesn't take unscheduled phone calls, and so on.

I fought back gamely and told her that what I had to say was of extreme urgency and importance and that I wouldn't be calling unless it was essential that I talk to her …

I wore her down. Eventually she said, 'Hold on, I'll see what I can do.'

Two minutes later Jocasta Shoemaker was on the line.

'This better be good, Mr Dyke. Some of us have real work to do.'

'Frank Wallace has gone missing.'

She didn't pause for breath.

'As far as I was concerned, he always was. What's changed?'

'He's setting me up for something and I think you and your company are involved, too.'

'What do you mean?'

'I'm not entirely sure.'

'That's a very persuasive argument. When *will* you be sure?'

I raised my eyebrows towards Belinda, who I guessed could hear both sides of the discussion.

I told Jocasta Shoemaker that I'd kept Wallace in a safe place but he'd absconded. I'd tracked him down to a location where there was nothing but the remains of a piece of charred paper containing chemical equations.

'Of what?'

'To be determined.' I paused. 'Listen, I know all this sounds off the wall but I think Frank is gearing up for something. I don't know why he's involving me, but I'm pretty certain you're involved as well.'

'We're well able to protect ourselves, Mr Dyke. Did you ever find out who were the mysterious people watching his house?'

'You're certain it's not you?'

'Goodbye, Mr Dyke.'

'Before you go, answer me this: is there something big happening soon? I mean, for Shoemaker Systems. Something that Frank might know about.'

She didn't reply straight away and in the pause Belinda punched me playfully on the arm. She knew I'd hit on something.

Jocasta said, 'What line are you on?'

'My mobile.'

'I'll call you back.'

I hung up and grinned at Belinda.

She said, 'How did you know?'

'Smoke and fire. You don't get one without the other. Frank's been retired a while and been writing his articles. So why now? What's pushed his buttons this week? He's on a timetable.'

My phone rang and I replied.

Jocasta said, 'We're on a secure line.'

'Who's going to be listening in? Frank?'

'I don't have time to go into everything, but perhaps you should know we do have a major event coming up. I can't give you all the details but I suppose it's possible Frank has found out through his contacts in Intelligence.'

'What sort of event?'

'I'm not going into specifics, but it's a signing. It's very important to us, and it's very important to the country.'

'You're kidding.'

'Do I sound like it?'

'Whenever people say what they're doing is important for the country, I reach for my sick bag.'

I felt her bridling even down the phone line. I pictured her tossing her lush black hair and raising her chin haughtily. It wasn't an unpleasant image.

She said, 'Your opinions are actually of no value to me. It happens to be true.'

'Okay, what could Frank Wallace do to prevent you getting what you want?'

'If you find him, perhaps you could ask him. Personally, I don't see what he can do, other than write more articles and do his best to drum up ill will towards us, and me in particular.'

'He doesn't like you, does he?'

'I took away his playmate. Excuse me for wanting to get married.'

'We're getting off track here. How much could he know about this signing? Assume he's learned about it from an ex-colleague, maybe even someone in your own organisation … how much information is he likely to have gathered?'

She sighed. 'A little. Not much. We're trying to keep a lid on it but of course as a company we have to make some commercial capital from the contract. Some people have been told, but with an embargo till after the event.'

'A secret intelligence agency having to blow its own trumpet. And they say irony is dead.'

'Are we finished here? I have a meeting I'm supposed to be in.'

'Aren't you a tiny bit worried about what he might be planning?'

'Not with a super-agent like you on the case. Why should I be?'

'I'll be in touch.'

'Please don't be.'

She hung up.

Belinda said, 'She's a charmer, ain't she?'

'She's worse in person. Except for the hair. The hair is good.'

I started the engine and fastened my safety-belt.

Belinda said, 'What are we going to do now?'

'I'm going to find Frank Wallace, of course.'

'And then what?'

'Give him a damn good telling off for wasting my time.'

CHAPTER NINE

I DROPPED BELINDA off with a promise to keep her up to date with developments, then drove back to Crewe. I bought a sandwich from Marks and Spencer and chewed it carefully in my office, staring out of the window at the pedestrians who were totally unaware of my deep thoughts.

When it was late enough I got back in my car and drove out to Dan's house on the outskirts of the town. He was up and looked alert when he opened the door, and dressed as though he was ready to go out. His hair was shorter now than it had ever been and he was filling out because he'd finally started eating properly. He was an inch shorter than me but still topped out at six feet and his face had the geometry of my own, though with his mother's eyes, dark and somewhat wary.

I brandished the burned sheet of paper. 'Fancy a bit of paid work?'

He took it and turned it over. There was nothing on the reverse side.

'What is it?'

'My keen detective's brain tells me there are chemical formulae printed on one side. I thought you might be able to find out what they mean.'

He shrugged. 'Okay. You want it now? Only I'm going out.'

'Would you say that to a real client?'

'A real client wouldn't knock on my front door or wake me up when I'm sleeping.'

'Okay, as soon as you can.'

'Are you allowed to tell me what it's about?'

'The last remaining vestige of Mr Invisible. He's left us a Clue.'

'Sporting of him.'

I walked further into the house while he took the paper upstairs to his office. I thought he might start work on it immediately but he came down a moment later.

He said, 'Craig's here.'

I looked out of the window and saw the white Porsche pulling on to Dan's short drive. A man of about thirty with blond gelled hair climbed out of the driver's side. He paused for a moment and surveyed his car, from the bonnet to the short boot, then, satisfied, pressed the electronic key and the vehicle locked.

I said to Dan, 'What does he do?'

'Owns a restaurant in Wilmslow.'

I nodded. 'It figures.'

Dan had crossed to the door and opened it and a moment later Craig came in. He leaned forward—I guess to offer Dan a kiss—but Dan backed away from it and cut his eyes sideways to me. Craig followed his look.

Dan said, 'Craig, this is my dad. Dad, Craig.'

I stepped forward and shook his hand.

'Nice car.'

Craig glanced out of the window, his gaze lingering on the sleek lines for a moment. His face was smooth and tanned and he wore clothes that hung perfectly on him—a Ralph Lauren pullover under a short blouson, neatly pressed chinos and what appeared to be new Nikes on his feet. There was a single white diamond in his left ear.

He said, 'Thanks. I've only had it a month. Still can't believe I've got it, to tell the truth. Always been a dream of mine to own a Porsche.'

'What does it do?'

He proceeded to give me some technical details about nought-to-sixty speed, torque and engine size. I wasn't really listening.

Dan interrupted. 'Craig, he's not bothered. If I didn't know better I'd say he was winding you up.'

A diffident smile settled on Craig's features.

'Sorry, I can be a real petrol-head bore. Bad as Dan with his computers.'

'Every man needs a hobby.'

'Oh yes, so what's yours?'

'Catching bad people and putting them in jail.'

He burst out laughing but stopped dead when he saw the look on my face.

'Seriously? You're a policeman? Dan hasn't told me anything about you.'

'That's because if he did, I'd have to kill you.'

He laughed again, but this time with less gusto. He looked nervously at Dan.

'Are you ready then?'

Dan said, 'Don't pay any attention to him. He's playing mother hen. Most of his work involves catching people who've defrauded the Benefit of ten quid.'

I looked hurt. 'A vital contribution to the economy of the UK.'

Craig was totally out of his depth now and was edging

towards the door. Dan fetched his coat from the kitchen. He opened the front door so that Craig could escape, then turned back to me. He seemed about to say something — probably recriminatory — but in the end shook his head and followed Craig outside, pulling the door closed behind him.

I watched them talk briefly over the top of the car, Craig glancing towards the house, then they climbed inside and Craig reversed on to the main road and drove away.

My mobile phone rang in my jacket pocket and I pressed the icon to reply.

It was Frank Wallace.

'So, Mr Dyke, how are you enjoying the work?'

I SAT ON Dan's sofa. If this was going to be another of Wallace's disorienting conversations I wanted to be comfortable.

I said, 'Where are you? Belinda was worried. Thought you'd fallen down the bath plughole.'

He laughed delightedly. 'Now, Sam, don't play games with me. She was glad to get me out of the house. I know when I'm not wanted. She was very sweet, though.'

'So what are you up to now?'

'Did you find the note?'

I was wary … I didn't want him to know his daughter had hired me to find him. But how else would I have traced him to the house containing the burned chemical formula?'

I said, 'The thank-you note?'

'You are a card. No, the one in the house. Don't tell me you didn't look in the waste bin.'

'How do you know I was there?'

His voice took on a harsh edge. 'Don't treat me like an idiot, Dyke. I know Emily came to see you. I don't need two guesses to know what she wanted. Especially when you and

Belinda set off like gladiators into the wilds of north Manchester … give me some credit.'

'Did you stay in the house?'

'What's it to you?'

'Just interested. It looked empty.'

'Why do you think I chose it? Emily's nosier than her mother was, God rest her soul. I couldn't risk her tracing me, or using someone else to do it for her.'

I looked at the number that was being displayed on my phone's screen. It was a mobile number. No chance of tracing it this time.

I said, 'Why did you use a land-line in the first place? You've got a mobile phone.'

'But then you'd never have traced it and found the clue, would you?'

'Does Emily know you're using her to play games with other people? She's worried about you.'

He laughed again. 'God, you're so obvious. You'd never have made it in Intelligence. Playing the guilt card on an old man … you should be ashamed of yourself. Anyway, I'm bored with this conversation now.'

'I still don't know what you want, Frank. What's this all about?'

'I've told you before—Jocasta Shoemaker and her company are on the wrong side of history with their current strategy.'

'What on earth does that mean?'

'It means time will prove the way they operate won't be countenanced by the British public once they learn how the Intelligence and security services are run in this country.'

'Get a Twitter account and let them know. Use Facebook. You don't have to wage this vendetta against one company and one person.'

'Ah, but that's where you're wrong, Mr Dyke. That's exactly what I *do* have to do. The point is it *is* personal. Personal to me and personal to her. We're playing out a great tragedy here—the Revenger's Tragedy, know it?'

I said that I didn't.

'Never mind. It ends in death and destruction, like all those Elizabethan plays. If it is Elizabethan, I'm not sure. I'll have to check. But it's the only way they *can* end.'

He fell silent and I heard him breathing hard, as though explaining his credo had exhausted him. Not for the first time I had the sense that I was talking to someone for whom the future was very short.

I said, 'I suppose the chemical formula doesn't mean anything, does it? Just another of your games.'

'You think so? Can you risk not knowing? Get that clever son of yours to find out. Oh, you have. Nice car his boyfriend's got, by the way.'

'You know I'll find you in the end.'

'You're a hell hound on my trail. Know it?'

Before I could answer he hung up and I realised I was squeezing my phone very tightly.

WHICH MEANT ANOTHER phone call to Shoemaker Systems and another argument with bobbed-hair Ann about the urgency of the call.

Finally Jocasta Shoemaker came on the line, her temper even shorter than usual.

'I'm giving you an awful lot of leeway, Dyke. What is it now?'

'I'm starting to rather enjoy our chats.'

'You're not funny and what's more, you're not timely. What did you have to say?'

'I've spoken to Frank Wallace. I think it's worse than we

thought.'

'You mean worse than *you* thought. I haven't been doing any thinking about this at all.'

'It's not just about his articles and bearing a grudge against you.'

'What do you mean?'

'He wants revenge. Proper revenge. And I think he's clever enough to get it.'

She was silent for a moment and I imagined her looking out of her twentieth-floor windows at the Thames and the inconsequential human lives beetling along beneath her.

Finally she said, 'I don't do this kind of thing on the telephone. Come in tomorrow.'

She had the typical London-dweller's view that popping into Town was the work of a moment.

I said, 'Let me check if my diary's free.'

'This was *your* idea. Don't go all coy on me now.'

'I can be there late morning. Tell your man Gale I'm looking forward to seeing his selection of action man poses again.'

'Tell him yourself. He's listening on the extension.'

CHAPTER TEN

I'D GIVEN BELINDA five hundred pounds from Frank Wallace's retainer but I still had a fair amount left from the fifteen hundred in cash I'd kept behind. So I turned up at the train station the next morning and laid my money down … but even so, I couldn't bring myself to pay the extortionate amount for a First Class seat.

So I sat with My People in Standard Class and drank strong tea with a chocolate cookie the size of a dustbin lid.

From Euston a different cabbie took me on a largely identical route to the Isle of Dogs and a different one of the Robo-Receptionists gave me my pass and the plastic wallet to put it in. As soon as I was in the lift I daringly put the pass in my pocket so that Gale couldn't snatch it from me again. That would teach him.

I felt like Bill Murray in Groundhog Day as Ann met me once more when the lift doors opened and led me to the same seat looking out at Canary Wharf. I couldn't be sure, but I thought the same traffic was passing on the street below and I was certain I even recognised one or two of the pedestrians …

Jocasta Shoemaker was definitely different, though. She

was wearing a black tailored suit and her hair was pushed back from her head with an alice band. Perhaps Anglo-Greek fashion wasn't yet aware that this was an outmoded look.

I try to keep up with women's fashion as much as the Sunday supplements allow.

She didn't so much greet me as summon me, standing fifteen feet away and raising her chin, then turning and walking back to her office. I followed like a good dog.

Inside her office Gale was sitting browsing through a sheaf of papers. He glanced up at me but didn't offer to shake hands. I don't think he approved of my presence, and he definitely didn't want me to catch him posing again. His attire today was a bright white shirt and a dark blue tie over dark blue trousers. Somewhere a dark blue jacket was feeling lonely.

Jocasta gestured towards the leather sofas and I sat and she sat opposite. Gale was positioned on a third sofa at right angles to us, like a tennis umpire. He put down his papers and folded his arms. I didn't need to be an expert in body language to tell he was pissed off.

Jocasta said, 'Here we are again. You with a tall tale, us with no idea of what you expect us to do. How are things different?'

Before I could reply Gale interrupted.

'What did Wallace say? What does he want?'

I turned to him. 'Do you want me to reply to your question first, or your boss's? I can be rude to either of you, but I'd prefer to be rude to you, if that's okay.'

He opened his mouth then closed it and looked away. A muscle twitched in his cheek.

I turned back to Jocasta and said, 'I think it's a mistake to treat Frank Wallace as just a nuisance. I'm convinced he's got something in mind other than publishing a few damaging articles to ruin your reputation. He wants revenge for what he thinks you've done to this company.' I waited for her to object but instead she stared at me impassively: she'd heard this before. I went on, 'Whatever he's doing, it's very well planned. He hired me just to get to you — probably because he knew you wouldn't talk to him — and now *he's* playing hard to get, phoning me, acting as though he knows everything I'm doing, teasing me.'

Gale snorted. 'He's such a flirt. You two should just get a room.'

I ignored him. Jocasta at least seemed to be listening.

I said, 'This major event you've got coming up — what can you tell me about it?'

'Nothing. There's a strict embargo on it. Content, timing, location. If I told you anything I wouldn't just lose the contract, I'd probably wind up doing life in the Tower.'

'Then what would Frank know?'

'As I said before, he must have a contact in government, in one of the agencies. He comes from a time when the security services were a lot smaller than they are now. He'll have met and worked with scores of people from different agencies who are probably still around. Isn't that right, John?'

Gale unfolded his arms and placed them on his thighs. I realised that with her relative inexperience in Intelligence she probably relied on him for counsel and expertise. He said, 'Most of his contacts will have dried up by now, dead or retired. And if they knew what's good for them they wouldn't say a dicky-bird about this project.'

'It only takes one.'

'That's right, Dyke. One more sad loser with an axe to grind. Jocasta, remember what we talked about.'

She nodded and turned to me.

'Despite what you might think, we have in fact discussed this. We strongly disagree with Wallace's suggestion that he didn't like the direction I took the company in after Kelvin died. As one of Kelvin's oldest friends and colleagues, he was consulted before anyone else. He agreed that the move from a corporate to a broader, international consultancy approach was the only way forward.'

'He was agreeing with the boss. You're hard to disagree with.'

'Thank you for the compliment, but if you knew Frank Wallace you'd know that's wrong. If he had a position he could argue it as well as the next man. He didn't stand on ceremony.'

Now they were both looking at me and I knew they were going to make an offer or drop a bombshell—one or the other.

I said, 'What do you want?'

'There are two things going on here. First, your lack of trust in our description of Frank and his belief set. You think we're lying about him. To be honest, I don't care whether you believe us or not. That's up to you and there's nothing we can do about it. But it's connected to the second thing, which is what he's *actually* up to.' She paused and glanced at Gale. 'You'd be surprised to hear I didn't know him that well. Yes, I knew him through Kelvin, and I was here for a number of years before I became chairman, so you'd expect that I'd have some grasp on his character, on what drives him. But that's not true. When I came on board he was already a distant figure, usually working from home or on foreign territory. We met almost accidentally when our paths crossed in the office, but he had little time for me and I respected that. I could hardly blame him given his position in the company and my relative newness. The bottom line is

I'm beginning to doubt I understood him at all. You might be right and he's out to get me in some way.'

'That took some guts to admit.'

'I'm not a stupid woman, Mr Dyke.'

'So what is it you're asking me to do?'

She glanced at Gale, who took over the briefing. He leaned forward in his seat and pointed at me.

'You're such a hot shot you can find out whether he was shitting us all those years. *If* he didn't believe what Jocasta was doing with the company, and I emphasise *if*, there aren't many people he'd have shared that with. Most of the people he worked with have moved on or retired. Whatever, they're out of our orbit. But there is someone you can talk to: Greg Last. He was one of ours until a couple of years ago, then he began to think gardening would be more fun than bugging hotel rooms so he retired. He knew Wallace as well as anyone. Ask him what Wallace thought of the changes Jocasta made. And while you're at it, ask him what Wallace might be up to.'

'What do you think he'll tell me?'

'I haven't a fucking clue. Except he'll tell you we're not all as nuts as Frank Wallace.'

Jocasta cut in. I thought she was becoming aggravated by Gale's combative attitude and I sensed she wanted to mediate.

'Personally I think Greg will back up what we've been telling you about Frank's commitment to the changes we made.'

I leaned back in my chair, wondering what all this was intended to prove.

I said, 'Why are you so keen for me to believe Wallace was gung-ho for your new-fangled ways? Who gives a damn? I'd be more useful to you trying to find him.'

Gale said, 'You want to be put on the payroll, is that it? Bit of lucrative consultancy work?'

I ignored him and directed my attention to Jocasta Shoemaker.

'I've come all this way from the wastes of the icy north and you want me to go talk to someone who knew Wallace twenty years ago. It's not exactly Code Red, is it? Do you just want me out of your hair?'

'If you'd done more work in Intelligence, Mr Dyke, you'd know this is how it proceeds. You gather information. Intelligence. You analyse it. Then you work out your plan. What else do you want to do, run around London hoping to barge into him on the street?'

She had me there. I actually had nothing to go on at the moment, so talking to someone who knew Wallace would probably have been the first thing I'd want to do anyway.

She added, 'If you like we'll pay you for a couple of day's consultancy. How does five thousand pounds sound?'

'Like more than it's worth for a conversation. But I suppose those are London rates, aren't they? Keep your money. As a matter of fact I already have two clients on the go.'

'Who?'

'Frank Wallace and his daughter.'

'You can't be serious.'

'I can be and I am. This expression you see on my face is one of distrust. I think you're doing your best but put yourself in my position. Frank hired me because he thought you were up to something. For all I know, talking to this Greg Last is just a distraction to keep me away from the real stuff.'

Gale had been keeping himself in check; but now he couldn't help himself.

'You think *you're* being distracted? How do you think *we* feel? One of the biggest contracts we've ever signed is on the horizon and we're talking to Joe Soap from No Hope about an ex-employee and his revenge fantasies?'

'All right, John.' Jocasta raised a hand slightly and Gale sat back. To me she said, 'Will you talk to Last?'

'Nothing would give me greater pleasure.'

'I'm told he lives in Chesham now. I'll get Ann to arrange it and text you the details. The ticket's on us.'

As I left Shoemaker's office I tried to convince myself that I was doing the right thing, being constructive and organised and logical.

But I couldn't shake the conviction that someone was manipulating me and I didn't know who.

CHAPTER ELEVEN

FIRST I HAD to do some shopping. I hadn't anticipated staying the night but there was no point going back to Crewe only to return the following morning.

I found an Oxfam shop and bought a cheap plastic sports bag with Head written all over it, then went to Boots and bought shaving gear, toothpaste and a toothbrush.

I still hadn't received a text with directions from Ann, so I consulted Google to find out where Chesham was and it turned out to be in Buckinghamshire, north east of London and reachable by a single tube journey from Euston Square. So I took a cab to Euston and booked myself into the Hotel Russell, a grand Victorian pile with high ceilings and hard tiled floors and marble columns by the handful. Wallace's money would pay for it. I'd stayed there before when I was on a course for Customs & Excise and knew its layout. What's more, it was only ten minutes' walk from Euston Square.

By now it was heading for late afternoon and I was wondering what to do for the evening, apart from eat in the large and echoing dining hall. I was lying on my bed staring at the ornate ceiling when my phone rang.

Dan.

'Do you know what you're getting involved in?'

'Do I ever? And hello to you, too. How's Craig and his car?'

'Don't start. Listen. That company you put me on to, Shoemaker, you do know they're real scumbags, don't you?'

'Define scumbag. And remember, you're talking to someone who counts several scumbags amongst his best friends.'

'Well Shoemaker Systems is only part of who they are. That's the visible part, the public profile. But a few years ago they started a so-called charity called The Sophocles Trust, and that's the real beauty.'

'Where did you get all this?'

'In the newspapers, believe it or not. All the work's been done by journalists and published but no one cared. Anyway, according to their mission statement, The Sophocles Trust works to bring together right-wing politicians and businessmen so they can throw expensive parties and congratulate themselves on thinking the same way.'

'I get the impression you're paraphrasing.'

'Not by much.'

I sighed. Naturally I knew that businesses who occupied themselves with security issues and governance and legal tap-dancing were more often than not home to people whose ideas about social engineering were anathema to me. And if Jocasta Shoemaker were a gun-toting, hellfire-spouting ultra-free-marketeer, that was her right.

I didn't have to like it, though.

Dan went on, 'You wouldn't believe the people who've spoken at their seminars or put themselves on the list of donors. It reads like a register of every right-wing nut you've heard of in the last ten years, here and in the US.'

'I never knew you were so political.'

'Things change. You read a bit. You got your politics from your dad, didn't you? I got mine from the Internet. Didn't have a dad, see.'

This was a dig at me for not being around when he was growing up—largely because I didn't know he existed. He didn't do that often, but when he was fired up about something, and I wasn't, the difference of opinion was often put down to my absence during his growing years. How could I know how he felt when I hadn't been there?

I said, 'What does this change? We knew Shoemakers weren't Mother Theresa. They're entitled to have political views.'

'But it's scuzzy. See, they have big shindigs in posh hotels in faraway places—so far away, journalists and TV people usually don't hear about them. Politicians from the UK and the States come along and meet businessmen, hedge fund managers and billionaires from Dubai and listen to talks sponsored by oil companies and accountancy firms. There's all this money sloshing around and all these ideas about de-regulating government and cutting taxes … they're all in it for themselves, every single one. It's just barbaric.'

My son, the social campaigner.

I said, 'What about that other thing, the formula?'

'Oh, yeah, I nearly forgot. It's nothing.'

'What do you mean?'

'It's the chemical formula for shellac. Do you know what that is?'

'It's a kind of wax product. So nothing dangerous, then.'

'Not unless he's going to wax something to death.'

I sighed. As I'd thought, it was apparently another of Frank Wallace's games.

Dan said, 'So, are you going to carry on working for these capitalist leeches?'

'While they continue to pay me.'

There was a sullen silence. Then he said, 'I've sent you a link to the article. Just read it. Might give you some perspective on the kind of people you're getting involved with.'

'I've always known what kind of people I'm getting involved with.'

'All I'm saying is, be careful. I think you're walking into deep water and you think it's a puddle.'

CHAPTER TWELVE

THE METROPOLITAN LINE from Euston Square took me to Chesham in just over an hour. I'd finally received a text from Ann giving me an address and a time when Greg Last would talk to me, which was eleven o'clock.

The train left the darkness of London's tunnels and emerged eventually into Home Counties lushness, with playing fields, golf courses, tennis courts and rows and rows of neat houses marching away into the countryside like good suburban soldiers.

From the station it was a short walk to Last's house, a detached thirties place with a neat lawn in front, a gravelled path and the sense of a large garden stretching behind into woods. I arrived as he was opening one of the twin garage doors, revealing a ride-on mower and other garden tools arrayed neatly inside.

He saw me and came out, squinting.

'You must be Dyke. Sent on a mission to debunk Frank Wallace. Good luck with that.'

But he said this with a smile and held out his hand, which I shook. He was stocky and pale skinned, with freckles and thinning ginger hair. His eyes were sharp and deep blue and looked me over quickly. He exuded competence.

Inside he offered tea, which I refused, and then he took me through to a fancy conservatory at the back of the house overlooking a lawn barbered to within an inch of its life. I had a sense of his wife doing something in the kitchen but he didn't introduce me. We sat in bamboo chairs with deep cushions and I felt for a second like someone in a book by Somerset Maugham.

I said, 'Thanks for seeing me. You probably have no idea what this is about and I wouldn't blame you if you kicked me out.'

He leaned back and folded his hands together over his stomach.

'You've got to be kidding. This is the most excitement I've had in ages. I like gardening as much as the next man, but once you've got the knack of pulling up a weed there's not a lot more to learn.'

I nodded towards the outside. 'Looks like it keeps you busy.'

'Only because I've got fuck-all else to do. Look, let's cut the jabber. All I know is that Frank is up to something and Jocasta Shoemaker wants you to talk to me in case I might know what it is.'

'What did they tell you, exactly?'

'That knob-end Gale called me yesterday and said they were sending someone down to talk to me about Frank, and was that all right. I asked what the problem was with Frank and he just said he was causing some trouble. That's all I know. So, what kind of trouble is it? And who are you again?'

I told Last who I was and that Frank Wallace had hired me essentially to deliver a message to Jocasta Shoemaker, the message being that he was going to revenge himself for what she was doing to his and Kelvin Shoemaker's company. Now Jocasta Shoemaker thought I should talk to someone to get the picture from the other side of the fence, seeing as I'd found it so difficult to believe her and John Gale.

Last grinned. 'That fucking Frank, he's up to something. He doesn't give a shit about what Jocasta sodding Shoemaker did to the company. After Kelvin died he kind of gave up, lost heart. He didn't care any more.'

'He told me he didn't like the fact the company was working more for governments than private businesses, that government intelligence work shouldn't be carried out by private companies, i.e. Shoemakers.'

'Oh for Christ's sake, read your history. Private companies have been working for governments since the year dot. Look at Pinkertons — someone in your own area of expertise. Allan Pinkerton was Lincoln's chief gatherer of intelligence during the Civil War, using all his private business contacts and networks. It probably goes back further than that, if I could be arsed to do the research. The Romans and Greeks used private individuals to do government work, didn't they? You can't keep them separate. Secret work is secret work and it doesn't matter who's paying you.'

'You're right. But from what I've been reading it's got worse. Intelligence officers move straight into private agencies as soon as they leave MI5 or 6. And then they move back again when they've had enough of dealing with stroppy clients. So the distinction between private and public intelligence gathering is becoming blurred.'

'I'll concede that. After all, I did the same, left SIS for private work. Started with Frank in MI6, then followed him to Shoemakers a year after he went.'

'Was it just the money?'

'Look around—this place is a mansion compared to where I was brought up, south of the river. But me and Kate have been here over thirty years, well before my time with Shoemakers. I didn't need the money—I needed a challenge. Like Frank.'

'What kind of a challenge?'

'You have to understand the kind of work we did. Mostly it was sitting in a sound-proofed room in an embassy in some shit-hole Communist satellite state, reading transcripts of conversations we'd bugged and looking for patterns, repetitions, possible code-words. Computers were just starting to be used for the brute work, but in the main it was me and Frank, reading stuff with a cynical and paranoid eye.'

'You must have thought you were doing some good, though.'

'That's why you carry on. Just when you think you're wasting your time, something pops up and you realise there's something on the go. Some unexplained troop movements. A supply run to an armaments stash which you know is unscheduled. The promotion of a major to a theatre where they already have more majors than they know what to do with. Then you know you're making a contribution, keeping democracy safe for the West, or some bullshit like that.'

'Was Frank as cynical as you?'

Last opened his mouth to speak, then checked himself and looked out of his conservatory window. The sun had risen higher in the sky and the lawn was an unnaturally bright green, as though luminous paint had been tipped over it.

He turned back to me.

'Frank loved the Blues, you know. All the old singers, Ma Rainey, Blind Blake, names you've never heard of. When we were back in London he'd go off hunting for old 78s and even wax cylinders of the really early stuff, if he could find them. Went to auctions and antique shops whenever he could. He was so enamoured with the music he used to play games with me, like trying to have a conversation when his half of it was entirely Blues song titles.'

'He's taken it up again.'

'Really? You poor sucker. But he used to tell me it wasn't sad music, like you might think if you know nothing about it—it was a music of hope, of looking forward to a better life, somewhere. I can't square that with being cynical.'

'You sure he didn't just have a sentimental streak?'

'Maybe. I wouldn't say he showed it much, particularly at work. He did maths at Oxford, you know, and was an excellent chess player, so he was always looking several moves ahead. I think for him, most of what we learned from analysing traffic was just … obvious. Kind of, "Well, they would do that, wouldn't they?" I don't think he was ever really surprised because he always saw it coming. I don't know if that's cynicism or realism. But it made him a first-rate analyst because he was as devious a bastard as the people we were listening to.'

Although I'd refused a drink earlier, a woman I took to be Last's wife appeared in the doorway with a tray of tea and biscuits. Last motioned her to come in. She was a slim woman with carefully-coiffed greying hair and eyes that never quite met your own. She carried an aura of sadness with her as heavy as the tea-tray.

'Kate, this is Mr Dyke. Doing some work for Shoemakers.'

I stood up ready to shake her hand, but she wiped her

palms on her pinafore and then held them up to show me.

She said, 'Sticky,' gave a wan smile and left the conservatory.

When she was out of earshot Last said, 'She hates me having anything to do with the old times. She didn't know the half of what I did, but she thought I was in constant danger from fucking Communist assassins. She doesn't mean to be rude.'

'No offence taken.'

'Look, there's something else you need to know about Frank Wallace. Never mind all this stuff about him avenging Kelvin Shoemaker and the rotten state of his fucking company.'

I put a sugar lump in my tea. 'Go on.'

'He was good at the analysis bit of the job—came like second nature to him. But the only thing he liked more than the Blues was getting his hands dirty.'

'In what way?'

Last leaned forward in his chair, his eyes gleaming.

'Back in the day it was all more rough and ready than now. We used to plant bugs ourselves, find ways into embassies, or buildings next to embassies, drill holes, hang fake pictures with cameras in, all that kind of shit. Your basic bugging. And Frank loved it. He loved all the trade-craft, all the official palaver about dead-drops and passwords and so on, but he liked the unofficial stuff, too … the stuff that was unacknowledged. Making hidey-holes in suitcases for bugs, picking locks, inventing ways of getting intelligence that hadn't been thought of before. He'd always used his brain and then he found he was very good with his hands. Did you know he put in the safe in Kelvin's office? Kelvin wouldn't trust anyone else to do it.'

Last was staring at me now and I wondered whether he

was trying to tell me something about Wallace that he couldn't say outright.

He smiled to himself and went on. 'I lost count of the number of buildings we broke into in town. Not just the embassies, but places where they'd hold meetings because they thought the fucking embassy was bugged—which it usually was. Safe houses. Hotels. Empty office blocks and so on.'

'You make it sound like fun. What would have happened if you'd been caught?'

'A quiet word would have been had with a senior police officer in a club somewhere and all charges dropped.'

'All very cosy. Fun and games.'

Last frowned and sat back again. I thought I'd pressed a button.

'Most people don't understand what's going on in the world, Mr Dyke. The newspapers and media spread happy-clappy bullshit while hiding their own complicity in maintaining the status quo. You're from Yorkshire, aren't you?'

I nodded.

'Things have been tough up there since Thatcher closed the mines and told the miners to piss off. I'd expect you to have a sense of reality about who rules the country and what they trick the rest of us to do to keep them in power.'

'I do, and I don't like it any more than you. But looking around here you seem to have done all right out of maintaining the status quo. I haven't seen any copies of *Marxism Today* lying around.'

'And you won't. I've had enough of isms to last me a lifetime, left and right and down the fucking middle. I won't apologise for the life I lead here. I've earned it through hard work, not through complying with an ideology.'

We paused and stared at each other. I thought we'd come to an understanding, even though we hadn't said it aloud. But then I might have been mistaken.

Last sighed. 'Look, I think what I'm trying to say is Frank was corrupted by his time in MI6. He lost sight of the big picture and got caught up in his own version of paranoia. By the time he joined Kelvin Shoemaker he'd begun to see conspiracies everywhere. It was no surprise to anyone that he took against Jocasta personally. After all, Kelvin had been his best mate. But as far as I know he didn't have any objections to what she was doing with the company. It wasn't as if she was doing it by herself—Kelvin had actually started down that line already, tapping up his government contacts, telling us to get onside with our former SIS colleagues. She just carried on in the same vein and put more energy into it than he did. We didn't know it, but his health was probably in decline well before he actually died.'

'How did he die?'

'Bit of a blur, that. Apparently he'd not been feeling well for a month and went in for tests. He never came out. A shock to all of us.'

'Anybody looked at? You know, being in the secret world and all? Any poisoned umbrellas?'

'I don't think so. Jocasta took charge of his health and was the one who sent us bulletins about his progress. When he died there was a curt email sent to the whole company and then we didn't see her for a month. So it was all hush-hush. There wasn't any investigation as far as I know. I seem to remember an undiagnosed heart condition was the line.' He paused, thinking, his eyes distant. 'My point about Frank is that whatever he's up to now, it'll be driven by conviction. It may be misguided, but I don't think he's crazy. There'll still be a rational part of him beavering away inside there.'

I nodded to the garden again.

'Was there ever a chance of him retiring to this kind of life?'

'What, Frank? Maybe, if Helen hadn't left him. That hit him hard. She left him with Emily to look after, too, just a baby.'

'How long had they been married?'

'About five years. I think they reckoned having the baby would keep them together but it did the opposite. She dropped the kid and six months later fucked off. We never knew where she went. Then a few years ago we learned she'd died. Single. Poor woman. Frank wasn't easy to live with.'

'Did he ever try to find her?'

'Not as far as I'm aware. Once she'd gone I think he wanted shot of her. He doesn't like losing at anything, so he didn't want her in the background reminding him of his failed marriage.'

He stood up and I knew the meeting was finished. He edged around the low glass-topped table and walked me to the front door.

'I liked old Frank. We worked together for a long time and when we retired we just cut each other dead. I haven't heard from him from that day to this. Still, if you need anything else, give me a call. I hope you find him in good working order. I don't like to think of him getting hurt, whatever he's up to.'

I walked away from the house and into the suburban street. It was sunny and tranquil and quintessentially English. Frank Wallace could have been a next-door neighbour to Greg Last if he'd wanted, could have led a cosy retirement and put the world of conspiracies and spying behind him. So why didn't he? Was he really that concerned

about his legacy at Shoemakers?
Or was there something else?

CHAPTER THIRTEEN

I WAS SITTING on the train watching London thicken around me when my mobile phone rang. I was in the quiet carriage so I let it ring but saw the caller was Emily Wallace.

As soon as I arrived at Euston Square I walked outside and rang her back.

She said, 'I've had another call from Dad. This morning, when I was at work.' Her voice sounded uncertain, as if she might burst into tears again.

'What did he say?'

'He was cagey. Wouldn't tell me where he was. Said he was all right, and what he was doing was for me.'

'What do you think that means?'

'I haven't a clue. He didn't explain anything. Just wanted me to know he was all right.'

'And what about you?'

'What about me?'

'Are you all right?'

She burst into surprised laughter. 'The patient is doing as well as can be expected. Truth be told, I'm a bit wobbly. Dad's all I've got. I don't like to think of him going off the rails.'

I didn't know what to say to that because I couldn't offer any solace.

I said, 'Where are you?'

'Still at work.'

'Next time he calls, ask him to meet you. Then call me.'

'He won't fall for that. He already knows you and I have talked. He'll suspect something.'

There'd been a change in her voice, as though she'd remembered something that had drained her energy.

I said, 'What is it? What's the matter?'

She sighed. 'I might be making this up, but he sounded fatalistic. As though nothing could change what he's going to do.'

'And he didn't give any clues what that might be?'

'Of course not. He's far too sharp for that. So, are you still trying to find him? Did you manage to trace that number?'

I didn't want to tell her about finding the page of burnt chemical formulae, even though it seemed harmless, so I said we were still working on it.

She said, 'Oh. And where are *you* now?'

'Outside Euston Square tube.'

'So you think he's down here?'

'Not necessarily. I've been to see Shoemakers again and they've put me in touch with someone who knew your dad.'

'That'll be Greg Last, I bet. They loved him, the tame little pet.'

'He and your dad worked together. They seemed to have liked each other.'

'Dad tolerated him. Wasn't really the sharpest knife in the drawer, he used to say. But he could play the corporate game. Deal with the clients, wear a nice suit.'

'He was very complimentary about your dad. Didn't want him to get hurt.'

She was quiet for a moment.

'Yes, sorry. I never met him so I shouldn't throw stones. Just find my dad, will you?'

'I will. No one can escape me. I'm resolute and determined.'

She laughed grimly, then said, 'Incidentally, did you see today's *Guardian*?'

'Too busy to read.'

'Get it. Might help you understand why Jocasta Shoemaker will seem a bit pissed off next time you meet her.'

I STEPPED BACK inside the station and bought *The Guardian* from a stall. There was nothing on the front page, but on page four there was a picture of Jocasta Shoemaker leaving a charity event, looking glamorous in a plunging-necked black dress and long silver ear-rings.

The headline was less frivolous: *Shoemaker in IS deal*.

The story was that Shoemaker Systems was on the verge of signing a major deal with both the UK and US Intelligence Services to provide consultancy across a range of security issues. There were no other details and all three parties involved had provided No Comments when asked. The journalist suggested that this was a step up for Shoemaker, as previously they'd been best known for offering security and intelligence services primarily to multi-national businesses. It was part of a growing trend, the journalist said, for national governments to outsource their core operations, leading many commentators to believe that the boundary between government and private intelligence gathering was becoming porous. As Snowden had demonstrated, individuals' personal information was already the playground of the NSA and GCHQ—involving commercial companies in its harvesting and dissemination could only lead to more intrusion into privacy and with potentially fewer safeguards in place.

I looked at the journalist's name: Tristan James, security correspondent. Behind his bland journalistic prose I could hear Frank Wallace's bitter anger.

He'd begun his campaign.

HAVING A SUDDEN burst of fame can sometimes be useful when you want to speak to people. From my room in the Hotel Russell I phoned *The Guardian* and asked whether I could talk to Tristan James. I could have tweeted him using a link given at the end of the article but that felt too weird.

I said to the receptionist, 'Tell him it's Sam Dyke. He might remember me in relation to the Stratford Greif affair a few months ago.'

He did remember me and was happy to talk to me, though not on the phone.

'Can never be too careful. Don't know who's listening in.'

He sounded young and intense, but then everyone was starting to sound young to me. We agreed to meet in a pub he knew on the Tottenham Court Road.

Before he hung up he said, 'What's it about? You got more info on the Greifs? That was some stunt they were going to pull off. Did you really chase him down the platform at Piccadilly?'

'That's over, Tristan. This is about Frank Wallace.'

Before he could say anything I closed the connection. That would teach him.

I called Ann at Shoemakers and she told me that Jocasta really *was* too busy to talk to me right now, but that I could try later. I suppose her being busy was connected with the *Guardian* article. I told her I'd like to speak to Mrs Shoemaker in person the next day and could she squeeze me in? She could.

At that point I didn't want to talk to anyone else for a while, so I laid back on my spongy bed and read through the rest of *The Guardian* until it was a decent hour to eat, then went down to the immense, clattering restaurant of the hotel and had a rather nice escalope of pork in a mustard sauce. No one spoke to me except the waiter and I kept people at bay by staring into space meaningfully and glancing at my watch as though I was expecting company.

I'd finished eating by seven fifteen and went back to my room to brush my teeth and pick up my phone, which I'd put on charge. By seven forty-five I was on another tube train. The rush was ending now but there were still dozens of passengers in each carriage. I wondered whether I'd even recognise Frank Wallace if I caught a glimpse of him behind a newspaper, or watching me surreptitiously from above a laptop screen, wearing a trilby instead of his flat cap, carrying a briefcase instead of a walking cane.

But I did recognise Tristan James from the small photo next to his article in the newspaper. He sat with his back to the wall in a dark corner of the pub, which was full of young people with braying voices and fashionable clothes. I sat opposite him. Up close I could tell he was in his mid-thirties, though he seemed younger. He had curly blond hair and smooth skin and didn't look as though he'd been closer to the Middle East or Afghanistan than a two-week holiday in Tuscany.

I said, 'Get you a drink?'

He gestured towards the glass in front of him on the table; it contained a mix of colourful chemicals passing themselves off as alcohol.

He said, 'Half-price cocktails till eight. I'm good.'

As it was now close to eight-thirty I knew I wasn't in the presence of a big drinker—though one foresightful enough to arrive early for our appointment just to get a cheap drink.

I said, 'Good article in the paper today. Can I ask how you found out about the contracts?'

He raised his eyebrows slightly and reached for his drink. His hand was steady—I hadn't scared him in the slightest.

'Well that's a question you know I can't answer.'

'Ah, protecting your "source". Who we both know was Frank Wallace.'

'If you say so. I can't possibly comment.' He put down his drink and glanced around at the people in the pub. 'What's your interest in this anyway? We looked at you for a profile after that thing in Piccadilly, something in the magazine—Day in the Life or similar. In the end we thought you might be too boring. Or too macho. We'd have half the women columnists on our back for encouraging masculine ideals or something. The other half would be wanting to sleep with you.'

'That's my curse—too male for my own good.'

He grinned and suddenly looked older. Crows' feet appeared at the corners of his eyes and the skin crinkled on his cheeks.

He said, 'Look, you tell me why you're interested in this Shoemaker story and I'll see what I can tell you. You mentioned Frank Wallace on the phone. Who's he?'

'Seriously?'

'I couldn't find him in our database. And Google wasn't my friend this time. Without those two on my side I'm stumped. Modern journalism, eh?'

I hesitated. I didn't want to put Wallace's name out into the media-sphere just yet. I still had a sneaking attachment to him and a residual antipathy towards Jocasta Shoemaker and her company. And he was still my client, sort of, though I supposed I'd done what he'd actually paid me to do—tell Jocasta he was seeking revenge. Maybe our contract was fulfilled.

And there was Emily to consider, too. The last time we'd spoken, just a few hours before, there'd been a warmth in her voice by the time the conversation had ended. I remembered her standing in my office doorway, pert and blonde, looking over-exaggerated in her white puffed-out parka, and it was an image that made me smile and feel good towards her.

I said to James, 'Forget Frank Wallace. That was a shot in the dark. I'm interested in the story because Shoemakers have asked me to help them out with some consultancy.'

He laughed. 'One of the biggest security companies in the world needs help from you? I don't want to sound rude, but you realise how ludicrous that sounds?'

I shrugged. 'It's something happening in my neck of the woods, north of Watford. What can I tell you? They don't have an office in Crewe.'

He was shaking his head. 'You country folk with your country ways. You think I was born yesterday? Sorry, lazy cliché. So you're doing what, due diligence on Shoemakers to see if you want to do business with them? Checking out their pipeline of work? Then you just happen to be in London when this story breaks and want to talk to me to see if I know any more … You haven't thought this through, Sam. I've been fed garbage by people much more subtle than you. People trying to plant a story so that they can deny it later and look good to their boss. People trying to flatter me to find out what I know and whether I should know it. Basic political shit. You've got all the subtlety of a ten-ton mallet.'

He was right. I'd taken him too lightly, persuaded by his

youthfulness that he didn't know his job.

'All right, I'll tell you something so long as you don't use it. Not yet, anyway.'

He looked at me warily. 'Go for it.'

'Shoemakers have been threatened. An ex-employee says he's going to spill the beans on all of their dealings, everything they've been involved in.'

'Why would he do that?'

'Revenge on Jocasta Shoemaker for imagined slights.'

'Shoemakers are in the public eye. Most of their dealings are recorded somewhere. You have to dig to get at them, but they're there. So there's not much to expose. Where's the threat?'

'No company likes its dirty linen hung out to dry in Fleet Street, especially when their profession is secrecy and they're about to sign huge multi-million pound contracts. Which reminds me, how did you find out?'

He looked at me steadily. 'Okay, I'll play. The contracts? There's been rumours for a while but no one was saying anything. As you say, secrecy carries a premium, especially these days. Then I got an anonymous email with a bunch of attachments, documents containing minutes of meetings, agendas, heads of agreement. I say the email was anonymous, but actually the sender used the email address of my boss. Very clever.'

'The documents you received—they could have been forged.'

'I looked into them, as much as I could. Looked at the agendas, persons present, then checked them against the known whereabouts of the people named. Were they in London or abroad on government business? And so on. It was all kosher. Then I tried to get a quote from Jocasta Shoemaker and wound up talking to this dick called Gale, who told me to fuck off. That's when I knew we had something. How could we ignore it? We had to publish. It's news, though not exactly earth-shattering.'

'Do people care now about government and security companies being in bed with each other? Don't they expect it?'

'Maybe some do. Not all. Our click-through rate tells us people are still interested. They care about what their government is doing. This kind of thing … it's all leading to more privatisation of government functions, more commercialisation of what should be owned and run by the state.'

'Ah, yes, I was forgetting you work for *The Guardian.*'

'Sod off. That's irrelevant. Snowden was right—it's about democracy and what it means. It's nothing to do with left-wing attempts to undermine legitimate government.'

'So these revelations today—what impact do you think they'll have on Shoemakers? Will the contracts go ahead?'

'Of course they will. This is a brief embarrassment to them, but only in terms of the timing. It would all have been made public eventually, but only when all the parties wanted it. We've looked up their skirts before they'd put their knickers on. They'll cover up soon enough.'

'Unless there's another email and more attachments with more revelations.'

'Indeed. I can live in hope.' He took a sip from his cocktail and pulled a face at it. 'Christ, that's sweet. Look, I seem to have given you more than you've given me. Care to redress the balance?'

'What do you know about The Sophocles Trust?'

'Hmm, the suspect answers a question with another question. A clever gambit. The Sophocles Trust was founded by Jocasta Shoemaker. Do you get it? Jocasta was the name of Oedipus' mother in Oedipus Rex, by Sophocles. I guess she couldn't resist the idea.'

'What does the Trust do?'

Tristan James looked at his watch.

'It's getting late and I have miles to go before I sleep. I'll tell you this much—do you remember Atlantic Bridge? Big news story that blew up in the early noughties.'

I remembered something about it. A government cabinet member had allowed a friend to run a so-called charity from his Parliamentary office. The charity was called Atlantic Bridge and was essentially a club for rich right-wingers to get together with like-minded politicians and decry the state of the world. Influence was peddled, jobs handed out along with funding. It fell apart when the press got hold of the fact that the charity was being run from inside Parliament.

'You're telling me The Sophocles Trust is similar to Atlantic Bridge?'

'I'd never accuse Jocasta Shoemaker of having an original thought.'

'So she does what—hosts it? Funds it? Makes fairy cakes for the rich folk to eat?'

'All of the above. And it's all perfectly legal. It just … smells funny, don't you think? You'd have to wonder whether these major contracts shortly to be signed with the Intelligence Services of two major Western powers have come about because of the schmoozing undertaken under the aegis of The Sophocles Trust.'

'I can tell you're a journalist.'

He was standing up to go. 'How's that?'

'You're the only person I've ever heard use the word aegis in conversation.'

He grinned and shrugged. 'My curse—literacy.'

I stood up and shook his hand.

'This work you do, security correspondent … do you ever feel—how can I put it—endangered? As if someone might be following you?'

'If I were really tough I'd say yeah, it goes with the territory or some such macho bullshit. But to be honest, no. Most of what I do happens here, in London, sometimes in Washington. But we've got stringers in all the dangerous places. So I get to sleep at night.' He looked at me oddly. 'Why? Do you think you're being followed?'

I looked past him, into the darkness of the pub.

'I don't think so. I know so.'

CHAPTER FOURTEEN

I'D SWEAR ONE of the Robo-Receptionists at Shoemakers gave a flicker of recognition, maybe even a smile, as she printed out my pass. But I limited myself to a 'Thanks' as I took it from her. I didn't want to excite her too much.

This time Ann wasn't waiting for me as the lift doors opened but I knew the routine and went along the corridor and sat in my usual chair until Jocasta came out and summoned me.

Inside her office there was another woman, who Jocasta introduced as Heather from PR. She was in her late thirties and was wearing a serious face, as though the revelations in the newspaper the previous day had led to the loss of thousands of lives and worldwide catastrophe. I guessed it was her role to spin the news or limit its spread in some way.

Gale stood by the window, looking over his domain. He didn't acknowledge my entrance.

Jocasta said, 'You saw what happened yesterday? The article?'

I nodded.

'Do you think it was Frank?'

'I'd be stupid to think otherwise. The question is, how

did he get hold of the documents?'

Jocasta turned to Heather, who had a leather-bound portfolio that she was protecting by holding it to her chest with folded arms. She said, 'The documents were filed on one of our servers. He must have had a password to get into it.'

'There was no other way?'

'I suppose he could have hacked it, but as you can imagine, our own cyber-protection is extremely strong.'

Still at the window, Gale said, 'The passwords were changed yesterday afternoon.'

'I hope you've flogged the offending clerk.'

He looked at me. 'He was hanged this morning at eight o'clock. To encourage the others.'

Jocasta said to Heather, who had been glancing nervously from Gale to me and back again, 'Send out the press release. I'm still not available for comment.'

'If the MOD calls … ?'

'I'll speak to Terry Bennett but no one else. He's onside with this. Tell everyone else I'm in meetings. If there's one thing the government understands, it's meetings.'

Heather nodded and gave me a half-smile as she left. The door closed silently behind her.

I said, 'Will it cause a lot of damage?'

She snorted. 'What do you think? We market ourselves as a security company that two national governments can trust and we can't even keep our own secrets, never mind anyone else's.'

Gale walked towards us and sat down on one of the leather sofas. I began to wonder whether he ever left this room. He said, 'It'll blow over. We've already primed a bunch of people about the signing—they'll just be pissed off that they weren't first with the news. They'll assume someone else broke the embargo.'

'I take it *The Guardian* wasn't one of the sources you told.'

'Too right. Let them do their own grubbing. They probably think there's another Pulitzer on the way if they keep digging, but they've got another thing coming.'

Jocasta took a seat opposite Gale and leaned back, staring at the ceiling. She was looking older, her strong Greek features becoming more defined and sculpted, like a statue exposed to a sharpening wind.

She said, 'Why are you certain it was Frank's doing?'

'Because I spoke to the journalist who wrote the story.'

Her eyes snapped to me.

'What did he say?'

'He had an email ostensibly from his boss containing all the documents—the minutes, the contracts and so on. But he didn't know Frank's name.'

'Or said he didn't.'

'I believed him. I sprang the name on him early and he didn't blink. Told me he ran a search on the name on the office system and found no record.'

Gale said, 'And you're such a good judge of people, as your engagement with Frank Wallace showed.'

'Will you boys stop comparing your dicks? John, what do you want to do?'

'We still don't know for sure it was Wallace who accessed the records. I can't believe that the passwords weren't changed between him retiring and yesterday, which means that someone else gave him the information, or he hacked us. Where we stand now, what harm has it done? A bit of early publicity. Could have done with a nicer spin on it, but that's *The Guardian* for you. Any opportunity to stick in the knife.'

'So you think we shouldn't do anything other than send

out the press release? Let it all calm down?'

'Hey, I'm internal security, not public relations. I don't even know why I'm in this meeting, except to annoy Dyke.'

Jocasta frowned. 'Okay, you're here because you're the only other person who knows what Mr Dyke has been telling us. If there's any connection between yesterday's article and Frank Wallace, we need to know. It's my job to deal with the rest of the directors. ' She turned to me. 'What do you think we should do?'

'First, don't ignore Wallace. Give him something, let him know you're taking him seriously.'

'Easier to say than to do. We can't get in touch with him even if we wanted.'

'He'll call me again. He'll want to know what we're thinking.'

'And you'll tell him?'

'As much as I have to.'

'And what *are* we thinking?'

'That it's hard to take him seriously if he's pointing a gun at our heads. Metaphorically. He has to stop leaking information, then maybe we can come to some arrangement.'

She looked at Gale. 'What do you think?'

'He said first—what's second?'

'I'll talk to Emily, his daughter. Find out whether he was good enough with computers to hack your system, or whether he had a password or a back door in.'

'And that helps how?'

'At least we'll know whether there's someone inside taking the opportunity to give out information, or whether it's actually Frank keeping his promise to dish what dirt he knows.'

She rubbed her hands on her thighs, then turned them

over and looked at her palms as if there might be a clue on them.

She said, 'I won't let this get to me. Kelvin wouldn't get stressed and neither will I.' She turned and looked intently into my eyes. 'How did we get here? Two weeks ago I was on the verge of the biggest deal of my life. Now I'm haggling with a pensioner with a grudge. Do you honestly think I've done something to deserve this?'

'Life's a bitch.'

'I know what you're thinking—a business deal means nothing compared to the sense of loss and desolation that someone like Wallace is probably feeling. The reputation of his friend and the legacy of his work are being abandoned for a quick buck. I should just suck it up and we'll muddle through and he'll be forgotten as soon as the contracts are signed.'

'Never occurred to me.'

'Have you ever thought about the hundreds of people who work for me? All of them depending on me and my colleagues to make the deals that guarantee them a job? If you want to talk about stress, there it is.'

'And you take on these burdens for free. No remuneration involved, no pension, no social advancement.'

Gale said to her, 'He's from the socialist north. You won't get any sympathy from him.'

'I don't want fucking sympathy, John. It would just be nice if someone saw it from my perspective for a change.' She stood up and smoothed down the front of her dress. 'Don't worry, I'm not going to cry. I'm not that much of a girl.'

I said, 'You wouldn't be running this place if you let your emotions get in the way, would you?'

'What does that mean?'

I shrugged. 'What I said.'

She stared at me but I kept my face expressionless and eventually she moved towards her desk. She leaned over and pressed an intercom button.

'Ann, bring the keys to Singapore House, will you?'

Then she stood up and came around her desk towards me.

'You haven't said anything about Greg Last. How did you find him?'

'Exactly as I expected. Stood up for Frank.'

'Really? I'm not sure Frank would have done the same for him.'

'But from what I told him, he thinks Wallace is up to something. He agrees with you that Frank didn't mind when you changed the company's strategy—but he implied he liked a game of chess.'

'What the hell does that mean?'

'I don't know. Except that in chess you try to persuade the opponent you're doing one thing when in fact you're doing another.'

Gale had remained on his sofa during all this. Now he stood up and pulled down his tunic by gripping it from the waist. I was surprised he hadn't had 'SS'—for Shoemaker Systems—embroidered on his shoulders. He said, 'So you reckon he's bluffing? All this stuff about telling our secrets is just a blind to confuse us?'

'Maybe.'

'In that case, you're suggesting the leak of information to the newspapers came from inside the company.'

'Uh-oh. That leaves you in the shit, doesn't it?'

His face darkened, but before he could say anything there was a knock on the door and Ann came in with an envelope. She crossed the floor without looking at Gale or me and handed the envelope to Jocasta. Then she turned and left.

Jocasta held the envelope out to me.

'You won't go on the payroll, but the least you can do is use the company flat. It's out past the Elephant and Castle, Singapore House. There are two keys in here—one for the outside door, one for number 60, the penthouse. The fridge should be stocked. There's wifi, the code is on a piece of paper inside this.'

Gale said, 'Don't leave the toilet in a mess.'

I took the envelope from her and pushed it inside my jacket pocket.

'I hope you don't think you're buying me off.'

'I wouldn't buy you off, Mr Dyke. If it came to that, I'd buy you *out*.'

'You haven't said what you'd like me to tell Frank if he calls.'

'Tell him nothing. I won't be blackmailed. If he agrees to stop leaking information maybe we'll talk. Maybe.'

'I don't think he'll be happy with that.'

'And I don't think I care. He's one man. We're a large organisation that's about to get even bigger. I know mice can frighten elephants but I'm not an elephant. I've got bigger balls.'

CHAPTER FIFTEEN

I HAD A FANCY sandwich from Prêt-à-Manger then went back to the Hotel Russell and checked out. The receptionist looked a bit startled by the sight of Frank's bank notes but recovered well and gave me a nice smile along with my receipt.

I headed north on foot again and, walking along from Euston station, and using more of Frank's money, I found a store where I bought underwear, socks and another couple of shirts. I could last a few more days with these basic supplies and you were never short of eating places in London.

Next I made my way to the Elephant and Castle via the Underground and, after a bit of walking around and looking upwards at various buildings, found Singapore House, which appeared to be a converted bottle factory. Looking up I saw that the original windows of each floor had been enlarged and expanded outwards so the building looked as if it was wearing a huge glass visor. The place had been redeveloped with an expensive clientele in mind.

I didn't need to use the key because there was a security man on duty and the glass entrance door was open. He gave me a considered look as I crossed the grey carpet towards the lifts but I had the door key in my hand and that must have been good enough to satisfy him.

When I opened the door to Apartment 60 it stretched out before me like the passenger hall of a fair-sized airport. I entered on to a slightly raised dais, with doors to the right that when I checked led to a huge bedroom and a sparkling bathroom appointed with Villeroy and Boch fittings.

Stepping down from the dais I entered a living room bigger than the floor-plan of my house, with an open entrance to a separate kitchen to the left. There were wooden floors throughout, polished to a honeyed glow. The wall of the living room featured the windows I'd seen from the ground, now giving a magnificent view west towards Westminster, the tower of Big Ben prominent above the Houses of Parliament, and north towards London Bridge, the whole picture framed by the three full-length windows in a kind of triptych.

On the far wall there was a fifty inch television with a surround-sound bar suspended beneath it. You watched it by sitting in one of three long sofas, preferably with your pinot noir perched on the square glass coffee table that squatted between them. Next to the kitchen was a door that led to stairs going up. I dropped my Head sports bag to the floor, where it lay on the gleaming boards like a gigantic slug, then mounted the stairs and found myself on a roof-top terrace that was twenty metres on each side. A long table surrounded by six all-weather chairs sat in the middle. I walked to the railing and looked across the city and listened to its muffled sound. I almost felt like a native.

Downstairs once more I crossed to the windows again. I was getting used to extraordinary views of London but not to the level of wealth they represented. Shoemaker's cash had bought this place. They'd taken it gratefully from a series of paranoid businessmen who wanted their secrets guarded or their enemies spied upon. I wasn't sure where I fitted into this life. Or whether I did. I'd been born in a terraced house in a small village in Yorkshire, son of a miner whose living was taken from him before I was out of short pants. These surroundings, this view, this level of privilege made me feel uncomfortable, as though I knew at the level of blood and bones that I didn't belong, that I would never belong.

And I hated myself for knowing that.

I turned away and took my bag into the bathroom, where I unpacked my toothbrush, toothpaste, razor and shaving foam. I also had a nice little wrapped soap that I'd stolen from the Hotel Russell.

In the bedroom I took out my new underwear, socks and shirts and placed them neatly in an empty chest of drawers whose drawers slid silently closed as if unwilling to disturb me.

By now it was the middle of the afternoon and I guessed that Emily Wallace would be back at work, assuming she'd taken a lunch break. I had no idea where she worked or what she did but imagined it was in the corporate sphere—there was something controlled and disciplined in her, something amenable to rules and regulations, that suggested a job in a creative industry or even the sciences wouldn't fit.

I wasn't sure what I was about to say because essentially I was going to use her to get to her father. And that made me feel uneasy.

She answered on the second ring.

'Mr Dyke. Can we make it quick? Got a rush job on.'

'Okay, short and sweet—can I see you tonight?'

There was the briefest of pauses.

'Oh, caught me by surprise there … I suppose so. Is it about Dad?'

'In the main.'

'That sounds ominous.'

'I'd like to see you face-to-face and as we're both in town it seems crazy not to.'

'So you're taking me to dinner?'

'I guess I am.'

'Meet me at Angelo's on Baker Street. I'll book a table if you like. Will you take a cab?'

'Tube.'

'Get out at Baker Street and walk south, past Nandos. You won't miss it. Eight o'clock?'

'I'm there.'

We hung up at the same time and I wondered why it felt like I'd just made a date with my client.

BY EIGHT O'CLOCK Angelo's was busy but when I went through the door I saw Emily Wallace immediately. She was wearing a purple blouse which showed off her blonde hair to good effect, and she was waving a curled hand towards me. As I came closer I realised that she was better looking than I'd remembered, and I'd remembered her as being very pretty. Now she was bordering on beautiful. When had that happened?

She said, 'You're two minutes late. I was beginning to think I'd been stood up.'

'I wouldn't do that. Not without a good excuse.'

'Like what?'

'Oh, *The Maltese Falcon* on TV. Leeds playing in the cup final.'

'I like a man with priorities.'

A man came and left menus the size of barn doors and

Emily and I discussed the relative merits of different shapes of pasta. Then the man came back and we ordered our pasta shapes and associated tomato sauces and a bottle of average-priced wine which would have bought me three bottles of good wine in Bargain Booze in Crewe.

When the wine came and I'd tasted it and murmured approval, she said, 'Any more news of Dad?'

'Nothing official, no.'

'What does that mean?'

'The article in the paper yesterday—I'm pretty sure it was Frank who passed over the documents.'

She looked glumly into her wine glass.

'I thought so too. How do you think he got hold of them?'

'There are two theories: one, he's still got a password to get into the system; or two, there's someone in the company who sent them.'

'If it's someone in the company, couldn't they have sent them direct to *The Guardian*? They wouldn't need to send them to Dad first.'

'Good point. But it's not likely we've got two disaffected people trying to get Shoemakers in trouble. My guess is Frank's still got a password or a way to get into the server. How was he with computers? Would he have been able to hack in?'

'No, but I would.'

SHE LEANED FORWARD over the table, her blouse opening slightly at the top to reveal a gold chain. I smelled a floral scent that hinted at the Caribbean.

She said quietly, 'You never asked what I do for a living.'

'I see that was a mistake. I'll have to go back to detective school.'

'I develop web-sites, or at least the back ends. Databases

and so forth. But I've got shall we say a wider skill-set. I'm not suggesting I could have got through their security, being who they are, but it's the kind of thing I'd have had a go at. Dad was okay with ordinary applications — Microsoft Office and so forth — but hacking is beyond him.'

'So did you?'

'Did I what?'

'Hack into Shoemaker's servers.'

She recoiled. But then a smile crept over her face.

'That would be a wrinkle, wouldn't it? You go hunting down my dad when all the time it was little ole me you should have been tracking.'

'At least that would be more fun.'

Any reply she might have made was interrupted by the arrival of our starters: something involving small sea creatures for her, a brick of paté and two matchsticks of thin toast for me.

When we'd finished and the remains had been taken away, she poured herself another glass of wine and sat back to nurse it.

She said, 'You're quite glamorous, aren't you?'

'In a rough-and-ready, northern way?'

'I Googled you when I got back from Buxton. All that press coverage you've had in the last few months. Must be good for the investigation business, but you still have that poky little office in Crewe. Not even a sexy secretary to flirt with.'

'I don't need a secretary when I can flirt with clients.'

She raised her eyebrows and took a sip from her glass. I found myself paying attention to the way her mouth pursed to take in the wine, then the rapid flick of her pink tongue across her lips to ensure she'd got every last drop.

She caught me looking.

'Have I spilled?'

'No, I was just admiring your technique.'

'Not as much as I've been admiring yours.'

Thankfully the main courses arrived then and we could return to discussing our pasta shapes.

Dessert was ice cream, of course, and then strong Italian coffee to finish. I fished out more of her father's money to pay the waiter.

She had a coat in the cloakroom and I helped her put it on, my hands lightly brushing her shoulders. It was the most physical we'd got all evening and it nearly took my breath away with its sensuality.

Outside the air was fresh but not cold, spring still holding out against approaching summer but not putting up much of a fight. And it was always warmer in London—all that pent-up energy soaked into the stones of the buildings releasing itself at night like a child's warm breath.

Emily was standing with her feet together, as if at attention, one hand holding the top of her coat together, the other holding her bag at her side. Her eyes glittered in the restaurant's lights.

She said, 'That was a nice evening. Weird, but nice.'

'I'm better at weird than nice. We didn't talk much about your father. I should have pumped you for information.'

'Oh, I think you pumped me for the information you wanted, Sam.' She pointed down the street. 'I'm this way. You needn't come, you're in the opposite direction.'

I held out my hand to shake. She took it then quickly leaned up and pecked me on the cheek.

'Take care. Call me when you hear anything.'

Then she turned on her heels and clicked down the pavement, towards the river. I watched her blonde hair bobbing for a while and then she was swallowed up by the swarms of pedestrians who were still walking the streets.

I thought about what had happened and wondered why I was having strong feelings for someone I barely knew. There was some kind of magic being worked but I didn't mind. It was good to have strong feelings again instead of the careful rationing of emotion I generally used to steer myself through life.

Back in the apartment at Singapore House I poured myself another coffee and turned out the lights so I could look west towards the seat of government, lit up like a carnival attraction. I wondered whether Frank Wallace was out there somewhere, watching me, plotting and planning, seeing the game ten moves ahead. Apart from giving the documents to Tristan James, he'd been quiet for a while. That suggested to me he was getting his plans in order, working out his next steps, making his preparations. And I had no idea what they might be.

The view from the window was still breathtaking at night. I'd read articles where people had said that the profile of London had changed rapidly in the last ten years. It was true. I looked over a London I'd never seen before - its history both ancient and modern written into its skyline. I felt very small and, for a moment, powerless. Frank Wallace wasn't going to blow up the Houses of Parliament or set the London Eye loose from its moorings. But he might be on track to hurt people and ruin their lives, and I felt I should do what I could to prevent that from happening.

CHAPTER SIXTEEN

SATURDAY MORNING WAS as bright as the previous day, so I went downstairs and hunted around for somewhere I could have breakfast. I didn't fancy the muesli and honey stocked in the apartment's capacious kitchen cabinets.

I found the perfect place amongst the Costcutters and charity shops on Tower Bridge Road, and had settled down at my Formica-topped table with a bacon sandwich and a stiff coffee when a thick-set man took the facing chair. He placed his elbows on the table and folded his arms on it. He looked to be in his forties and had a soft-featured face and short dark hair fringed with white over the ears.

I bit into my sandwich and stared him in the eye. No one comes between me and my bacon.

He said, 'Smells good. Better than that poncy stuff in Angelo's last night.'

'I don't know, I quite liked the ice cream. There's not much you can do to ruin ice cream.'

He nodded, watching me eat.

He said, 'Sometimes you have to be a bit careful, don't you, about what you bite off. You never can tell whether it's going to upset you later on.'

'I've got a very strong stomach. Nothing much upsets it.'

'There's always a first time, isn't there?'

He leaned back, taking his arms with him. He didn't seem to know what to do with them, so just laid them in his lap.

I said, 'MI5? MI6? Tax office?'

He grinned. 'Like I said before, I heard you like a laugh. Probably makes you feel a cut above the rest of us.'

That's when I placed his voice—the man who'd rung me late at night to warn me off hunting down Frank Wallace.

I said, 'I wouldn't be so coarse as to laugh at you. I have standards of behaviour, you know.'

'You do?'

'I wouldn't interrupt a man at breakfast, for one thing. I'd also try to effect a proper introduction, instead of all this secrecy and metaphorical clap-trap about meals and stomachs.'

'The famous northern bluntness.'

'No, everyday common courtesy. But you're from the south, aren't you? You're weaned off courtesy by five.'

'All right, you want me to be blunt. Frank Wallace. Stay clear. Can I be any blunter?'

'You said all this to me on the phone when I was in Crewe. You told me to turn off the light in my second bedroom—thought you were being clever but it's just rude.' He tipped his head in acknowledgement. I went on, 'Why are you interested in what I do?'

'You don't know what you're involved in.'

'Ooh, scary. Big stuff.'

He looked past me into the street. I shouldn't really have riled him but it was so easy. I find it satisfying to prick pompousness. One of the perks of the job. His diction was middle-class, educated, his accent a standard Received

Pronunciation, like an announcer on the BBC. I recognised the tone and the attitude from his phone call. He was probably a middle-grade civil servant tasked with throwing a scare into the maverick investigator from beyond the pale. It had happened before and it would doubtless happen again. I was sick of it.

I said, 'Does Terry Bennett know you're here?'

This was a name I'd heard Jocasta use to Heather from PR and I didn't know what leverage he had over the pallid functionary opposite me.

In reply he raised his eyebrows and dipped his head again.

'*Chapeau.* That means well done. Bit of French for you. You've done your homework. Unfortunately, Terry has no say in what I'm telling you.'

'Ah, interdepartmental friction. Five against Six? Old guard against new? Oxford U versus Manchester Polytechnic?'

'You're not doing yourself any favours. Just accept a word to the wise and back off.'

I finished my sandwich and started on my coffee, which had attained the requisite level of cool.

I said, 'I'm confused.'

'Must be a familiar feeling to you.'

'Excuse me if I tell you things you already know, but Shoemaker Systems are about to enter a contract with the government of this fair isle and the rebels across the water. I know—and I'm betting you know—that Frank Wallace is claiming he's about to blow all that sky high with revelations of skullduggery, probably involving the leaking of information about The Sophocles Trust and its malign influence on the big decision-makers. How am I doing so far?'

'Ball park.'

'So if I'm tasked by Shoemakers—and by proxy, you folks—to find Wallace, how does that hurt? Or more precisely, *who* does it hurt?'

'None of your concern.'

I sipped some more. The coffee was terrible but I had to put on a show of thinking things through.

'I reckon there's a war of the roses going on here. One group wants the contracts to be signed and everything to go ahead without interference. Let's call them the Terry Bennett Faction, or TBF. The other group are saying, fuck this for a game of soldiers, we don't want no outsiders coming into our turf, stealing our jobs and our women and making us look like layabout shirkers. Frank Wallace can do his worst if it means we get to stay in charge. Let's call them the United Kingdom Intelligence Party. You can work out the acronym yourself.'

The man had folded his arms again but his face was expressionless, which was hard on my sense of humour.

He said, 'Is that it? Finished?'

'It's the usual problem with any large institution: you've got upstart modernisers struggling against entrenched die-hards who don't like change because it's too hard.' Still no response. I changed tack. 'Do you have any idea where Frank is? You must have been tracking his credit cards or phone calls. Otherwise why am I paying all these taxes?'

'Not at liberty to tell you that.'

'Which means no, you haven't a clue. He was one of you up until a couple of years ago so he knows the ropes. He's using cash and throw-away phones. Wearing hats so you couldn't see his face on video surveillance tapes. Probably using public transport instead of his own car. Nine million people in the naked city and you can't find one of them.'

'Your references are very outdated for a man of your youth.'

'I'm a student of history. So, brass tacks. What will happen if I don't comply? I have a client, you know. I can't just abandon him or her.'

'I doubt that anything serious will happen. But the Queen won't be happy.'

'Bang goes my knighthood.'

'More than that. If the Queen's not happy, we're not happy. You ought to be more worried about us. You probably think of yourself as a bit of a hero after what happened at Piccadilly Station. But we've got very short memories when it comes to gratitude. Just ask the Gurkhas.'

I stood up and gathered my cup and plate to return them to the counter. He rose to face me, putting his forlorn hands into his pockets.

I said, 'I haven't heard any compelling arguments to come over to the dark side. I've got a job to do, just like you.'

'That's your message?'

'No, my message is, *Rien ne va plus*. All bets are off. Bit of French for you, you condescending prat.'

I HAD BARELY let myself back into Apartment 60 when the phone rang—not my mobile, but the land-line perched on a side table in the living room. I knew who it was before I answered.

Frank Wallace said, 'So what did Gerry want?'

'Hi, Frank, how are you?'

'Yes, yes, yes … never mind the usuals. What did Gerry say?'

'Was that his name? He didn't tell me.'

Frank snorted. 'No, he wouldn't. Thinks he's playing it cool. He'd just started in Five when I met him. Gerald Doyle.

Looked down his nose at everyone. But he's still a message boy.'

'He told me I should stop looking for you.'

'Is that what you're doing?'

'For your own good. At least that's what everyone's saying.'

'How *is* Jocasta? Bearing up?'

I took the phone and walked to the windows overlooking the spread of London, wondering whether he could see me standing there.

'Where are you, Frank? Haven't you done enough now? A big splash in an important newspaper, people looking at Shoemakers a bit sideways … what more do you want?'

'You know what I want, Mr Dyke.'

'I know what you *say* you want, but I can't see the rationale behind it. They tell me you're a chess player. Well all this is too obvious, a frontal assault. Pawns and bishops all going hell for leather. I don't believe it.'

'You're saying I'm bluffing? I won't carry through?'

'Put it this way, I can't believe you're petty enough to want revenge on a woman doing her job the best she can. People keep telling me you were as gung-ho for government contracts as everyone else at Shoemakers. Or at least you didn't argue. Went with the flow.'

'It's called depression. How did *you* feel when those gangsters burned down your house? Takes a while to get up the gumption to carry on, doesn't it? You let people lead you by the nose for a bit—sit down, have a cup of tea, you'll get over it … all that rubbish. That was me. I'd put a lot of myself into that company and I lost both it and my best friend at the same time. You try going through that lot and coming out the other side with your wits intact. It wasn't till afterwards that I got angry, when I sat down and thought about what they were doing.'

'You could have spoken to them, to Jocasta. She doesn't appear to be entirely unreasonable.'

There was silence. I didn't believe I'd persuaded him one way or the other but at least he was thinking.

He said, 'Come talk to me, face-to-face.'

'I can't do that, Frank.'

'Why not? Don't you trust me?'

'You haven't given me any reason to.'

'I want to show you something. Just you. Jocasta mustn't know anything about it. It'll explain some things, make my position clearer.'

It was my turn to think. Was he still my client? Did Emily's status as the second client overrule his claim? How far was I beholden to Jocasta Shoemaker?

He said, 'Well?'

'I suppose you've got a time and a place.'

'Funny you should say that.'

'You always think one step ahead, don't you?'

'Tain't nobody's business if I do.'

'That's a song title, isn't it? Don't you ever tire of that game?'

'Not yet. Do you want this address or not?'

'Tell me.'

He told me and we hung up.

I was getting irritated by this routine. Everyone seemed to be watching me while I didn't have a clue where anybody was or who they were. I knew it wouldn't stay like this — things changed, people made mistakes, got sloppy. The trick was not to give up, no matter how uncomfortable you felt.

And anyway, my mild feelings of discomfort were still better than how I would feel twenty-four hours later.

CHAPTER SEVENTEEN

THE PHONE IN the apartment had numbers in its memory, including direct lines to Jocasta Shoemaker, John Gale and some other names I didn't know. I suppose the people who were given the use of the apartment were important enough to be able to speak directly to them. I dialled for Jocasta, wondering what I was going to say. At that moment I trusted neither her nor Frank so I wasn't sure who I was informing on.

She answered brusquely and I remembered she didn't like using the phone, even though it was a direct number. 'Yes?'

'It's Sam Dyke. Frank's just called. He wants to set up a meeting with me for tomorrow. He wants to show me something.'

'What?'

'He wasn't specific.'

'Are you going?'

'I said I would.'

'Then why are you calling me?'

'I don't know. Perhaps I thought you might be interested.'

'Don't be childish, Dyke. Of course I'm interested but you made it very clear you already have a client, so I have no power over what you choose to do.'

I said nothing for a while.

She broke the silence first. 'What? What do you want me to say?'

'I thought you might have some words of encouragement.'

'Okay, break a leg. Is that good enough?'

'Is there anything I can tell him? From you? Anything you'd want him to know?'

She laughed. It was a bitter sound, as though she was peering into a grave.

'Tell him I'm a big fan. Especially of his timing.'

'So you've nothing to offer.'

'Not that I can think of just now. I told you my thoughts on the matter yesterday. Where is it anyway, this meeting?'

'Why do you want to know?'

'Just curious. I'm interested in his trade-craft—where would he choose?'

I told her what Frank had told me and as soon as I hung up I regretted it.

FOR THE REST of the day I was at a loose end. I went out again and walked along Tower Bridge Road to the bridge itself, standing amongst the tourists taking photos of themselves. Was Frank amongst them, taking photos of me framed against the great towers? The crowds were both fluid and prehensile, gathering you up like an elephant picks up a banana in its trunk and depositing you elsewhere. I let myself go with it until I found myself disgorged, standing alone by the side of the road like an abandoned orphan.

I headed west and walked down past HMS Belfast, a

forbidding grey hulk, then went on up towards London Bridge. Despite the blue sky and temperate weather the river was grey-green and choppy, the river buses rolling slightly as they ferried their wind-whipped passengers past the famous sights—which mainly consisted these days of pubs and restaurants, so far as I could see.

I turned away from the river and pootled around looking in shop windows until it was time for me to have lunch. More of Frank's money bought a home-made steak pie and chips in a pub on Long Lane and afterwards I ambled aimlessly again, buying another pair of trousers and more underwear, for emergencies. I also spent an hour in a bookshop and came out with Robert Hughes' *The Fatal Shore* and the latest Ian McEwan. I couldn't remember when I'd been so carefree and unpressured.

Towards the end of the afternoon I made my way 'home' and laid my purchases on the bed, then went through to the living room and turned on the massive television using an instruction manual I found in a drawer. The people on the news were enormous and garish. It's strange when the images of people's heads are larger than your own. When the talent and dancing shows started up I hunted through the satellite channels and eventually found a James Stewart movie from the thirties. That kept me distracted until the early evening, at which time I would normally have been interested in eating again.

But I wasn't.

I realised that I wanted the day to end and the next one to begin. I went to bed and read more about spies in Thomas' book on British Intelligence.

It did nothing to assure me of the Service's actual level of intelligence and I finally went to sleep in a brooding and considered mood.

CHAPTER EIGHTEEN

IT WAS AN old cinema out near Spitalfields, the letters on the hoarding over its entrance—dating from somewhere in the 90s—advertising Bingo and a forthcoming concert by Max Bygraves.

I stood at the end of the road and watched it for half an hour before I turned the corner and approached. It was Sunday lunchtime, which meant the traffic had lessened somewhat and there were few pedestrians about.

There was a side alley running the length of the cinema and I followed instructions by squeezing down it, pushing past brambles and avoiding dog turds that looked as though they'd been deposited by lions, not local Chihuahuas. The paintwork of the cinema was a pale cream and was peeling off in flaky patches to reveal a garish pink beneath it.

At the far end the Emergency Exit was ajar by one foot. I pulled it further open and went inside, into a damp, mildew-laden atmosphere that I supposed was the reek of decaying carpet and cinema seats. I edged carefully along a dark corridor and met another door—the exit that led from the auditorium in case of fire—and pushed it inwards.

Surprisingly, the space that opened up beyond was

relatively spacious and clean. There was a dim light coming through gaps in the roof and I could see all four walls and the layout of the area. Immediately to my left there was a short flight of carpeted steps leading up to the stage. A tattered fire curtain still hung down to it from above, hanging lower where a few of the hooks had broken away from the material. Directly ahead of me the seats in the auditorium had been ripped out to make way for Bingo seating and dozens of plastic chairs were stacked in tall chevrons on either side of the arena, some of them leaning dangerously against ranks of tables, their legs folded beneath them. The floor had been covered with cheap wooden laminate that creaked as I walked towards the rear of the auditorium. I neither saw nor heard any movement or sound.

I reached the swing doors at the back and went through into the foyer. The glass entrance doors were boarded up from the inside and the ticket-booth and popcorn stall were both dusty and cobwebbed. The foyer was dark and grim, like a cathedral crypt that had fallen out of use. Beyond the booth another door marked 'Private' swung on its hinges. I went through it and turned immediately left, heading up the stairs to the projection booth.

The booth had been stripped of its equipment years ago, the only remains being the two plinths on which the projectors would have stood. I bent down and peered through one of the slits through which Flashdance and Top Gun were projected thirty years before. I could just make out the stage and the fire curtain.

I hadn't noticed the mobile phone on the table at the back of the booth until it began to ring. I picked it up and pressed the green button.

'Glad you could come, Mr Dyke. Shame you didn't come

alone.'

'I don't—'

There was a muffled boom from the auditorium. I took a step and ducked down again to look through one of the projection windows. I saw the fire curtain billowing out towards me. I realised that I'd heard a scream that began when the explosion occurred and was still piercing the air. Papers fluttered in the auditorium, disturbed by the aftershock.

I turned and ran from the room, taking the steps two at a time. I covered the foyer in four strides and then was racing down the sloping aisle towards the stage. The screaming had stopped. The curtain was now hanging straight, but as I arrived it was ripped back and Gale stepped out. I leaped up on to the stage. He halted as I approached but his eyes were fierce and aggressive.

'Dyke, where's Wallace?'

'What happened back there?'

He hesitated, then drew back the curtain again and turned away, talking over his shoulder.

'That fucking Wallace set off a device. My man Givens comes through the door and the fucking thing goes off in his face. He'll be lucky to keep an eye.'

I grabbed him by the arm.

'Second question, what the fuck are you doing here?'

He stared at me, saying nothing. Then turned to go into the darkness at the back of the stage. I heard someone whimpering and as we came close I saw a young man staggering in a corner, his hands to his face. Blood was leaking through his fingers. I reached for my phone.

Gale said, 'The fuck you doing?'

'Calling an ambulance. Any objections?'

'Don't be fucking stupid. We've got our own men.'

'And your own hospital?'

'You might say that. They're on their way.' He turned to Givens. 'Let me have a look at that.'

The man removed his hands from his face and I saw that it was raw down one side, the skin puckered and bloody. Both eyes looked to be functioning, though, and they looked at me with the fear of a dog that's been whipped.

He was in such pain that his system had switched off and he'd stopped whimpering. I hoped Gale's private ambulance arrived soon, before the real pain kicked in.

Gale said, 'Good lad. Won't be long. Stay there. Don't get in any fights.'

I said, 'When did you call the ambulance?'

Gale looked at me with suspicion.

'Soon as it happened. It's on speed-dial. I give a location and a code word and they know what they're coming to.'

'It took me about twenty seconds to get down here after the explosion—you were bloody sharp.'

'That's the difference between a trained man and a monkey in a leather jacket. What's the point you're making?'

'Just that you fucked up this meeting between me and Wallace. He knew you were here.' I took the phone from the projection booth out of my pocket. 'He rang me just as you arrived. He knew there was someone else here. I never even saw him.'

'Well we know he's a clever bugger, don't we? He must have watched you come in, then waited to see if anyone was with you. Rang you and set off the device from the safety of a pub down the road. The coward's game.'

I pushed past him and went across the stage to the door that led outside. It had a fire-bar across its middle. The smell of burned plastic hung in the air. The inside of the door was scorched and there were pieces of twisted plastic and circuitry scattered on the floor, as though Wallace had concealed his explosive device in a small transistor radio.

I went back to Gale.

'So, what … you find this door open, barge your way in hoping to find Wallace, pushing Givens in front of you, and then something just explodes in his face?'

'That's about right. Though I didn't push Givens in front of me. He offered to go first. Young and thrusting, what can I tell you?'

'Where was it, this device?'

'How do I know? I was still the other side of the door, checking the alley.'

'So you never saw it.'

'Didn't have to, did I? Door blew back in my face. Probably protected me.'

I stared at him and he stared right back, waiting for the next question.

I said, 'We've got to tell the cops.'

'We'll handle it. Stay the fuck out.'

'Your own private police, too?'

'Contacts. The corridors of power. You wouldn't understand.'

'You still haven't explained why you were here in the first place. I told Jocasta Frank wanted to deal with me alone. Didn't she hear that bit?'

'She heard everything.'

He was using his staring-hard-at-me face again.

I said, 'I get it. You decided to be the lone wolf. Try to catch Frank by yourself and screw me.'

'I think you pretty much screwed yourself by agreeing to the meet in the first place.'

'You realise this was a test?'

He adjusted his stance. Had he been wearing his tunic

instead of a protective waistcoat, I'm sure he would have tried to pull it down.

'A test of what?'

'To see whether we could be trusted. Shoemaker and me. You've proved neither of us can be. So you're the one who's screwed us over, Gale, not me.'

He couldn't answer that so he didn't try. He turned and went back to Givens, laying a hand on his back and talking quietly to him.

I wondered if anyone outside the cinema had heard the explosion. In retrospect it had been relatively minor, not as loud as a firework. And if they had heard, would they give it any importance? Maybe it was just something falling over. Or perhaps it was a car crash somewhere. Would it be easy to place the explosion inside the cinema? Who was around to know?

I walked away from Gale and took out the phone that Wallace had left for me. I used the History function and found the last number that had called and tried to ring it back. Unsurprisingly, the number wasn't recognised.

I thought about young Givens and what Frank had done to him. What perhaps had been a game was now more serious. Givens might have been killed or permanently blinded. There might have been more people in the area when the device went off. It might even have been me in its path.

I quit the cinema the way I'd entered and left Gale to deal with the aftermath, whether it involved police or not. It was his mess—he could fix it.

Then I took out my own phone and called Jocasta Shoemaker. I'd copied the direct number from the phone memory in Apartment 60. She answered straight away.

'Well, what did he want?'

'He wants to give you some serious grief.'

There must have been something in my voice. She paused.

'What do you mean?'

'Gale turned up and spiked the meet. I never even saw Wallace. You've got a man down.'

'What?'

'Frank set off a small explosive. One of your men is injured.'

'Where's Gale?'

'He says he's dealing with it. I left him there.'

She sighed, then said, 'Come down to my place. This afternoon.'

'Why should I do that?'

'I hate phones. And we should talk.'

She took my silence for agreement and gave me an address and directions. I told her I had no car.

She said, 'Hire one. What are you, twelve?'

I hung up and walked away. I dropped Wallace's phone in a skip outside a house being revitalised for the next property boom. I found the nearest tube station, went down into the dark and got on the first train that came.

I sat on one of the sideways-facing seats, staring at the tube map on the opposite side of the carriage for a long time before I realised that my hands were shaking.

CHAPTER NINETEEN

I USED MY tablet's Internet connection and found a Hertz and they gave me a small sporty Citroen with sharp brakes that nearly pitched me through the windscreen at the first corner. Then I used the tablet's GPS function and CoPilot to guide me out of London, south towards Sussex.

Hayward's Heath was on the way to Brighton and the road was busy both ways. The software predicted a journey of about an hour but didn't take into account the traffic in London, so it was an hour and a half before I drew close, the middle of the afternoon. Eventually the directions took me left off the A23, through the town and its nest of red-brick estates, and out into the countryside again. A couple of turns later and I was descending a single track, over a small hump-backed bridge and arriving in the midst of a clutch of buildings—a stable block, a couple of neat barns and a large converted farmhouse. Behind the stables I could make out a swimming pool, still covered, and a tennis court. The Shoemakers had done well for themselves.

A large black Range Rover was parked outside the farmhouse and as I pulled up next to it Jocasta Shoemaker came to the door. She was wearing a sweatshirt and jeans and her hair was long and loose.

She approached me and gestured with her chin to my Citroen.

'We'd have sprung for a bigger model.'

'Not necessary. I'm not on your clock. Though I appreciate the apartment.'

She nodded. 'Kelvin's idea. We bought it off-plan. We couldn't afford it now.'

She turned and I followed her inside, into a dark kitchen that was mostly wood except for a black granite counter-top and a dusky red Smeg fridge. When I passed through the door she closed it behind me and turned a lock.

She glanced at me. 'I was burgled a year ago. The country's not always as laid-back as it seems. I'm a bit paranoid now.'

'Tell me. My entire house was burned down a few months ago.'

'Jesus. What happened?'

'Some bad guys were making a point.'

'Did you catch them?'

'With a little help from the cops.'

She nodded. 'They have their uses.'

The kitchen opened out down a step into a wide living room flagged with broad York tiles. She went through and stood in front of the fireplace, where a single log guttered.

She said, 'Gale called. What a fuck-up.'

'He's not that bad.'

'Christ, you two. I meant the situation.'

'You shouldn't have told him where the meet was.'

She looked at me but said nothing in reply. Then she tilted her head back towards the kitchen. 'Do you want a drink? Coffee? Something stronger?'

'You don't seem that interested in what happened

today.'

'Gale told me.'

'His side of the story.'

'Is there another?'

'There's always another. Did he say how Givens was?'

'He'll live. We'll look after him.'

'Your private medical arrangements.'

'They come in useful from time to time. The point is, there's no fuss. The police weren't involved, it was a private matter.'

'You should still report it.'

'I'll have a word. Training accident.'

I looked at her and she held my gaze.

I said, 'You can get away with this?'

'There's a lot of government time invested in the success of our bid.'

'But some people aren't keen.'

She frowned. 'Meaning?'

'I had a visit. Someone called Doyle. Wanted me to back off finding Frank. I had the sense he was enjoying your discomfort.'

She was dismissive. 'Oh, him. He's a runner. A small rump of old boys in the Ministry don't want to be tainted with commerce.'

'He seemed to know a lot about me.'

'Well they are spies, you know.' She moved away from the fire and seemed to hesitate. Then she looked at her watch. 'Oh, sod it, I'm going to have a drink. Are you sure you don't want anything?'

'A beer, if you have one.'

She walked back to the kitchen and I heard the fridge opening and the top of a bottle being popped. There was more clinking and she came back in carrying a glass of red wine and a German beer in its bottle. She handed it over then sat down.

I don't know what I expected, but I thought there might have been a more dramatic reaction to the events of the day.

I said, 'You know Frank isn't playing. He wanted to speak to me today, show me something. When he saw Gale and his man he set off a device. Greg Last told me he liked toys.'

Although she was leaning back in a deep chair her body language suggested she was still tense. Her free hand pulled at the seam of the chair's arm.

She said, 'I know what Frank wants.'

'Really?'

'He wants me to fail because he did. He can't stand the idea of my succeeding. Every spy I've ever met in this business has been jealous and petty. And their bosses are worse, with an abiding belief in the efficiency of the class system in identifying good candidates for secret work.'

'He doesn't think he failed. He thinks you did.'

She gestured through the windows to the meadowland beyond. I could see the high fence of her tennis court and the edge of the covered swimming pool behind a barn. A pair of french doors led from this living room to a wide patio with steps leading down to a formal garden. I almost expected to see a couple of yokels with straw hats tending the roses.

She said, 'Does this look like failure to you? What definition is he using?'

'You're operating in different moral universes.'

'Perhaps. Tell me, do you think I'm attractive?'

That forced me to take a swig of my beer. I considered for a moment, then said, 'On an aesthetic level, very.'

She nodded, taking my opinion seriously.

'Yes, a lot of men do, apparently. It helps me do my job.'

'It's a macho world.'

'Indeed. And you men can't seem to control that heat-seeking missile you've got between your legs.'

'Your point is?'

'I'm trying to work in a rational way, the way I was brought up, the way Kelvin taught me to behave. But I work with men who put up a good front of thinking objectively while at the same time making every single decision on the basis of one emotion or another—perhaps fear, perhaps suspicion, perhaps lust.'

'Frank told me on the phone that when Kelvin died he was numb. He only got angry later.'

'Exactly! He's acting irrationally but he's giving himself a logical reason for his behaviour—he's punishing me, wanting to see me suffer, because he did. Because I "took" his company away from him.'

'Do you blame him? You dropped in without any experience, without any history in the game. Even if he didn't want the job himself he might have expected some consideration.'

'He got shares. A good amount.'

'Not the point, is it? His ego was damaged.'

'You don't like me much, do you?'

'What's that got to do with it? As a matter of fact I admire your guts. It can't have been easy taking charge of a company like Shoemakers.'

'It wasn't. A nest of vipers barely describes it.'

'You might have expected some push back from the old lags.'

'I did. I worked damned hard to get them onside before Kelvin passed away. I worked hardest with Frank, though you wouldn't believe it.'

I'd finished my beer and I didn't know what to do with

the bottle. All the tables and chairs seemed polished to perfection and I didn't want to risk leaving an unsightly lower-class ring on a surface.

She stood up again and took the bottle from me.

She said, 'What do you think Frank will do now?'

'He'll phone me again and whine and moan. Then he'll want to set up another meeting. I still don't know what he was going to show me this morning—though I can't imagine it'll be anything different to what he's already said. But it's no good for him if we don't understand why he's doing this. He wants to explain.'

'What if we don't want to listen?'

'Won't make any difference. The explanation is only part of it. What he really wants is his revenge.'

'He wants the company to go down?'

'No, sorry. It's more serious than that.'

She brushed past me on the way to the kitchen then stopped and turned as if she'd suddenly understood what I meant.

'You think he wants to hurt me?'

I nodded. 'The fact he set up an explosive device this morning suggests he's tipped over the edge. I think we should call in the police, let them find him. He's too smart for me.'

She raised her eyebrows.

'No police. I want your word on that.'

My turn to pause. I had my own position to consider, such as it was. I couldn't neglect the fact a crime had been committed by Frank, though strictly speaking I wasn't present when it happened and couldn't be absolutely certain he was responsible. I wondered if silence would make me an accessory in some way. Shoemaker Systems wasn't even a client, so I couldn't claim any form of client privilege.

Jocasta said, 'If it makes you feel better I'll tell my Intelligence contacts about it, let them deal with the Met. They'll love that. They've got nearly as much to lose from all this as I have.'

'You'll have to keep me out of it. Training accident.'

'Exactly.' She became suddenly brusque. 'If that's settled I think you should leave this alone now. Send an invoice or whatever for the car hire and any other expenses. We'll take it from here.'

'You can't fire me—I don't work for you or your company.'

Her lips became thin. 'Maybe not, but we can make it hard for you.'

'I have a client. They may not see it that way.'

'Emily? She'll run out of money to pay you. Didn't she do something in computing? Anyway, she'll soon see what a bang-up job you're doing and try something else. How much do you think she really wants to find her father?'

'More than you, evidently.'

She smiled mirthlessly and returned to the kitchen. I followed her out and passed her on the way to the rear door.

She called to me as I was climbing into the Citroen.

'Mr Dyke?'

'Yes?'

'I didn't tell John Gale about the meeting today. I wouldn't have double-crossed you.'

'Interesting.'

'I'll talk to him.' She looked at me levelly for a moment and I thought she was going to add something more. But she shook her head slightly and said, 'When you get over the bridge turn right—it's a quicker route back to the main road, no matter what your GPS says.'

CHAPTER TWENTY

I LEFT THE apartment that night and travelled back to Cheshire on a late train full of football fans returning from a game. We were a grim crew, our heads full of what we'd seen and the disappointment it represented.

I tried not to think of London and Wallace and Jocasta Shoemaker. And especially not John Gale. I didn't want to worry about how he knew of my meeting with Frank Wallace and what he intended to do by interrupting it. And what was Frank going to show me? More documents? Some grainy black and white film taken from a hidden camera showing Jocasta Shoemaker in the midst of making a shady deal? I couldn't imagine what it was and in fact I was tired of all of them and the Great Game. Spying wasn't a game; to my mind it was less important than that.

Of course I still had a client—Emily Shoemaker was paying me to find her father but I had nothing to work with. Perhaps, I thought, I should get on the next train back and do some sleuthing. I should be asking questions of everyone who knew Frank Wallace, trying to uncover where he might hide out … but that would be pointless because Frank would expect that and would be holed up somewhere he'd never stayed before. He'd have changed his habits as well as his appearance. Without access to his credit card account I couldn't even track his expenditure ... but that would doubtless draw a blank: he was too wily to leave a paper trail.

So the following morning, Monday, I went into my office and stared into space for a while. I'd tried ringing Dan but had had no reply. He was a grown man now so I let it be. I hoped he wasn't having too much fun driving around in Craig's Porsche.

Which reminded me. There was something I could do.

I made a couple of phone calls and wrote some notes and then did nothing with them but put them away in a drawer. I wasn't happy about what I'd found out but I didn't yet know what to do with it. I thought I might know later on.

By which time it was lunch. I was about to leave the office when a call came into the machine on my desk and I let it ring till the answerphone kicked in, then listened.

'Sam, it's Belinda. I don't know where you are but no change there. Give me a call, catch up.'

I could have answered before she finished speaking but I didn't have the energy, so I let the machine record it then went out for a sandwich.

WHEN I GOT back I drew up my invoice for the services I'd failed to render to Shoemaker Systems and placed it in an envelope. I'd included the hire of the Citroen and my train tickets to and from Crewe. I might have added the sandwich I'd eaten on the train but I didn't think they should be made to pay for that. Though somebody should.

I found myself thinking about Emily Wallace. She was a light presence in my head—funny, glinting like a sharp knife, sensual but distant. I couldn't work out what exactly she wanted. Her father was bordering on the wrong side of sanity but you couldn't say he was missing. If she was worried about what he might do, she should call in the police. I was a weapon of last resort in this situation and I had a sad suspicion she was wasting her money by paying for my time—especially as I was just sitting around thinking about her instead of her father.

I was in this febrile mood when of course Frank rang.

I'd heard several versions of his voice by now: serious, light-hearted, curious, delighted. What I hadn't heard was angry.

As soon as I answered he said, 'What, so you're giving up now? What's the matter with you? I thought you were supposed to have gumption.'

'Frank, you're a dangerous man and you should come in for your own good.'

'Dangerous? You don't know the half of it.'

'You almost blinded that youngster who'd done nothing to you. In fact you might have killed someone.'

'It goes to prove you're not taking this seriously enough.'

'You're kidding, right? Talk to Emily. Tell her where you are. She's worried and she's paying me money to find you. Money I doubt she can afford.'

'Are you going to hang up on me? Don't you dare hang up on me.'

'You've crossed a line, Frank. I can't help you any more. You've taken a legitimate complaint about Shoemakers and their involvement in government intelligence work and turned it into a one-man terror campaign. If the press gets hold of what you've done to Gale's man, you'll be found and you won't get any mercy—from them or from the courts. And no one will listen to what you have to say.'

I almost heard the gritting of his teeth.

'Finally, you're getting it.'

'What do you mean?'

'You've been thinking this was the ravings of a disappointed man, haven't you? That I'm bitter and twisted because I was shut out from Shoemakers' inner circle. I'm here to tell you you're wrong. I couldn't give one shit about Givens and his poorly face. He's just one of the pawns. Sacrificed to get your attention. I'm after the queen. She's the one with the power and I'm going to wipe her from the board.'

'You see, that's the kind of talk that doesn't go down well with the press. You ought to reconsider your communications strategy.'

'Are you mocking me?'

'No, Frank, I'm firing you. I've had enough of these aggravating telephone calls. You only talk to me to gloat or to promise ... well, I don't know what you're promising. Jocasta Shoemaker's given up on you. You've shot your wad with your revelations to the press. Even Emily wants you to go home so she can lead a quiet life.'

'Not true.'

'How do you know? Do you ever listen to her when you call? She's worried about you and wants you to give it up.'

'Too late for that.' He paused. 'You know, I'm disappointed. I read all that stuff about you in the papers and I thought you'd stick to it. Argue my case with that bitch. Help me get a hearing so that I didn't have to go the alternative route.'

'You've had your hearing, Frank. But no one was listening. Largely because they've heard it all before.'

He laughed suddenly, a hollow sound without soul.

He said, 'Oh, boy, you've done it now.'

'Not more threats ...'

'Wakened the sleeping giant. Never go into diplomacy, Mr Dyke. You'd be laughed out of the Corps.'

'See you soon.'

'Not if I see you first. Boom boom.'

He hung up on another song title—John Lee Hooker. I knew that one.

I realised I'd trodden a dangerous path by aggravating him. Perhaps I should have tried the conciliatory route but if I wanted him to show his hand I first had to force it.

Which of course was a ridiculous move to make when you're dealing with a psychopath, as I soon found out.

FIVE MINUTES LATER I was talking to Ann at Shoemaker Systems. She refused to connect me with Jocasta but she'd take a message.

I thought long and hard for ten seconds before saying, 'Tell her that Frank Wallace is officially angry. I might have had something to do with that. I'm not sure what he'll do next but she should watch her back.'

Ann was writing this down. When she'd finished she said, 'I'll get the message to her as soon as I can.'

'I know—she's in meetings all day.'

'Actually, no. She's working from home. She turns all her phones off and only looks at her email twice a day. You've missed the first possible connection. I'll send it for the second, this afternoon.'

'I have every faith in you, Ann.'

'Mr Dyke, you're making everyone's jobs here much harder. Please try not to contact us again.'

I hung up feeling bad. I didn't like to upset people who had little control over what their companies or their bosses did. It wasn't fair.

But there had been something in Frank Wallace's voice

that told me everything had gone up a notch. By trying to play clever mind-games with him I'd likely made him more dangerous. I'd lost control of myself, lost my sense of perspective. I'd wanted to tell Frank what I'd really thought of him but telling him directly wasn't the best way to do it.

If he was a hornets' nest, I'd just stirred it with a big blunt stick.

CHAPTER TWENTY-ONE

AS I EXPECTED, I didn't get a reply from Jocasta. She was so bound up in the contracts and, presumably, the politicking around Givens' injury that she wouldn't find the time to speak to me.

I thought about Givens and what his life would be like for the next six months—the plastic surgery, the counselling, the re-living of the explosion and the subsequent nightmares … it wasn't going to be easy for him.

Several times I was tempted to pick up the phone and call the police, tell them what had happened and see how it was handled. Would they say they knew all about it and it was being dealt with? I shouldn't worry? Or would they react with anger because I hadn't reported it earlier?

And what was my part in it all? Did Frank really blame me even though Gale had come of his own volition? How had he even known of the meeting if Jocasta hadn't told him? Perhaps he had a way of following me, too. That was what Shoemakers did, after all—spy stuff.

There were so many imponderables and unanswered questions that I couldn't get the situation straight in my head. Wallace had become almost an imaginary character in my mind's eye—all-seeing, all-knowing, inescapable. I felt myself becoming paranoid, turning around suddenly on the street to see if he was following; staying away from windows at home and when drinking in cafés; stopping to look at reflections in shop windows in case I might catch him lurking on the far side of the road …

Tuesday morning I rang Emily Wallace and was re-directed to her work phone. When she answered I had a sense of a busy office behind her: I saw strip lighting, grey cubicles, people walking back and forth importantly with pieces of vital paper in hand.

I said, 'It's me. Reporting in.'

'Really? Have you found him? How is he?'

'No, no … nothing like that. I'm back home. I think I'm going to have to give up on this case, Emily. Your father seems to know everything I do and Shoemakers are being difficult. I can't get any traction anywhere. Besides, he's evidently well physically.'

There was a silent 'if not mentally' hanging in the air that neither of us addressed. I couldn't bring myself to tell her what he'd done to Givens. That was something to be dealt with when he resurfaced or when Shoemakers found him. Assuming they were looking. If they'd spoken to their Intelligence contacts as a way of smoothing over the Met, presumably they'd be on the case as well. I was likely to be a spare wheel with all that manpower on the job.

Emily had been quiet. Now she said, 'So that's it? You're giving up?'

'Like father, like daughter.'

'What?'

'Your dad said the same thing to me.'

'He rang you again? Why didn't you tell me?'

I hesitated, editing the events as I went along. 'Nothing

to tell. We arranged a meeting but it didn't happen. So I'm no wiser.'

'I think I had a right to know. As your client.'

'You're right, I'm sorry. I wasn't thinking.'

'And after that conversation with him, you're abandoning me. How did he sound?'

I sighed. I didn't want to get into this. But she was right, I should at least have told her I'd spoken to him, even if I couldn't tell her the rest of what happened the previous Sunday.

In the end I decided I shouldn't protect her from a truth she'd learn eventually. I said, 'He's running close to the edge, Emily. He sounds perfectly sane but I have to tell you, I think he's losing his grip.'

She was quiet for a moment. 'I thought it would come to this. He's been getting more strident in the last few months.

'I'm sorry.'

She drew a deep breath. 'You can't stop now, Sam. He needs help. I can't do it—can't find him, I mean. Please, help me.'

'There's nothing I can do.'

'Just think about it. Please.'

I walked around my office and stared at the empty desk, the computer that was switched off, the calendar with no dates pencilled in.

But I couldn't alter the fact I had nothing to work with. Nowhere to start. No one to speak to.

I said, 'Let me sleep on it. At the moment I can't think where I'd begin. Maybe something will come to me.'

'I'll pay you upfront, if that will help.'

'That's all right. Your dad paid me enough to be going on with.'

'Come down and see me.'

'I'm not sure I should, just yet.'

'I want to see you, Sam. Can't I make it any plainer?'

'I'll be in touch.'

There was resignation in her voice. 'All right. I'll be here.'

She hung up and I sat down, my heart thumping a little faster and my mouth dry. This was getting interesting.

CHAPTER TWENTY-TWO

ALTHOUGH SHE DIDN'T like it when Sam was off on a case by himself, Belinda knew that she couldn't be in his pocket all the time. She had her own—occasional—cases to engage with and she actually enjoyed the quiet life. Her days in the Army had been one long to-do list and she liked the fact that now she could more or less pick and choose what she did, so long as the money kept coming in.

It was a week since they'd broken into the house in Manchester and found the formula but Sam hadn't spoken to her about it or the case. She wondered if she'd screwed up so badly that he wouldn't talk to her now for fear she'd blab or make another mistake.

But then he wouldn't have taken her to Manchester to look at the house if he thought badly of her. And he wasn't like that anyway. He didn't hold grudges and when things went wrong he just moved on. He was so damn rational.

Most of the time.

That was part of the fun of working with him. He could be hot-headed and act like a dog pulling a bone from a nest of tree roots, but he was smart and put things together in a way she didn't always anticipate. So she learned from him all the time.

She was in her kitchen preparing a salad when her doorbell rang. It was late afternoon and she wasn't expecting visitors.

Peeking through her spy-hole she saw a face she didn't want to see: Frank Wallace, dressed in his Barbour jacket and flat cap and probably carrying his walking cane.

She opened the door, knowing that she was frowning.

She said, 'You forget something?'

He shrugged and smiled. 'I wanted to talk to you about Mr Dyke. Can I come in?'

Belinda stared at him long and hard, then thought, *If he tries anything, I can take him.* She was trained in an Israeli hand-to-hand combat technique that protected her from most assaults, even from men bigger than herself.

She turned away to walk down the corridor and leave him to close the door.

She was about to tell him to do this, glancing back over her shoulder, when she heard a slight hissing noise. Within seconds the strength had gone from her legs and the hallway appeared both blurry and distant at the same time.

She knew she was about to hit the floor before she felt it.

And then she didn't feel it.

SHE HAD NO idea how long had passed but she knew it was dark, so it was probably a few hours later. She had a thumping headache. Her hands were bound behind her back and she knew at once she was lying on a thin carpet in the boot of a car. There was a gag in her mouth, she was wearing a blindfold and her ankles were also bound. The smell of petrol was overwhelming and for a moment she thought with horror that Wallace had set the car on fire after dousing it with petrol.

Then she realised they were moving at a steady pace and in a straight line. They were probably on a motorway. Possibly on the way to London down the M6.

She didn't think Frank was going to kill her because he would have done it by now.

But that didn't mean she wasn't scared.

After half an hour or so the car slowed and turned gently off the main road. She guessed they were coming into a service station. She closed her eyes and made herself relax, waiting for the boot lid to open.

When it did, she raised herself from the floor of the boot to lash out with her feet.

But met thin air—he'd stayed well back.

And then Wallace's voice said, 'I thought you'd be awake by now. Say bye-bye.'

And then the hiss came again and she went numb even as fear began to mount in her chest.

CHAPTER TWENTY-THREE

LATE AFTERNOON MY office phone rang. I'd had no calls for two days so I had a sinking feeling when I answered.

Wallace said, 'Would you like to speak to Belinda?'

'Frank, what are you talking about?'

'Simple question: would you like to speak to your investigative partner, Ms Belinda McFee?'

'What have you done, Frank?'

'Stop using my name like you're speaking to a child. Don't talk down to me. Now, for the last time, would you like to talk to Belinda?'

'Yes, I'd like to speak to Belinda.'

'Too bad, she's otherwise engaged.'

'Where are you? What have you done?'

'Well if I replied to either of those questions there'd be no fun, would there? Suffice to say I'm in or around London. Now, have a think about what you want to do next. Calling the police is absolutely *verboten*, of course. Speak later. *Ciao*.'

The phone went dead and I rang Belinda's number immediately. It went straight to answerphone on her landline and then voice mail on her mobile.

I locked up and ran down the stairs towards my car.

IT WAS JUST getting dark by the time I arrived at the end of Belinda's street. I parked and watched the house for a while as the street lights grew in strength around me and the other houses began to switch on their own interior lights.

Belinda's house remained veiled in darkness.

I tried her phones again and got the same responses from both. After fifteen minutes I couldn't wait any longer and walked up her short path and knocked on the door: it didn't swing open.

Fortunately I knew she kept a spare key beneath the plant-pot in the basket hanging to the right of the doorway. I lifted the plant-pot and grubbed out the key and let myself in.

I called her name but knew instinctively the house was empty. I switched on the hall light and then went through each room and the cellar—nothing to be found. No signs of a scuffle, no note, nothing out of place.

If Belinda had been taken by Frank she either went willingly or he'd drugged her in some way. She would have fought like a tiger if she'd been taken by force and something would have shown—a scuff mark, the raised edge of a rug, a drop of blood on the wooden boards.

I switched off the lights, locked the door and put the key back, then returned to my car.

I found myself sweating and my pulse was raised. I was completely powerless, which of course was what Frank Wallace wanted. He was proving a point to me, though why he should use Belinda to make it, I didn't know. Did he still expect me to press his case with Shoemaker Systems after the events of Sunday morning? Did he think I was so moral-free that I could continue to do the job he'd paid me for?

My phone rang.

Wallace said, 'So she's not answering her phone and she's not in. Where do you think she might be?'

'If you harm a hair on her head —'

'You'll do what? You can't even find me at the moment, so carrying out any kind of threat is a bit beyond your means.'

I closed my eyes and tried to calm my heartbeat. I hoped that he wouldn't harm Belinda because she was blameless in this. She'd even tried to help him when we thought he was in danger.

'What do you want, Frank? I can't tell Jocasta Shoemaker that you're a reasonable man open to discussion when you keep doing unreasonable things.'

'So I'm unreasonable, am I?'

'I'd go so far as to say irrational right now.'

He laughed grimly. 'I've never been so rational in my life.'

'Emily wants you to come home. She's worried for you.'

'Don't do that, Mr Dyke. Don't use family ties as a bargaining chip.'

'So emotional blackmail is okay for you but not for me?'

'Nice try, but the circumstances are different. Do you know the song "Nobody knows you when you're down and out"?'

'Eric Clapton, *Layla*.'

'A late-comer. First recorded by Bessie Smith in 1929. It's about having no friends to go to when you're feeling bad.'

'Is that what you feel like, Frank? Feeling bad and no friends to help out?'

'It's a great song, that's all I'm saying.'

'Well thanks for bringing it up.'

'All life's in the Blues, Mr Dyke. That's why it's priceless. That's why we've got to preserve it.'

'There are lots of things worth preserving, Frank. No argument from me.'

'Very good. Right, what would you do to get Belinda back unharmed?'

'I'm sorry, I don't play those kinds of games.'

I hung up.

I'd taken a calculated gamble. If it went wrong, I hoped Belinda would forgive me.

If she was still alive to do so.

CHAPTER TWENTY-FOUR

I HAD A restless night and the next morning Wallace rang again.

'Had a good night's sleep?'

'The answer's still the same, Frank. No game playing.'

'All right, all right … don't hang up. I admire you sticking to your guns.'

'I don't believe you'd hurt a defenceless woman.'

'Let's hope you're right, eh? Now listen up, I'm going to give you an address.'

He read out the address of a building in London and asked me to say it back to him, which I did.

He said, 'You'll find her there.'

'Is she all right?'

'Last time I looked.'

'So what's the point of it all? You've probably frightened her to death and you've got nothing from me.'

'But that's where you're wrong, isn't it? You're back in the game now. Admit it, you want to get your hands on me. Hurt me.'

'You're a sad old man.'

'You've got the address. Remember the numbers

195318520. Be there before five o'clock or else the fun will start. And give my regards to Belinda. Welcome back.'

He hung up. I repeated the numbers in my head and wondered what he meant by 'the fun will start'.

Then I looked at the National Rail timetable online, drove back to my house to pick up some things and called a taxi to take me to the station. The first train I could catch would get me to Euston just after four o'clock. It should be plenty of time to get me to the address he'd given me.

I didn't know what I'd find in London and I wasn't particularly looking forward to finding it.

THE ADDRESS WAS out in Streatham, a good half hour taxi ride from Euston station. It was four-forty when the cabbie dropped me off and returned to Euston for some of those juicy commuter fares.

The building Wallace had steered me towards was a single-storey square block standing by itself in a back street. It was the kind of building you might have expected a photo-copying agency to set up in—not a house, not an office block: a functional unit.

Looking both ways up the street, wondering if I might see Wallace ducking into a doorway, I knocked on the plastic entrance door and then tried it. Locked. There was an old-fashioned key-pad on the wall next to it with firm alpha-numeric push-buttons to press. I typed in 195318520, the number Wallace had given me, but nothing happened. I tried again, the first edge of panic beginning to attack my nerves.

Again the door refused to move.

I thought back to when he'd told me the numbers—I was sure I'd remembered them correctly. I tried again with the same result.

I moved down the side of the building trying to peer through the windows but there were closed blinds at every one. I could see nothing.

I went back to the door pad and thought. Wallace was a game player but I didn't really think he'd harm Belinda. So whatever he was doing, there'd be an easy solution—something that he knew I'd get quickly.

The key-pad had both numbers and letters. He'd told me to remember the numbers 195318520, but he hadn't said those were the ones I needed to gain access inside. And he'd said them in pairs, not single numbers: nineteen, five, three, eighteen, five, twenty. That's how I'd remembered them so easily. I looked at the letters … what if it were a straightforward code? In the alphabet, 19 would be the letter S, 5 would be E, 3 would be C … I knew where he was going. I typed in S-E-C-R-E-T and there was an electronic click.

This time the door opened when I pushed.

The first space I entered was like a doctor's waiting room with a row of plastic chairs against one wall and a waist-high counter against the other. An empty wire filing basket sat on the counter.

Facing the counter was a door marked 'Toilets' and behind it was a door calling itself 'Private' but I ignored the description and went through anyway.

The next room was larger than you'd think from the outside but was completely unfurnished. Grey Venetian blinds covered each window and there was a thin carpet underfoot.

In the middle of the room Belinda was strapped to a chair, her hands bound behind her back and with a strip of thick grey tape over her mouth.

I walked closer, then stopped. She shrugged helplessly.

I said, 'Are you booby-trapped? Are you going to

explode when I untie the ropes?'

She shook her head wearily so I peeled back the grey tape as slowly as I could manage and she took in a sucking breath.

'That bastard Frank, I'm going to break his legs.'

I untied the ropes around her wrists. They came loose and she rubbed her forearms. Then she bent to untie her ankles.

'Came to the door last night, large as life. Hat, cane, just like before. Asked could he come in, I said, Yes, of course — turned round to go back in the house and he gassed me. Last thing I remember is a weird hissing sound.'

'Have you been here since then?'

'No. I woke up in the boot of a car, then they gassed me again and I think they'd put me on the back seat.'

'They?'

'Well, despite my svelte figure Frank's hardly strong enough to carry me by himself, is he?'

'Any ideas?'

'None. Dead to the world, me. So anyway we get here, or somewhere close, and when I wake up this time there's a black bag over my head. That was some scary shit right there. But he tells me not to worry and we sit in the car for a few hours listening to Blues CDs. Well, I thought, he's resorting to torture. Then the music goes off and the door opens and I'm picked up, put in this chair and tied up again. They take the hood off and I sit here waiting.'

'How long?'

'About an hour.'

'You must be starving.'

'And about to pee my pants. Thank God I went before he came to the door.'

'Did you hear any conversation? Did Frank talk to anyone?'

'Not that I heard. They could have been passing notes or using sign language, though, couldn't they?'

I helped her stand up and held on to her while she regained her balance and strength. She exercised and trained so it wasn't long before she was able to take her own weight.

I said, 'We've got about ten minutes. Frank's got something set up for five o'clock.'

We both looked around the room. It was the kind of space that might have been sectioned off by cubicle dividers or even temporary walls. There were two radiators on each outside wall and two doors at the back of the room. One had a running man Exit sign over it, the other was either a store-room or perhaps an office.

Belinda said, 'Sam,' and I saw she was looking behind me.

I turned and saw a stack of cardboard filing boxes with white sides and brown lids—two piles with two boxes in each pile.

She said, 'I think Frank brought them in behind me. I heard them being dumped on the floor. I've got to find a toilet.'

'Through the door, opposite the counter.'

She left, heading to the reception area. While she was gone I opened a box and started going through it. Inside were a number of cardboard folders. It soon became obvious that they were Shoemaker System files—or copies of them. So much for the paperless office.

Belinda came back in and opened a box and for five minutes we sat on the floor and read through the files. Eventually she said, 'What have you got?'

'Contract information.' I leafed through the one in my hand. 'Companies in Syria, Libya, the Yemen.'

'Me too. And invoices. All signed off by Jocasta. To the

supply of Intelligence and Security services. Frank's sending you a message.'

I'd stopped reading the one I had and was leafing through the rest in the same box. 'She's pushing the envelope. I don't know whether these are legal or not. Is Syria considered someone we can do business with again? But at best it's a potential conflict of interest with the contracts she's going to sign with the UK and US.'

'Why is he showing these to you and not telling the press?'

'He wants me back in the game. That's why he kidnapped you, to get me down here again.'

'Oh, thanks for coming, by the way.'

'That's all right. I didn't think he'd hurt you but I had to make sure, didn't I? Anyway, he's giving me these to try to convince me that Jocasta Shoemaker isn't on the side of the angels, whatever she says to the contrary. And he's telling me rather than giving them to the papers because … well, actually, we don't know that, do we? These look like the originals but he might have copies. They could be splashed all over the news tomorrow.'

We put the folders back into the boxes and replaced the lids.

I said, 'We've got a couple of minutes. Do you want to stick around to see what Frank's got set up?'

'Not really. What do we do with the boxes?'

'Leave them here. We can't take them with us and I certainly don't want to be caught carrying them.'

'He's going to a lot of trouble to keep you involved.'

'Sadly, I've never felt so wanted in my life.'

WE LEFT THE building as I'd found it. The door closed behind us with an electric click so there was little chance of anyone blundering inside and finding the evidence. We walked across the road and waited.

At five o'clock, a light went on in the building and I heard faint music coming from inside. Belinda and I looked at each other and then crossed the road to listen at the door.

Belinda said, 'One of his Blues records.'

'I think it's "Baby Please Don't Go".'

'You're a font of knowledge.'

'I know the cover version. I think it was Van Morrison.'

'At least he wasn't going to blow us up.'

'This time.'

We walked back to the main street and I hailed a cab and we went back into town.

I said, 'What kind of food would you like?'

'An Indian would press my buttons about now.'

So we asked the cabbie to take us to a good Indian restaurant and let Frank's money treat us to a rogan josh and a chicken biryani, plus naan bread. During the meal I filled her in on what had been happening with the case.

She said, 'You went quiet on me for a few days. I thought I'd screwed up once too often.'

'You didn't screw up. Frank's an expert. He set me up. He always planned to go missing after he'd launched me at Shoemakers. That was the plan—to use me as a messenger because they wouldn't listen to him. They're barely listening to *me* because I'm tainted by association. So don't worry about it. He'd have found a way to sneak out somehow.'

'You're very kind.'

'Listen, I've screwed up way more than you on this case.'

I told her about the explosion at the cinema.

'Wow, and they've got their own ambulances and doctors? Is that even legal?'

'I suppose it's a branch of private health care. A supersecret branch.'

'If they have their own ambulances then they probably have their own hospital, or some kind of unit somewhere.'

'We've seen the kind of clients they have in those boxes. They paid the big bucks. Anything's affordable if you've got the cash.'

Outside the restaurant I peeled off five hundred pounds from Wallace's retainer and gave it to her—she had nothing except the clothes she was standing in and, as I'd done the previous week, would have to kit herself out with some essentials.

I said, 'If you like we can call the police and report a kidnapping. In fact we should, to get it on record.'

'What good would it do? I'm exhausted and I don't need all the hassle right now. From what you've said no one's been able to find him anyway and we could do without the publicity. Well I certainly could: Novice Private Investigator found tied and gagged in need of pee. Put it down to a learning curve on the job.'

'Okay, if you're all right with that. Get some sleep tonight then go home tomorrow. Try not to think about what happened, if you can.'

She grinned and squared herself before me. 'You don't get rid of me that easy, Sammy. I'm in it now. This dosh will get me a few nights in a cheap hotel. If you think I can back off after what Frank Wallace did to me, you've got another thing coming.'

I raised my hand to hail a taxi, then turned to her.

'Okay, here's the thing. I'm back in the Hotel Russell. Get a room near Euston. Buy a throw-away phone and text me— just write "Hello, sexy", like it's a spam text and I'll know it's you. Hopefully it'll throw Frank off if he's reading my messages. Text me when you're in but don't tell me where you are — at least I'll know you're safe.'

'Without my own phone I haven't got your number.'

I wrote it down on the back of the restaurant bill and she tucked it inside her jacket, which Wallace had thrown over her in the car and which we'd found in the corner of the room where she was kept captive.

As the taxi pulled up, she reached out her arms and gave me a hug.

'Thanks, Sam. I was scared.'

'Me too. Glad you're okay.'

She climbed in the back of the taxi and waved as it drove off. I waited for another taxi to take me to the Hotel Russell. Standing in the street, I glanced around as though I might catch Frank Wallace watching me. I hoped I wasn't getting into paranoid habits, though it wasn't a stretch to believe he knew what I was doing.

I rang Emily Wallace on her mobile and was put straight through to voice mail. I didn't know what I wanted to say so just told her I'd arrived in London and would talk to her when I could.

Once in the hotel I threw my travel bag on the floor, stripped and showered. As I came out of the shower, towelling my hair, the phone pinged. Belinda had found a room and was safe.

I was still staring at the screen when the phone rang in my hand.

Frank Wallace said, 'Hello, Mr Dyke. Welcome back. I hope you enjoyed the reading material.'

'What does it mean?'

'If trouble was money ...'

He hung up before I could reply. I guessed he'd given me another song title. Did it mean anything? That Shoemakers were in trouble and Wallace intended to profit from it? That the case files in the boxes showed that Shoemakers had themselves profited financially from the trouble their unsavoury clients were in? Or was it the first title that had sprung to his mind? I couldn't tell.

In any case, I hadn't liked the hint of levity in his voice. I was coming to realise it usually meant trouble, with or without money attached.

CHAPTER TWENTY-FIVE

THE ROBO-RECEPTIONIST definitely smiled at me as she printed out my I.D. and tucked it rather lasciviously into its plastic wallet. I must have passed some kind of initiation test. Getting a response from the receptionists had been like the Labours of Hercules so perhaps I was now accepted into the clan.

For once Gale wasn't in attendance, for which I was glad. I'd called that morning on the pretence of having an invoice to present and had managed to wangle a two-minute conversation with Jocasta. Perhaps she felt guilty about the curt farewell she'd given me on Sunday, though I doubted it. When I told her that Wallace had kidnapped Belinda as a way of apparently bringing me back into play, her tone changed. She told me to come over immediately. She didn't know who Belinda was but perhaps the involvement of an innocent third party had woken a dormant sense of responsibility.

In her office I explained in more detail what Frank had done with Belinda and how he'd led me down to London to rescue her. Afterwards we sat facing each other across the glass coffee table. I wondered if I looked as tired as she did.

She said, 'That must have been horrible for her.'

'She's tough and she's bearing up well.'

'Give her my apologies and good wishes.' She leaned back in the sofa and said, 'A week tomorrow.'

'The contracts are signed Friday?'

She nodded. 'Every day brings a new wrinkle, something else to be ironed out.'

'We should call in the police. First Givens, now Belinda. Frank's running riot.'

'Is that what your friend wants?'

I hesitated. 'No. She thinks the paperwork would get in the way of finding him.'

'Sensible girl. If my people at the Ministry can't find him the cops won't stand a chance.'

'Our position is getting very tenuous if it all comes out later. Physical assault, kidnapping … You'll only have so much good will with your Intelligence people. If Frank does something outrageous and we didn't tell anyone, you'll be burned.'

'You too.'

'Yes, me too. But I'm not worried about that.'

'What *are* you worried about?'

'Frank Wallace. And his daughter.'

She looked at me coolly. 'I get it now. You think his motives are pure but his methods are wrong. You don't like what I'm doing, what my company is doing, but you think Frank should carry on writing his articles and argue his case in open forum.'

'Maybe. There's something I didn't mention when I described finding Belinda.'

'Yes?'

'Frank had left boxes of files for us to find.'

Her eyes grew alert. 'What kind of files?'

'Shoemaker contracts with clients. Going back five years or so. And invoices for work performed. Mainly in the Middle East.'

For a moment I thought she was going to throw me out of her office. Then she took the heat out of her expression.

She said, 'That's private property. Do you have them?'

'They're safe.'

'I want them returned at once.'

'I'll see what I can do.' I leaned forward. 'You have to understand that I don't really care about your business. I don't like what I know of it, but there are lots of things I don't like. Pistachio ice cream. Modern dance. James Blunt. What I want is for Frank to be caught and held to account for the damage he's done, and for Emily Wallace to be able to sleep at night because her father's safe. Even if he's in prison somewhere.'

I took an envelope from inside my jacket and handed it to her.

'This is the invoice for the car hire and some incidentals. All I'm asking is that you and Gale keep out of my way and don't interfere while I find Frank. You benefit from getting the job done, I benefit by not being hamstrung. Any help you can give me, fine. If you don't want to, also fine. Just stay out of my way.'

She glanced at the envelope but didn't open it. Instead she tore it in two and placed the halves on the table.

'I'll do better. What say we pay you—no, hear me out— we pay you a daily rate on a consultancy basis. You don't have to treat us as a client if you don't want to. There are no strings attached, no objectives or targets or outcomes. Just a stipend for your time.'

'Why would you do that after what I've just said about your company?'

'Perspective. There are other people involved—your friend Belinda, Emily Wallace. I had to speak to Darren Givens' wife this morning. I told her we'd pay any surgery bills she cared to send. I don't think it helped much.'

'He'll probably be scarred.'

She glanced at me. 'Yes, thanks for that. Anyway, Frank seems to want you involved in this … this whatever it is. A manhunt?'

'He thinks I'm persuading you to cancel the contracts. He knows more of my whereabouts than I do of his, so I don't suppose he's worried about being caught.'

'Can you find him? When the Intelligence services and, presumably, the Met can't?'

'He'll give himself away eventually. He talks too much not to. The thing is to stay in touch and keep thinking. If he knows I'm here—and he will—then he'll assume we're in negotiations about the contracts. He'll think his campaign is working.'

The nervous tic she was using today was to twirl her wedding ring around her finger. Kelvin Shoemaker had been dead three years and she still wore it. But why not? Perhaps it was a reminder of something other than just her husband. An earlier time, perhaps a better time.

She said, 'Do you think his campaign is working? Do you expect me to cancel the signing? Because I'm telling you now I won't.'

'I came to visit you that first day thinking you were the bad guys and Frank was wearing the white hat. Then it changed and it looked like you were innocent and he was nuts. The more this goes on the more confused I've become. To be honest, I don't trust either one of you now.'

'Ah, welcome to the world of big business.' She stood up suddenly and crossed to a door I hadn't previously noticed.

It was behind her desk and had only a keyhole in place of a handle. She took a key from her desk and unlocked the door, pulling it towards her by tugging on the key. 'Come on up. I want to show you something.'

THE DOOR LED immediately to a short flight of steps going up. I'd assumed that Jocasta's office was on the top floor but evidently there was another storey to the building.

We went through another door and were in a large conference area: there was a massive beechwood table surrounded by upward of twenty rotating leather chairs, with two octopus hands-free telephone units, one at each end, and power points in banks of five scattered down the centre of the table.

To one end of the room was a small seating area of armchairs and sofas, next to a long cupboard supporting two expensive drinks dispensers and trays of biscuits. At the opposite end was another seating area around a smaller table where, presumably, conference attendees or clients could do their online work in privacy.

And there were the windows.

All four sides of the room contained floor-to-ceiling windows of the type I was now used to in Apartment 60. The views were stunning—along the Thames west towards Tower Bridge and east towards London City airport; north towards Canary Wharf and its high-rise cluster, south towards Greenwich and the Observatory.

Jocasta said, 'This must be my favourite place in the whole world. Except for Kos.' She turned to me and smiled. 'Where I was brought up.'

'You don't have an accent.'

'My parents consulted on what to do for me to grow up properly bi-lingual. It seemed that the first seven or eight years I should be brought up here, then go to Greece to acquire the language there. It helped that my father was English and my mother Greek. So I never really lost touch with either language.'

'And then you came back.'

She walked close to the window that looked west, into the heart of London.

'I was a student at L.S.E. doing research in geopolitics.'

'I only understood half of that sentence.'

She glanced at me again. 'Don't be coy, Mr Dyke. You're sharper than you make out.' She turned back to the view outside. 'Kelvin came to give a talk on security in the modern world. I wrote to him afterwards and interviewed him for my thesis. I never finished it. He offered me a job as an analyst in his new company and we ended up working together closely.'

'Wasn't he married?'

'He had been but she died in 1980. He'd been alone since then. There was a child, a boy who went to college in America and stayed there and has no interest in this business. Trained as an architect. I say "boy", he's in his late thirties now. He lives in Georgia and I understand he renovates houses. He has his own family and career and we're not in touch.'

'Could I speak to him?'

She became defensive. 'Why would you want to?'

'Background.'

She didn't seem convinced but in the end shrugged.

'I'll get Ann to give you his number.'

I moved on.

'So there was an age difference between you and Kelvin.'

'Yes, twenty-five years. Do you find that shocking? He was the most interesting person I'd ever met. Experienced and wise and with energy that came off him like light.'

'How long were you married?'

'Just six years. During that time the company grew exponentially and we had less and less time together—he had to supervise the setting up of our foreign offices while I stayed here. People like Frank Wallace are reluctant to admit it, but for most of the last two years of Kelvin's life, I was running the business. It was no surprise to me when Kelvin left me the controlling shares. The chairmanship was ratified by the board anyway, so I felt no qualms about taking over.'

'Did you know that Frank felt so strongly about your appointment, or about the direction you took the company in?'

At first I thought she was ignoring the question, lost in writing her own autobiography.

'There was a new world opening up. Opportunities that people like Frank Wallace didn't understand. Governments on both sides of the pond were becoming receptive to the use of private companies like ours.'

'They used mercenaries in Iraq.'

'Of course, though they wouldn't call them that. Those men call it The Circuit, don't they? Getting themselves hired through agencies to work as private soldiers.'

'It's either that or private investigation for most of them.'

She raised her eyebrows. 'Really? Like you?'

'I steer clear of anyone with tattoos and a moustache. A dead giveaway.'

She laughed lightly, her lips parting to show straight white teeth.

'I'll watch out for them.'

'You were telling me why Frank didn't like what you were doing.'

She sighed. 'I guess in the end he was too locked into an

old world. You know he's keen on the Blues? He was always prattling on to Kelvin about some old disc he'd found, as if he could inspire him to like the music with the same fervour. That defined his world-view—the past as a golden age, where everything was better.'

'He told Greg Last the Blues were optimistic. I can't see that myself.'

'I have no idea but I'm no expert. I can't stand that droning on.'

'You told me when we first met that Frank was happy with what you were doing with the company. Were you lying?'

She turned to face me, folding her arms across her chest.

'No, I was not lying. Did he express reservations? Yes. But he was never overtly aggressive or troublesome. It was more like he wanted to get straight in his head where we were going. Remember, things were changing. Security was becoming a global business and we were looking for global clients.'

'Who were not always salubrious.'

'You mean those from the Middle East?'

'For example.'

'If we didn't work for them others would. We didn't have as big a profile then as we do now, we needed the work.'

'Whatever it was.'

'Don't be so high-and-mighty. Have you never taken on a client you were dubious about?'

'At least I'm not a hypocrite about it.'

'I'm not so sure about that. You're sitting on an awfully high horse up there. Listen, we did the best work we could. It was usually straightforward security work for company directors. Sometimes banks, yes, sometimes the companies that cluster around oil producers—consultants, advisers, finance men. Occasionally we'd run due diligence on a company that was about to get in bed with a Middle East organisation. Nothing involving secrecy or Intelligence in the way you might mean it.'

'Do your new partners know about this?'

'Of course. They do due diligence too, you know. We convinced them that we're objective and even-handed.'

'And Frank? Was he objective?'

'For someone who'd worked all over the world, he was very small in his thinking. He refused to see how everything was connected. He was still bound up in the cold war. Us and Them. And you didn't do business with Them. Fortunately, the world's moved on.'

'Besides, you had bigger fish to fry.'

'When you work with governments you have much more power, yes.'

'And that's important to you?'

'Power relates to power.'

'What the hell does that mean?'

'That once you have clients at a certain level, you gain other clients at the same level. All of a sudden you're a major player. That's why this deal with the UK and US governments is so important. It makes us a world player in security.'

'You'll earn more money.'

'We'll know more people. And then we'll earn more money.'

AFTER I LEFT the Shoemaker building I called Emily. This time she replied but she wasn't at work—the ambient sounds in the background were different.

When I asked where she was she said, 'Out to see a client.

On the tube. We could get cut off at any moment. Glad to hear you're down in the big city again.'

'I need to talk to you.'

'Has Dad phoned?'

'No. Well, not for a day or two.'

'You can take me to dinner again if you like. I suppose Dad's still paying?'

'Name the place.'

She thought for a moment then suggested Strada, on the opposite side of the river from Apartment 60 by Tower Bridge. It was a medium-length walk from the apartment, where I'd agreed with Jocasta to hole up again while I was working on Frank Wallace.

Emily said, 'There's a great view of the Bridge when it's lit up at night. Romantic.'

'I'll look forward to it.'

'You should.' She paused. 'Is there something I should know?'

'Your dad's crossed a line, Emily. And the thing is, I'm not sure he knows there's a line to cross.'

'Sam—'

She was cut off suddenly, presumably by the train losing signal. I stood on the pavement for a moment, thinking and anticipating, then walked to where I could catch a cab back to the Hotel Russell to check out.

CHAPTER TWENTY-SIX

EMILY WAS RIGHT—the view from the panoramic window at Strada was spectacular, Tower Bridge gleaming in an iridescent, multi-coloured glow as if made from luminescent Meccano.

This time I arrived first so I could watch Emily's entrance, which was also pretty spectacular. The weather had warmed during the last couple of days so she wore a short black jacket which, as she took it off, revealed shapely shoulders under a navy halter top. Her hair had been cropped and shaped since the last time I'd seen it and she looked both older and more sophisticated, almost a different woman to the one I'd first met in my office. Perhaps a gift for chameleon-like adaptation ran in the family.

But her expression was grim, as though she'd dressed for the part but didn't want to be in the play.

She gave me a half-smile as she sat down and hung her jacket over the back of her chair. Then her lips thinned once more and her eyes found the table-top.

We said hello.

I asked how she was and she said she was fine.

I said this looked like a nice place and she agreed, adding

that it was expensive but popular.

Finally she looked up and her eyes were fierce.

She said, 'My dad hasn't crossed any line. He's not well and needs help. Can we agree that before we start?'

My hands were on the table. I turned them over, showing my palms as if to say I wasn't carrying any concealed weapons.

I said, 'Emily, he's hurt people.'

'What people? Who?'

'Remember I said I was supposed to meet him? Well I turned up but he didn't, because someone else arrived who wasn't meant to be there. Your dad let off an explosive device and a young man was injured.'

Her hand had flown to her mouth.

I said, 'He's all right, but he'll be scarred. On the side of his face. I've spoken to Frank since then and he doesn't seem to care. He just wants what he wants.'

After a moment Emily took a drink from the carafe of water that had appeared on the table. Then she said, 'You mentioned "people". Who else?'

'You don't need to know any more, Emily.'

'You're wrong, I do. What else?'

'A woman I work with … Frank kidnapped her and brought her down to London.'

Her eyes were now round. 'Why? What did he do to her?'

'Nothing. He told me where she was so I could come and release her. He didn't harm her though he led me to believe he would if I didn't come. He left some files intended to incriminate Shoemaker in some shady dealings.'

A waiter had appeared at our table with menus which we took and ignored immediately.

Emily breathed out as though she'd been holding it in

since I started talking. She looked past me at Tower Bridge.

After a while she said, 'He was a weird dad.'

'Most dad's are. I'm a case in point.'

'His job meant he was away a lot. I grew up in a series of Embassy houses all over Europe. But even if I was in the compound he wasn't always there. Then he sent me to school over here and afterwards I went to university and we haven't really been close since then.'

'Did you ever know what he did?'

Her eyes came back to me. 'No, never. Not in detail. I thought he was a diplomat of some kind. He was too gentle to be a spy. He'd arrive back from somewhere and you might have expected him to bring gifts and so on, wouldn't you? That's what most normal dads in his situation did. But he just went to his den and tinkered with stuff until he had to go away again. Some years there was a routine, when he was actually working in the Embassy, but mostly he was a distant figure.'

'What about your mother? How did she cope?'

'Well she didn't, did she? Left as soon as she had me.' An ironic smile pulled down the corner of her mouth. 'To be fair, she gave it six months. So she had a try.'

'Then who brought you up?'

'There were arrangements in the Embassies. Then I came to school in the UK so it wasn't an issue. Been independent since the age of about ten, one way or another.'

I reached over and took her hand. She didn't pull it away.

I said, 'I'm sorry this is working out the way it is.'

'How *is* it working out, Sam?'

'Your father is making a nuisance of himself and at the moment I can't see any way of stopping him. He's one step ahead every time. Isn't there anything you can tell me about where he might be staying? Was there a family home? Even the home of a relative or friend? Somewhere he'd think no one else knew about?'

She shook her head. 'Do you think I haven't been worrying this out? Remember, we never had much of a home over here until he bought that place in Buxton. After he left government service he just rented. We'd moved around so much beforehand I don't think he liked the idea of a permanent place. And even if he considered it, he was probably too late to get on the mortgage ladder. Too old, couldn't afford a deposit. He didn't really think it through.'

The waiter came back and we made some hasty decisions about our food. When he left I realised I was still holding on to Emily's hand.

I said, glancing down at our hands across the table, 'What's going on here?'

She grinned at me. 'Smile when you say that, stranger.'

I couldn't help myself: I did.

TWO HOURS LATER we were standing on the pavement outside a house in Camden.

She said, 'You could always come up. Check there are no burglars.'

Her breath was warm and sweet against my neck. My arm had found its way over her shoulders and down her back, where it rested, idling, minding its own business.

I said, 'Do we think it's a good idea? You're paying for my time.'

'I might want a rebate for tonight, then. Fooling around on the job.'

'It's vital information gathering.'

'If you come up I'm sure you'll find more information upstairs.'

'I'll do it just to show how committed I am to the work.'

'Good.'

She turned away and opened the front door of the house that, when I looked closely, seemed to contain half a dozen flats. She pushed a timed light switch and we hurried across a tiled hallway and were half-way up the second flight of stairs when the timer went out and we fell into darkness.

She said, 'Don't worry. I know the way.'

Her hand found mine and she tugged me upwards. There was a rattle as another key found another lock and then we were inside. She stepped carefully between the furniture and turned on a table-lamp. The room came to life. There was a sofa and a matching chair, some modern prints on two of the walls, a flat-screen television. The wall facing the windows was completely taken up with a floor-to-ceiling bookcase. I noticed ranks of books on music history, particularly the Blues—biographies of Bessie Smith, Billie Holiday, W.C. Handy, Leadbelly ... it was a collector's library.

Emily had been watching me. I said, 'Nice room.'

She said, 'The best room's through there.'

And pulled me into the bedroom, overcoming my weak powers of resistance.

I WOKE IN the night in the unfamiliar surroundings of a woman's bedroom. It felt ... feminine. There were smells and textures I was unaccustomed to. There was a flowered curtain over the window and it let in a dim orange glow from the street-light immediately outside.

I sat up in the bed and looked down at Emily's arm protruding from the bedclothes. It was frail, as slight as a child's. Her splay of hair fell over her face and moved gently as she breathed. I wondered what I was doing here. It felt as though I'd been seduced. I hadn't been unwilling but neither had I felt like an equal partner.

I slipped out of the bed and dressed in the darkness. My clothes were cold. It was about four o'clock, I guessed, but I could still hear London working outside. In an hour or two it would start waking up properly as delivery vans started their runs and newsagents rolled up their shutters.

I let myself out of the flat and went quietly down the stairs. As I was about to open the door someone unlocked it from the far side.

It was a young Indian girl wearing a nurse's uniform under a heavy coat. Her shift must have ended. She flashed a glorious smile up at me and slipped past without a word.

I held the door open and went outside, into the cold air. Even at four o'clock London was busy. But not busy enough to make me invisible to myself or, I suspected, to Frank Wallace.

CHAPTER TWENTY-SEVEN

I WAS ASLEEP in Apartment 60 at eight o'clock when my phone pinged with a text. I stirred enough to read the blurry words. It was from Emily. It read: *Grt evening. Sorry u cldnt stay. Dnt worry bout it.*

I told myself that I should learn text-speak … and then reminded myself that I hated it. Still, it was nice to get absolution from her for ducking out of the morning hellos and awkwardness.

Then I realised that before the phone had pinged, I'd been half-awake and thinking about her. Reminding myself of the smooth curve of her skin in the small of her back, of the slight down on her neck, the scent beneath her ear.

And even when I was shaving and brushing my teeth I was still thinking about her. Remembering things she'd said, seeing again the sparkle in her eyes over the table at Strada, feeling her naked foot touch my leg beneath it.

I caught myself smiling in the shaving mirror and gave myself a good telling-off. This was no time to be falling for someone's tender ministrations, especially when I was trying to catch and render harmless her father.

Who, on cue, rang. This time it was the land-line in the

apartment, not my mobile.

'Mr Dyke, I'm not happy.'

'I can't say I'm surprised.'

He seemed taken aback. 'Why do you say that?'

'Because you're always unhappy about something, Frank. It's your natural state.'

'But you don't even know what I'm unhappy about.'

'Oh, the state of English cricket. The falling standards of the BBC. The quality of letters to the Daily Mail. Do I sound as though I care?'

'This is the kind of flippancy I don't like in someone who's squiring my daughter around town.'

I felt myself standing to attention like a guardsman hauled before the Queen.

'So you saw that, did you?'

'I don't know what you think you're doing with Emily. She's a young girl without a lot of experience in the world.'

'She's old enough. She's certainly older than the age of consent. She seems to think you weren't that concerned about her welfare when she was younger.'

His voice went cold and hard-edged. 'She said that, did she? That's not good.'

'She's a grown woman, Frank. It's none of your business what she does or what I do with her. It's her choice. You didn't seem so concerned when she was expressing her worry about you—why should it be any different the other way around?'

'Because I'm her father.'

'So are you forbidding me from seeing her?'

'Do you think I'm capable of a deliberate murder, Mr Dyke?'

His change of subject was abrupt—even his tone of voice had shifted, to one of genuine curiosity.

I said, 'Are you thinking about it? You realise I'm still in the middle of negotiations. Or do you mean me, for seeing your daughter? This isn't Sicily, you know.'

'You can stop talking about her now.'

'Can we meet somewhere and talk like civilised human beings?'

'I'll give it some thought. How are they going, incidentally, the negotiations? Is Jocasta coming round to our way of thinking? I imagine you're weaving your spell on her. As you are on Emily.'

His tone was ironic and I suspected he knew I was no longer trying to persuade Jocasta to cancel the contracts. But he would have known that from my first meeting with her, when it came out that his objections were only recent and hadn't been put forward when he actually worked for the company. This was all part of his game-playing.

I said, 'Put it this way, she's listening. But it's a big decision.'

'Of course. Returning to my topic, do you think I could murder someone in cold blood?'

'Obviously I'd advise against.'

'I don't know whether I am—capable of it, I mean. I haven't given it much thought.'

'Don't get carried away with those kinds of thoughts. You can get wrapped up in them and start seeing the world in a wrong kind of light.'

He laughed unpleasantly.

'Oh, Mr Dyke—stick to private investigations and leave psychology alone. Please, for the sake of my sanity if nothing else.'

'Is that all? Or were you calling for a reason?'

'Now, now, don't get touchy. Yes, I had a reason to call you other than to berate you for walking out with Emily.'

'I'm all ears.'

'Good, well listen up. I daresay you've found out about Kelvin Shoemaker's strangely-timed death. Dear old Greg Last might have mentioned it, if not Jocasta herself.'

'By all accounts it was sudden.'

'Indeed. What you might not have known was that when he fell ill, Kelvin was taken to the private hospital that The Sophocles Trust had recently endowed, and, I should add, bought.'

'Are you suggesting that Jocasta had him murdered by her tame doctors?'

'It's not up to me to suggest anything, is it? It strikes me that for a detective, you haven't done much detecting. I think what I've just given you is known as a clue. You might want to follow it up.'

I DIDN'T BOTHER making an appointment this time—I just took a cab to the Shoemaker building and asked one of the Robo-Receptionists to tell Mrs Shoemaker's assistant that I was in the building and would appreciate a short conversation.

But I was nevertheless surprised when the lift doors opened five minutes later and Jocasta appeared, striding towards me like a Valkyrie in a calf-length skirt and high boots, her black hair waving in her slipstream.

She shook hands then took me aside. I thought she was going to sit me in one of the black couches that squatted against the foyer wall, but instead she took me past them and down a corridor that opened up into a large, bright canteen. It was around eleven-thirty—too late for breakfast, too soon for lunch—so it was relatively quiet. She queued up with me while we took coffees and biscuits, the staff keeping their eyes down and their voices respectful, then found a two-seater table in a corner.

She said, 'You seem to be spending more of your time hanging around here than out in the big wide world doing detective work. What do you want to know that you couldn't have asked yesterday?'

'I had a call from Frank.'

'I thought as much. What does he want now? My head in a basket?'

'Funnily enough, that might not be too far from the mark.'

She reacted physically—she straightened her back and cast a rapid glance around the room.

'Say more.'

'He asked whether I thought he was capable of murder.'

'What did you tell him?'

'I avoided the question. I didn't want to fuel his ideas.'

'But you think he's thinking about it.'

'Let's just say you should put Gale on red alert. Where is he, incidentally? Has he made a dash for freedom?'

'He has his own schedule and timetable. And there are preparations for next week, of course. He's working with official minders. There are going to be some heavy-hitters at the signing.'

'Then I hope it's going to be in a lead-lined bunker somewhere.'

She gave a lop-sided grin.

'Rather the opposite. For some reason the government types have decided that rather than keep it all hush-hush, given the recent publicity that Frank has given them they're going to be all open and above-board. After all, signing the contracts fits in with their ideology of reducing state involvement in matters that can be handled just as well by private enterprise.'

'I can't tell whether you believe that horse-shit or not.'

'I don't have to believe it. I just have to be there to sign. As it happens, I do believe it—there are things we can do better than the government agencies because we've actually got more expertise on hand.'

'Only because they've been firing people and you've been hiring them. They'll soon be left with a janitor to switch the lights on and off and a cleaner to dust the empty desks. Then they'll outsource those jobs to India.'

We stared at each other across an ideological divide represented, rather bleakly, by a synthetic wood table-top.

I said, 'So anyway, where is this charade to take place now? The middle of Trafalgar Square?'

'The next best thing—on a boat in the middle of the Thames.'

'What?'

'Someone had the bright idea that it would symbolise the Atlantic and signing the contracts there would be a kind of link between the two Intelligence communities. With us being the link, of course.'

'Public Relations gone mad. What does Heather think?'

'She's all for it. We've had such a bad press lately this might arouse some interest.'

'Anyway, I came here to ask whether you'd take Frank's threat seriously.'

'Was he being serious? Is he really going to try to kill me?'

'Who knows? But we can't ignore the possibility. You should have Gale get you some protection.'

'And what are you going to do for all the money I'm now paying you?'

'Stare into space for a while until something comes to me.'

'Do you have any idea where Frank is?'

'At the end of a phone.'

'You're very reassuring.'

'I try.'

She narrowed her eyes. 'You seem different.'

'In what way?'

'Softer. More … amenable.'

'As a tough private investigator I take that as an insult.'

'What happened? Are you all right?'

I didn't reply. I was thinking how falling for someone—someone like Emily Wallace—put things in a different perspective. Priorities shifted. Hard edges softened.

Jocasta's phone rang. She stared at the screen for a moment, then answered. She said, 'Just a moment.'

She looked around the cafeteria. It was empty except for two people in the furthest corner of the room, whispering to each other across their table.

Jocasta pressed a button on her phone and laid it on the table.

She said, 'We're both here, Frank,' and looked over at me with a shrug.

Frank's voice rang tinnily from the phone's loudspeaker.

'Ah, Mr Dyke. So good to speak to you again. What have you two been conspiring about?'

I said, 'Have you considered my request?'

'What's that?'

'To meet me face to face.'

'It's in the pending file.'

Jocasta said, 'Frank, where are you and what do you want?'

'Ah, now, that's not a fair question.'

'Are you going to talk to me sensibly and stop playing games?'

'I only play games when I'm bound to win, Jocasta. Am I going to win this time?'

Jocasta snorted, then picked up the phone and cut him off. She looked at me defiantly. I raised my eyebrows.

'Why did you do that? I thought we were on the point of having a conversation. The very thing you wanted to do.'

'I'm not playing games just to satisfy him. I'm not negotiating from a position of weakness.'

'Is that what it was?'

'Look, I've got to go. Thanks for the heads-up about Frank's aims and intentions. I don't believe them for a moment, by the way.'

'You don't think he wants to kill you?'

'No, I don't.'

'He might be a bit miffed that you hung up on him. Especially seeing it was his choice this time.'

'You saw—he rang me when it suited him. He could have done it any time before, couldn't he? Ask yourself why he didn't. Why he needed you as a go-between.'

She had a good point. Wallace seemed to be able to contact anyone any time he wanted. It struck me that perhaps she knew him better than she'd admitted.

She was about to stand up when I leaned forward.

'This morning he suggested that Kelvin wasn't treated well when he went into your hospital. He suggested that The Sophocles Trust might have been involved.'

She looked down her nose at me. It was a strong, proud nose that took some looking down.

She said, 'So now you think I and the dedicated doctors at Aries House murdered my own husband. He's full of bright ideas, isn't he? And you seem to be pretty good at believing them.'

'I have to ask.'

'Even if it were true, which it isn't, what bearing would it have on the contract signing or Frank's alleged intention to kill me?'

'Did you hear what you just said? It has all sorts of relevance.'

'For example.'

I could tell she wanted me to say them out loud so I'd hear how monstrous they'd seem.

I said, 'For example, did you come by the shares in Shoemaker Systems honestly? Or did you have him killed so that you could inherit them? That leads to the question of the will … was Kelvin of sound enough mind to leave the shares to you? Were you just working behind the scenes to enrich yourself by moving the company to a different business model? And so on.'

'I suppose I asked for this by offering to take you on in a consultancy role. Consultants are paid to think the unthinkable, aren't they?'

'I'm just thinking out of the box, running the idea up the flagpole to see who salutes.'

She stood up. 'Well don't let me detain you in dreaming up your fantastical ideas. Go to it. I don't think they'll find any purchase anywhere, but hey, it's your right to make a fool of yourself.'

She strode away purposefully, her hard heels rapping on the tiled floor.

I thought it interesting that although she'd poured scorn on the idea that she might have murdered Kelvin, she hadn't outright denied it.

CHAPTER TWENTY-EIGHT

IT WAS NOW approaching midday and people were starting to filter into the canteen for lunch. Most were men and women in smart clothes—jackets, creased trousers for the men, tailored suits for the women—but a group of half a dozen men wearing the same tunics I'd seen Gale wearing sauntered in as if they owned the place. I would have put them mostly in their mid-twenties, probably ten to fifteen years younger on average than the other employees. They joshed with each other as they queued for massive plates of protein and vegetables, then pushed two tables together so they could sit in the round with their backs to the rest of the employees. They continued their banter as they bent to their food.

Gale wasn't with them but I took them to be his own cadre, the team to which Darren Givens belonged.

I stood up and joined them, standing behind the chair belonging to a particularly beefy specimen. Like the others, his hair was military short and he had a ruddy, outdoors complexion. I suspected Gale recruited them for strength and obedience, like well-trained Labradors.

The banter stopped when they saw me.

I said, 'Hi. I guess you're John Gale's team.'

The man facing me across the table was dark-haired with clear, intelligent eyes. He put down his knife and fork and wiped his lips with a paper napkin.

He said, 'I don't recognise you, sir, and I see you don't have a pass.'

He was right. Because I hadn't been expected at Reception there was no pass ready to be printed out for me. And when I'd walked off with the boss there'd been no problem.

I said, 'I've been working with your boss and with his boss.'

'I'm sorry, sir, I'm going to have to ask you to get a pass before we can talk to you.'

'Why, what are you frightened of? If you'd been here ten minutes ago you'd have seen me in that corner talking to Jocasta Shoemaker.'

'But I wasn't, so as far as I'm concerned, you weren't.' He stood up and there was a stirring of chair legs around the table. 'I'm going to have to ask you to leave, sir.'

'I wanted to ask how Darren Givens was getting on. I was there when he was injured.'

Now there was a real stir and the ring of faces turned towards their leader. The man in the chair I was holding pulled it away from my grasp and looked up, frowning, as though I had no right to be in his space.

The man who had stood up walked around the table to confront me. He was two inches shorter but he acted as though he were taller, which was a good trick.

He said, 'Sir, you'll have to leave now. We can't talk about anything related to this organisation unless we know you're properly accredited.'

I said, 'Were you in the Army?'

His eyes flickered. 'No, sir.'

'Navy? Territorials?'

'No, sir. Please leave.'

'So you're completely untrained in any anti-terrorist protocols or behaviours. You can't even carry weapons, can you?'

I was getting to him. He'd started grinding his teeth.

'We're trained security personnel.'

'Trained in what? Watching TV monitors? Doing fifty reps with a bar-bell?'

'What's your point, sir?'

'I was just wondering why John Gale pushed an untrained and naive young man ahead of him into an exposed situation while he stood protecting himself behind a heavy fire-door. That's my point.'

The young man flinched and looked down at his mates at the table. One of them came to his aid.

He said, 'Givens was injured in a training accident.'

'That's the story for public consumption. Don't believe everything Gale tells you.'

They stared at me intently. And then I could tell from their eyes that something was happening behind my back. I turned in time to see Gale bearing down on me like a galleon in full sail, his hands frantically pulling down on his tunic. He arrived and juddered to a halt.

'The fuck are you talking to my men about?'

'Men? You mean this bunch of boys you've been feeding tripe to?'

'Get out of this building now. You don't come between my team and me.'

'Or what, you'll take my pass away? Oops, sorry, don't have one.'

By now other people in the cafeteria were taking an

interest in us. The conversation between myself and the young team member had been relatively quiet. Gale's arrival at full steam had ignited a sliver of concern amongst the other diners. Gale noticed the stir that was growing around us. But instead of stepping back to defuse the situation he came a pace closer and spoke very quietly.

'You don't know what you're playing with, Dyke. You have no fucking clue. Now back off and go get some sunshine on that ugly mug of yours.'

A witty reply was making its way to my lips when my phone pinged in my pocket. I raised a finger to Gale.

'One moment, please, I must take this.'

It was a text from Frank Wallace: *Go outside. I'll call.*

I put the phone back in my pocket and shrugged at Gale, then looked down at the table of young toughs.

'Don't let your food go cold, guys. And listen to this man here. He's the boss so he knows exactly what he's doing at all times. Even when it looks as though he doesn't.'

I strode away before Gale could challenge me or land another disabling verbal blow.

GALE WAS RIGHT on one thing—the sun was shining outside. But I didn't have time to appreciate it because I barely got through the glass doors of the Shoemaker building when my phone rang.

'Frank, are you watching me right now?'

'Trade secret, dear boy. That was awfully rude of Jocasta to hang up on me like that. What did she think she was playing at?'

'I'm not going to take your side against hers. Not at this stage. What do you want, Frank?'

'You'll be pleased to know I've been considering your request to meet me. And I'm going to grant it.'

I wasn't expecting this and he heard it in my silence. He produced one of his delighted laughs.

'I caught you off guard there, didn't I? Now, no funny tricks this time. We don't want another Givens incident, do we?'

'Where do you want to meet?'

'It's one of my old haunts, Greg Last would recognise it.'

He gave me an address and said it was in Dalston, near the station.

He added, 'Have you looked into Kelvin's death yet?'

'I don't see how it's relevant to what you're doing.'

'Some detective you are. Don't you know everything is connected, somehow?'

'I'll think about it.'

'Okay, play it your way. Tonight, eight o'clock. In the dusky dusk. Don't be late, and don't bring anyone along. We know what happens when you do, don't we?'

CHAPTER TWENTY-NINE

I'D ONLY BEEN to Dalston once before, years ago, when my Excise colleagues and I wanted to speak to someone urgently about the pirated software he'd been importing via Liverpool and selling in London.

It had changed quite substantially since then, mixing its original slightly down-at-heel Edwardian ambiance with a new modernity—upscale offices, renovated shops, lots of new glass windows on old stone buildings.

Past Dalston Junction station itself I walked for about five minutes then crossed the road and ascended a few steps to knock on the large wooden door of a small Victorian town-house with its blinds closed. The sun had just set and there was an eerie half-light in the street, that kind of light that almost has a weight of its own, like fog.

I heard the door being unlocked electronically and then it swung back, revealing nothing but more darkness and shadows.

There was no one in the doorway so I went inside and closed the door behind me. The lights came on at once.

The inside of the building had been ripped out. What should have been a narrow corridor containing stairs leading upwards, with doors to a parlour and dining room and a kitchen somewhere to the rear, had become a single large room. In the vast space in which I found myself, a thin spiral staircase painted bright red, like something belonging in a fire station, led upstairs. The room I was in was illuminated by a series of halogen spotlights hung from the ceiling and pointed at the walls, which were flat and pale. I wondered if the place had been converted into a specialist art gallery but there was no art on the bare walls and no furniture in the room.

Wallace's voice came from upstairs.

'I'm up here, Mr Dyke.'

I crossed to the spindly staircase and wound my way upwards, into yet another large, empty space.

But this arena was hidden in semi-darkness, with just one floor lamp illuminating Frank Wallace sitting in the corner on a wooden chair. He was dressed the same way I'd first met him — flat cap, Barbour jacket, walking cane. In the shadowed darkness I couldn't read his expression.

He said, 'This has all got rather messy, hasn't it? You must be regretting the day I found your door open and came inside.'

'You broke in, Frank. Don't keep on with that story, you're not fooling anyone, especially me. Now, are you giving yourself up?'

He laughed, genuinely amused. I caught a glint from an eye beneath the peak of his cap.

'And I should do that because you're in such a position of strength?'

'Because you're spiralling out of control. I'm sure your motives were honourable to begin with but surely you see that Jocasta's not going to listen to you. She's got too much riding on these contracts.'

He stood up and walked towards me, pointing his cane at my chest as if it were loaded. In the half-light he was an oddly threatening figure and I felt myself tense.

He said, 'What if I were to kill you and blame Jocasta for it?'

'Is that what you're going to do?'

'It's a possibility, isn't it? I'm sure I could fabricate a story about her passion for you and how it got out of hand. You're staying in her company flat, you've been seen talking to her, alone, several times in her offices. The lonely passion of Jocasta Shoemaker. You spurned her and she lured you here and then killed you. The Intelligence services would have to back off and I live to fight another day.'

'It must be tempting.'

He lowered his cane and returned to his chair, though he didn't sit. He stood behind it and laid one hand on its topmost bar, almost casual.

He said, 'There are too many problems with that scenario. Too easy to establish that yours was a business relationship, that you only met recently so her feelings towards you would be largely unmotivated. No, I can't make it work.' He grinned at me. 'So you're safe for the moment.'

He fell quiet and looked at me impassively. I wondered if he expected me to offer gratitude for his magnanimity.

I said, 'So what are we doing here, Frank? What was so urgent you wanted to see me today?'

There was a creak of a floorboard behind me, then a cold metal barrel was placed firmly against the nape of my neck.

John Gale said, 'Actually, it was me who wanted to see you.'

CHAPTER THIRTY

FRANK WALLACE SAID, 'See, isn't this fun? Lots of surprises tonight.'

I said, 'That explains the leaks. Jocasta had a traitor in the camp.'

Behind me, Gale said, 'Traitor is such a harsh word. I'd describe myself as a loyal employee who wanted to give some upward feedback to his boss.'

Wallace said, 'Unfortunately, she wouldn't listen, would she? Didn't listen to me, didn't listen to poor old Gale here. She perhaps forgot that I recruited Gale many moons ago. He owed me a drink, as the old-time coppers used to say.'

With Gale behind me, a familiar odour returned—it was the scent I'd smelled in Jocasta Shoemaker's office the first time I was there, thinking it was the office's filtration system adding a perfume to the recycled air. It had been familiar but I didn't know where I knew it from.

Now I remembered: it was John Gale's personal aroma, the one I'd first smelled when he'd put a knife to my back outside Wallace's house in Buxton. It had lodged in my brain but I hadn't attached a reference card to it.

I said, 'That night outside your house—it was all play-acting, wasn't it? The knife in my ribs?'

Wallace said, 'I told you—I had to persuade you to get onside with me.'

'Gale held the knife. You drove the getaway car, your face turned away so I wouldn't see you in the dark.'

'Excellent detective work!'

'And when he turned up at the cinema and got Givens injured—Jocasta didn't tell him I was meeting you there, you did.'

'You get there in the end, don't you?'

I said, 'Okay, so what's this about? How does this play in to the signing of the contracts?'

Gale said, 'It has no relevance, Dyke. I just don't like you, so you're going to disappear.'

'That's a bit short notice.'

'Sorry I didn't consult your calendar.'

Even though he was behind me and out of sight, I felt him tighten.

I said to Wallace, 'Can you trust him, Frank? This is just a personal vendetta between him and me. Do you really think he's on your side?'

Wallace pushed up the peak of his cap.

'He'd better be on my side, hadn't he? He's pretty well implicated in all this. Let's face it, he sacrificed young Darren Givens' good looks just so I could convince you I was serious.'

'Is that what it was—a demonstration of your sincerity?'

'I thought you needed more persuasion. And Jocasta, too, of course.'

'She's not going to change her mind.'

'Oh, she might. Eventually. When she finds out what else is in store.'

My heart chose this moment to start beating a little faster.

The way he was talking was making it plain they couldn't allow me to live. If I did, I would tell Jocasta about Gale, the leaks would stop and Wallace would lose his leverage.

I said, 'What happens when Emily finds out what you've been doing?'

'She'll understand my motives. She's smarter than you think.'

'I already know she's smart ...'

' ... except in her choice of father? I can hear your cogs turning over from here, Mr Dyke.'

His voice hard, Gale said, 'Can we stop all this blathering now? Let's get on with it.'

Wallace raised a hand in apology.

'Of course, you're quite right.'

He took a step towards me and raised his cane. I heard a hissing noise and knew the sleeping gas was coming my way—Wallace did like his toys, and the cane was an obvious candidate for a sleeping-gas dispenser.

I slumped forward and fell to my knees and stayed there a moment.

Gale said to Wallace, 'Now what?'

'He's a big man, he'll need longer. Wait till he goes, then we'll take him.'

'I don't know why we don't just kill him.'

'Patience. We'll keep him under wraps until we're all away. I'm only doing this for your sake. He was going to work it out sooner or later so we'll just keep him out of action.'

I slowly stretched out on the floor, placing my hands beneath me to catch my fall.

I'd been there thirty seconds when Wallace said, 'Okay, it's time.'

I heard Gale step up behind me and reach down to turn

me over.

They hadn't counted on the fact that I'd learned from Belinda's experience and made myself a couple of nose-plugs from cotton-wool, just in case Wallace wanted to try the same trick again.

So when Gale reached his arms down and pushed them under my ribs to flip me, I swivelled and caught him hard on the side of his face with my right fist.

He grunted and fell sideways heavily. He must have still been holding the gun when he bent for me because I knocked it from his grasp and it skittered across the floor.

But he was more nimble than he looked and was on his feet in an instant. I rose to face him.

I heard Wallace say, 'Oh-ho!' in a delighted tone, then Gale was on me, clubbing at me with a series of angled jabs like a demented cage fighter. He was using some kind of oriental martial arts that I didn't recognise but was probably very popular down at the gym. I fended the blows off as best I could using my forearms and open hands, trying to stay upright.

I stepped back to catch some breath and when he came forward again I caught him unawares with a straight left to the nose, which spouted blood immediately. He growled. I hoped he realised that oriental martial arts were no use against Marquis of Queensberry moves.

Apparently not. He'd been adjusting his stance, crouching lower, presenting a different profile. He was going to try another technique from his repertoire. But first he wiped blood from his nose and lifted his eyebrows towards me.

He said, 'A monkey with street smarts, eh? You're still a monkey.'

'Doing a two-day course doesn't make you a black belt.'

It wasn't much of a come-back, but it was the best I could do in my winded state.

Wallace's voice rang out and we both turned to face him.

'Stop right now!'

His face was red and his eyes narrowed. He was holding the gun in his hand.

He said, 'Earlier today I asked you, Mr Dyke, whether you thought I could kill a man in cold blood. Do you remember?'

'I do.'

Gale said, 'Stop talking, Frank, just do it.'

So Wallace shot him.

CHAPTER THIRTY-ONE

HE WAS STILL holding the gun steadily as Gale was blown backwards and hit the floor. He had grunted once and his hand had moved to his chest in a reflex. But the life was leaving him fast.

Wallace said, 'It appears I can. Kill a man, I mean. Good to know.'

We watched blood spread from Gale's body across the polished floorboards. It was viscous and moved slowly, pumped out by Gale's slowly fading heart.

I looked across at Wallace, who seemed fascinated by the sight of the dying man. I said, 'You don't have a donkey now. Who's going to do the heavy lifting?'

'I know, bit of a pain. He was useful for getting your Miss McFee into and out of the car. Telling me what's going on in the office, that kind of thing. But an awful bore, don't you think? Always on the edge of a melt-down. I warned him about his temper but he didn't listen. Why does no one listen to me, Mr Dyke? Don't I talk loud enough?'

'So is it me next?'

'Oh, I don't think so. Where's the need? You'll be better off convincing Jocasta that I'm serious about her. And my vengeance. Don't forget my vengeance. It is deadly and sudden and strikes with the wrath of Apollo. How does that sound? Appropriately apocalyptic?'

'I can't tell whether you're joking or not.'

'Oh, not joking. Never joking. Now, would you kindly remove the plugs that you seemingly have pushed up your nose? That was very clever, incidentally. I suppose you learned from Miss McFee's experience. Take them out, please.'

I pulled the bedraggled pieces of cotton-wool from my nose and dropped them to the floor.

He said, 'Disgusting,' and raised his cane with his other hand and gassed me.

I WOKE TO the sound of the door being battered down and the clumping of several hobnail boots coming up the spiral staircase.

I was face down on the floor. Gale was next to me. The gun used to shoot him was a few feet from my right hand.

Then the voices started shouting at me, telling me not to move, not to fucking move, just fucking stay there … until eventually I was given permission to move and was helped to stand while my hands were cuffed behind me. Both my forearms complained painfully—Gale must have caught them a few hard blows when he attacked me.

I was taken downstairs and then outside to a van and placed inside it, away from the scene and away from the eyes of nosy pedestrians. Through the high windows in the rear door of the van the sky seemed full of flashing lights in blue and red and there were lots of crackly conversations between men in uniform.

Eventually two men without uniforms came and sat in the van with me. One was older, balder, and wore an expression a hang-dog could only have aspired to. The younger man was bright-eyed and keen. They took some interest in how I looked, inspecting my feet, my face and my posture. I did nothing to help them out.

The older of the two men said, 'This looks bad for you, doesn't it? Anything you want to say now?'

'Not really. When will I get out?'

He looked snidely at his younger partner.

'Anno Domini 2030, with time off for good behaviour.'

I sat back on the hard bench and looked away and eventually the van started and drove somewhere not more than half an hour from the scene. At last it drew to a halt.

A sliding gate opened and closed behind us and then the van door was yanked back and I was led out of the van, into a tiled entrance of a large brick building and along a corridor. In front of a high counter my possessions were taken from me and my name and address were requested. I was then led to another room and my handcuffs were undone and a cup of black coffee was placed before me. I didn't touch it.

An hour later the door opened and the same two policemen came into the room and the interrogation began.

CHAPTER THIRTY-TWO

THE INTERROGATION WAS thorough and, as usual, boring for the prisoner. That is, me. Keep saying the same thing over and over while they look for a wrinkle, a slightly different way of describing what you've already described half a dozen times. Find that difference and pick away at it like a scab until it peels away, showing the truth underneath.

The moment I was picked up I'd been anticipating this session without any joy. It was always going to be dull, and it was.

They gave my story a good going over while making sure I was fed and watered correctly. They were nothing if not correct. They made notes correctly, they asked the correct kind of questions, they listened with the appropriate level of seriousness. All told it was a very professional job but they just didn't believe me. The weight of evidence was too strong, they kept saying. I should just tell them what really happened and then we could all relax.

I kept telling them the truth as it had occurred, omitting only a few key details. That meant explaining who Frank Wallace was, who John Gale was, what the nature of my case was and how the freedom of the civilised world depended on my being released to fight for justice … I think that was the bit they didn't believe.

It was a tiring twenty-four hours, and they could have kept me longer if they'd really tried hard, but a lawyer provided by Jocasta Shoemaker had me out by Sunday lunchtime. He was a glib, grey-haired man with a small repertoire of expressions but an air of seriousness that, I think, made the rest of us realise we were only playing at the law. He put us right and had me out on the street in a very short time. We shook hands on the pavement and I never saw him again.

I spoke to Jocasta from the phone in Apartment 60 on Sunday afternoon.

I told her what had happened in Dalston before the police arrived, then said, 'Thanks for the lawyer. I think he frightened the cops into letting me go. But it's probably screwed up your contract signing, hasn't it?'

'Not really. You told them it was Frank Wallace, right?'

'I had no option—it was him or me.'

'Did they believe you?'

'Hard to say. I don't know if Frank put my hand on the gun to give it my fingerprints. I won't have residue on me or my clothes, but Gale and I were obviously in a fight before he was shot: I gave him a bloody nose. The rest is circumstantial. Add the fact that Frank called it in and you've got a third party witness to the shooting. He could have told them anything.'

'I'm right in thinking you didn't shoot Gale, aren't I? I don't want to be spending all that money on our lawyers if you're guilty.'

'Frank shot him. I thought it was going to be me but it turned out he disliked Gale more. And it's more fun to try to pin the murder on me.'

'So as far as anyone knows it was a private dispute between him and Gale and you were unfortunately in the middle of it.'

I was in the bedroom staring at the ceiling, the phone at my ear, and now I swung my legs to the floor.

'You're re-framing this quickly, aren't you? I expect you'd call it taking charge of the narrative. But your man Gale was murdered—doesn't that mean anything?'

'Don't go romantic on me. I liked Gale well enough but it's hard to feel any sympathy for him after what he's been doing to my company. He lied to me, Dyke. And it seems he gave Wallace our secrets. Why should I be sad? He didn't have any family so I have no grieving relatives to deal with, other than that bunch of troglodytes he calls his team. And don't forget he seems to have put Darren Givens in the line of fire without any compunction. Good God, he was even happy to see you killed.'

'I think he'd been a loyal soldier.'

'Just loyal to the wrong commander.' She paused, perhaps aware that she was irritating me and that wasn't good for my health. She said, 'What are you going to do now?'

'Nothing. I want to sleep for a week but that's out of the question.'

'Let me know if there's anything else I can do. Get some rest.'

She hung up and I laid back down on the bed. I had a bad taste in my mouth—a hangover from the gas Wallace had used on me. They'd served me three squares on Saturday and breakfast on Sunday morning but I hadn't really been hungry and still wasn't. There was something in Frank Wallace's behaviour, and now Jocasta Shoemaker's, that turned my stomach. It was as though the rest of us humble mortals were only here to feed their ambition or witness their great deeds. Perhaps the absolutes in which they dealt—national security, individual privacy, corporate integrity—desensitised them to the tribulations felt by real people. The unemotional language of their clique pressed on them a way of explaining events that was bland and without feeling—collateral damage, rendition, and so on.

It was a way of seeing the world I understood—but had rejected. I refused to use abstractions that concealed the world's real meaning from me.

THAT NIGHT BELINDA came round with Chinese in several bags. By now I was starving so we set up in the fancy kitchen and tore into the shiny cartons.

I explained to her what had happened on Friday night. Her eyes were round.

'Jeez, Sammy, that was a near thing.'

'If I close my eyes I can still hear the gun-shot. And the whoomp as the breath left him. He would have died immediately, I think, at that range. Though his hand went to his chest just like in the movies.'

'What gun was it?'

'I didn't see it clearly. It was behind me to begin with and then it was sliding on the floor and then it was in Frank's hand. Pretty big. Perhaps a Glock. Maybe the 40.'

Belinda grinned. 'Investigator talk—I love it.'

'We're usually bad-mouthing clients. How are you for money, incidentally? I noticed the new threads.'

She'd turned up wearing Guess jeans and what looked like a new leather jacket.

'They have the greatest charity shops here. I thought Knutsford was good, but this place rocks. I may never go home.'

'Well if you're going to stick around, I've got a little job for you.'

'Cool!'

I told her what I wanted her to do.

CHAPTER THIRTY-THREE

THE MEETING IN Jocasta Shoemaker's office on Monday morning was grim.

There was no official replacement for Gale, though Jocasta told me on the way from the lift that she'd asked Human Resources to find one. For the time being his team had been asked to be self-managing and carry out their schedule as best they could. A man from the Ministry of Defence was coming in to brief them later that day on the arrangements made so far for the signings.

It all smelled like trouble to me but I said nothing.

There was, however, another man in her office when she led me inside.

She said, 'Mr Dyke, this is Terry Bennett. He's our sponsor, if you like. I'm afraid I can't tell you any more than that.'

'It's okay, I signed the Official Secrets Act years ago.'

Bennett shook hands. He was in his forties, with broad shoulders and a bright yellow tie and he looked fit. His grip was strong.

He said, 'Jocasta has caught me up on your role and what Wallace has been doing. She also told me what happened on

Friday. Shame about John Gale. He seemed competent but if he wound up playing for the wrong team he took his chances.'

'Are your people talking to the Met's people? Or should I expect a knock on the door from the flat-feet?'

'If what you told them is true I think we can back you up. If you're telling lies you're on your own.'

'I wouldn't expect anything else. So does it affect what happens next Friday?'

'I can't say I'm happy about it but it's a little late to pull up the drawbridge now. All hell would break loose. What's your take on Wallace? What's he up to?'

'What he's been up to from the beginning—disruption. Keeping us guessing. He's ideologically averse to what you and Shoemakers are planning and I guess he thinks he has nothing to lose.'

Bennett shook his head. 'He's not acting rationally. If he really wanted to raise issues around this there are better ways of doing it.'

'Not to his mind.'

'He could write to the press. He could contact his MP. Hell's bells, he could start a petition on Change.org.'

'Not direct enough for Frank. He's always been a can-do man. Hands on.'

Jocasta said, 'Have you any idea what he'll do next? Can he really damage us?'

'Maybe not, now. He's a wanted man. At least I think he is. I told the cops as often as I could that he was the one who shot Gale—I hope to God they're doing something about it. We'll see if anything turns up on the news or in the press.'

Bennett coughed. He looked embarrassed. 'Erm, I don't think that will happen.'

'Have you D-Noticed it?'

'We haven't gone so far as that … just pulled in a few favours. To keep it off the air till after next Friday.'

'Great … so Frank will be wandering around with impunity while we sit with our fingers up our backsides.'

Jocasta asked, 'What's the worse that can happen?'

'Who knows? Maybe he has plans to blow up your boat on live TV. Or stage a one-man protest on the riverside to distract attention from the excitement of contract-signing.'

Bennett said, 'Look, we've got this thing locked down. We'll have ministers from the UK and the States on a boat in the middle of the Thames, so don't you think we're taking a precaution or two?'

'There's no way you can change the venue?'

Bennett shook his head. 'The PM's got too much riding on this. Now it's out in the open anyway he wants to milk it. Spirit of transparency and all that. Nothing to hide. Just good business sense.'

'The man's an idiot.'

Jocasta smirked. 'But he's our idiot.'

Bennett looked annoyed and for practically the first time I felt as though I were on Jocasta Shoemaker's side. The thought wasn't attractive.

I said, 'You have to remember Frank's been operating in the clandestine world a long time. He's working alone so there's no communication with anyone else you can tap — except when he calls me. And I think he's using a different phone every time and throwing it away. I've had no luck ringing him back. So he's out there, motivated, canny, experienced and with a plan that none of us knows anything about.'

Jocasta said, 'You're scaring me. Do you have any idea what we can do?'

'As a matter of fact, yes.'

WHEN I LEFT the office I rang Emily Wallace. I'd been trying to get through since Sunday but each time I'd gone straight through to voice mail.

This time she answered.

'Sam, I'm so sorry. I was up to my eyeballs in work and couldn't get away. How are you?'

I thought it best not to describe how her father had shot a man to death in front of me on Friday night.

I said, 'I've had an interesting weekend. Perhaps we could get together and I could tell you about it.'

'When were you thinking?'

'When you're free. It doesn't have to be straight away if you're busy.'

'Okay, let me get back to you. Are you sure you're all right?'

'Yes, why?'

'You sound different—cagey.'

'No, I'm fine. Honestly. I just want to see you again. Perhaps have a refresher on what we did the other night.'

'Cheeky! Was rather nice, though, wasn't it?'

'That's how I remember it.' I suddenly realised something and paused. Then I said, 'You haven't asked me whether your father's called.'

'No, I haven't, have I? Should I be embarrassed? I'm afraid I've been rather too busy to think about him. You keep telling me he's talking to you so I suppose he's doing all right, isn't he?'

'I suppose so.'

'Anyway, damnit, did you call to speak to me or about my father?'

'You, of course.'

We chatted for a few minutes more and then hung up on

her promise that she'd ring me when she was free.
I hoped Frank had been listening in.

CHAPTER THIRTY-FOUR

I DIDN'T HAVE to wait long to find out.

I'd walked away from the Shoemaker building and had found the same coffee bar I'd used on my first morning there, and was settling into a window seat with an Americano, when my phone rang.

He said, 'So you talked your way out. I should have been more thorough. Given the fuzz no choice but to hang you.'

'You didn't really want to implicate me, did you? You're having too much fun giving me the run around. You didn't even leave the gun in my hand.'

He laughed. 'Schoolboy error. Now, down to serious matters. I don't know how often I have to tell you, but lay off my daughter. She's not involved in this aspect of my life.'

'Jocasta has an offer for you.'

There was a silence in which I could hear him breathing. I imagined him on the other side of the street, in disguise, looking at me in the café's window through ultra-strength binoculars.

He said, 'Go on.'

'She'll back out of these two contracts and focus only on domestic business if you stop releasing information to the press.'

He was quiet again. I could hear no ambient noise at all.

Then he said, 'I don't believe it. That's a complete one-eighty. She's not capable of it. Nice try, though, Mr Dyke. I see your experience at the hands of the rozzers hasn't impaired your native cunning.'

'You're a very suspicious man, Frank.'

'I have to be.'

'Will you think about it, at least?'

'I make no promises.'

'Incidentally, as an aside, why did you kill John Gale and not me?'

'Not suffering survivor syndrome, are you?'

'Not as far as I know. I've survived a lot and never suffered.'

'Hmm, I doubt that. But you're stern Yorkshire stock, aren't you, so you can probably put it in the rear-view mirror. In answer to your question, I didn't need him any more and he was becoming a liability. You won't believe the venom he showed towards your good self. You must have really got under his skin.'

'I saw through him as a petty martinet. He didn't like it.'

'Indeed, indeed. A martinet, good word. Very astute. It was his idea to kidnap you, by the way. I bought into it because I was afraid you'd see through him and his bluster. But in the end he was too much of a risk. No self-control. Now, thrilling though this chat is, I must hie me away.'

'Frank, can I ask you a question?'

'Fire away.'

'I've just told you about Jocasta's offer to cancel the contracts but you don't seem interested. It sounds like you don't really want to talk to her. So what is it you *do* want?'

'Well, first, I don't believe you. Second, I've told you

before—I want my revenge on that harridan who's ruining the company I hold so dear.'

'Bullshit. That's your standard line but I don't believe it.'

'Do I care whether you believe it? Let me think … no. Now, I really must go. As for revenge, as Muddy said, I can't be satisfied … '

The line went dead.

This whole thing was suddenly heading in a very strange direction and I felt like the ground I was standing on had just turned through a ninety degree angle.

AS SOON AS Wallace had hung up I rang his daughter again.

She said, 'Two calls in half an hour. Should I feel stalked?'

I smiled into the phone. I said, 'Your father just called. I thought you should know.'

'What did he say?'

'That I should stop seeing you. He knows every time I call your phone. How's he doing that?'

'I have no idea. Are you there, Dad? Call me. Talk to me. Let me know you're all right.' She paused a moment, then said to me, 'Do you think he's listening in?'

'Either that or it's a hell of a coincidence. Look, I know you were going to call me when you were free but I really want to see you.'

'Wow, a girl could feel flattered.'

'I have an ulterior motive.'

'Oh yes? Should I wear something flimsy?'

'That would be an additional bonus, yes.'

'So what is it you want first?'

'All the books on music in your flat … are they yours?'

'Some of them. Most of them my dad gave me over the

years. He'd read them then give them to me later. Why?'

'And you kept them because he didn't bring you gifts when he went away.'

Some coolness came into her voice. 'I suppose if you were psychoanalysing me you could say that. I didn't have much of his attention but I could have his books. Sorry, Dad, if you're still listening.'

'Is it okay if I come and look at them?'

'I suppose so … what are you looking for? Perhaps I could help.'

'It's not something I should say over the phone. Even if I knew what it was.'

'All right. It can't be tonight and I'm at work all day tomorrow. How about tomorrow night, about eight?'

'That would be great. And bear in mind the flimsy option.'

THAT WAS AS far as my plan had got, so I went back to Apartment 60 and did some research using its wifi and my tablet. I found out more about The Sophocles Trust and its constituent parts—the fact that its Chair was a former Conservative MP and there were a number of directors with noble and glorious careers behind them: the head of a national charity; a former governor of the BBC; the ex-head of a large Health Service Trust; the retired editor of a gung-ho, right-wing tabloid newspaper; a deputy director of the FBI … etcetera.

I supposed they were working for nominal fees and expenses, but it was possible other contacts and other monies would have derived from their position on the board. As the Trust was an international organisation they would have the opportunity to wine and dine people with vast resources behind them, to leave their business cards in the most exclusive, hand-crafted wallets.

I also found out more about the various bodies that Sophocles had endowed or bought out. There was the Sophocles Chair in International Security at an Oxford college, currently held by a previous director of MI5. There was the Sophocles Fund for Research into Advanced Intelligence Gathering Technology. There was a laboratory in Aberdeen that was endowed to explore the use of new technology like graphene in protective wear—trying to out-Kevlar Kevlar.

And there was the Sophocles Unit for the Treatment of Traumatic Injury, set up at a former paediatrics out-patient facility in Chalk Farm, and the place where presumably Darren Givens had been taken for treatment to his injured face. I'd looked this up a day or two earlier to satisfy my own curiosity.

I wondered if the staff called it SUTTI. I would.

I didn't know where all this information was getting me. As far as I could tell the donation of money or prestige wasn't anything more underhand than the funding supplied by Google and a thousand other charitable organisations to worthy causes. If they were making money they were entitled to invest it wherever they wanted.

I just couldn't help thinking there was something grubby about the whole system—frighten clients into spending squillions of pounds with your company, then invest that money into researching and supporting those ideas that eventually persuade clients to spend even more money with you. I supposed it was good business sense but I felt like I wanted to wash my hands after I'd finished reading.

However, I didn't.

I opened my browser again and went to Facebook, then searched for Craig Purser, Dan's partner. I found someone from Alderley Edge who was likely to be the right man and looked at his page, which fortunately gave me the information I needed.

CHAPTER THIRTY-FIVE

THE UN-MUSICAL CLAMOUR of the telephone in Apartment 60 woke me the next morning. I climbed from the bed slowly—fighting Gale had left my forearms blue with bruises that still ached.

Jocasta Shoemaker was incandescent with fury.

'Of course it's too early in the fucking morning for you to have seen the papers, I suppose.'

'Give me a précis.'

'Précis? I'll give you bullet-points and a fucking slide show. Wallace has palmed off more information to any journalist who'll listen.'

'Is it bad?'

'If it were true it'd be bad. As it is, it's catastrophic. There's a whole list of countries we're supposed to have done business with, some of them being on a proscribed list, others being on a not-very-nice people list. Plus, he makes a big deal of the private arrangements we've made with government departments in the US and over here. He's in danger of royally screwing us over before we've even begun.'

'So is any of it untrue?'

'Not untrue *per se* ...'

'So you can't haul the papers in front of the courts. They'll just plead fair comment and conceal their source. Given the people you've done business with, you can see their point.'

'Oh thank you very much. I didn't come to you for a moral verdict on me or my company, thanks all the same.'

'My mistake. I thought you wanted my absolution.'

'What I want is for you to find Frank fucking Wallace and ... I don't know, offer him a deal.'

'Can I remind you that you were the one who hung up on him?'

'Things change.'

'Will you cancel the contracts?'

She sighed with frustration. 'It might not be my choice after this. But no, I won't cancel them. I won't be blackmailed. But tell the bastard I want to at least talk to him before everything goes up in smoke. Can you do that?'

I sat down on the edge of my bed. It wasn't yet eight o'clock but I could sense the life in the streets below me.

I said, 'I've already told him you've offered to cancel the contracts if he'll negotiate.'

'You said *what*?'

'It's just a tactic to get him into a conversation. We can figure something out afterwards.'

'I didn't give you permission to tell him that. What the hell were you thinking?'

'It was a test. I don't believe he wants to negotiate but if he refuses at least we'll know where we stand.'

'How would it help?'

'We'll know he has an ulterior motive, that negotiating isn't on the table.'

'So what the hell is he up to?'

'I guess we'll find out, won't we?'

'You're not much of a comfort.'

'So fire me.'

'Just find him, will you? Counting today it's four days till the signing. I don't want to be dealing with all this nonsense at the same time as keeping the various Ministries happy.'

'I'll do my best.'

She'd calmed down and her voice was at normal pitch. Now I could hear the fatigue in it, the end of a tether being approached.

She said, 'I'm interviewing someone for John Gale's job later today. I haven't worked out what to say if he asks what happened to the previous incumbent.'

'Bennett managed to keep it out of the press then?'

'So far. We're running on empty here, Dyke, so anything you can do can only help. We need Wallace to be kept quiet until everything's signed. Then we can focus on what to do with him afterwards.'

'I'll see what I can do.'

She hung up and I lobbed the phone on to the bed.

Why did Frank do it? Wasn't he firing all his ammunition when he could have been keeping some in reserve for later in the week? Or perhaps there was even more to come in the following days.

I couldn't help feeling that from his perspective, he was still playing a game. We were all puppets being yanked this way and that by his tug on the strings.

And it wasn't over yet.

I SHOWERED AND dressed and prepared to go out. I wasn't entirely sure what I was going to do but staying indoors was not an option.

Before I left the apartment I picked up my mobile to call

Dan.

But instead of getting a dial-tone and then the notes as the number was dialled, I got a strange blank noise and a message on the screen telling me my SIM was no longer active.

I tried Emily's number and got the same response from my phone.

My shoulders slumped. I suspected that somehow, Frank had cancelled my contract. I had no idea why he would do that, seeing as my phone had been our principal method of contact, but maybe he was gearing up for Friday already and wanted to throw me off-piste for a while.

I was walking towards the phone in the Apartment when it rang. I picked it up—I would have sworn it was still warm from my conversation with Jocasta a short time before.

'Mr Dyke, the phone thing—that was just a little message from me to you. I think you were getting a little cocky.'

'So you're showing me how all-powerful you are?'

'Sort of. But I'm going to make things easy for you after this.'

'Why did you do it, Frank? You know I'll just buy another SIM card on Pay-As-You-Go, which you won't be able to interfere with.'

'Don't be so sure … anyway, that's exactly what I want you to do. You see, I want to meet Jocasta Shoemaker face to face and I want you to organise it. You told me she wants to cancel these contracts but I don't believe her. Or you. I'll have to see it in her eyes before I believe it.'

'Given what happened to Gale you'll understand her reluctance.'

'I give you my word that nothing will happen to her.'

'Is that worth a lot in today's currency?'

'I just want to see her and talk to her.'

'Frank, would it surprise you if I said I didn't believe you?'

'No, it wouldn't surprise me, but you'd be wrong.'

I tried to read into the tone of his voice the real motives behind his offer. I couldn't do it. I used to think I had a pretty good handle on what motivated people. Now motivations seemed a mystery to me. It was as though I'd been transported to a planet where the causes of human behaviour had been distorted out of recognition. It was no longer possible to assign a motivation to someone's actions because they were perverse or simply unknowable. Both Frank and, in a way, Jocasta Shoemaker, had undercut my certainty. They were playing chess at such a high level of abstraction that it might as well have been particle physics.

I said, 'It's going to be hard. She doesn't trust you and I don't think she actually trusts me.'

'Noted. But I believe you can make it happen. When you leave the flat buy a new phone and call this number.' He read out a mobile phone number and I repeated it back to him. He added, 'The new phone is to throw off anyone else they might have listening in to you. Your phone itself might be bugged, not just the SIM. I don't have to tell you not to involve MI5—that Bennett character can take a running jump. And if you let him in I'll know and it'll all be over.'

'How do you know anything now that Gale's gone?'

'I worked there a long time, Mr Dyke. I have my methods. Now, go buy that phone. Repeat back the number to me.'

I did so.

Then I hung up, left the apartment and bought a phone.

CHAPTER THIRTY-SIX

I TOOK THE SIM card from my old phone and put it in the new one to transfer all my contact numbers. Although the phone wouldn't connect to my provider it would still carry out menu functions. Then I caught a cab and went straight over to the Shoemaker building.

From the lobby I got one of the receptionists to call Ann and she arranged a pass for me, which the receptionist handed over almost sulkily, as though I'd gamed the system.

When the lift doors opened on the ground floor Ann was inside, frowning. The doors closed behind me and we went up together.

She said, 'Is everything all right?'

'What do you mean?'

'There's a lot of shouting and people going back and forth this morning. I'm supposed to be Mrs Shoemaker's Personal Assistant but all that means is I make appointments and take phone calls. My last job I virtually ran the office. Here I'm kept in the dark most of the time.'

I glanced at her. She was younger than I'd realised, perhaps early twenties.

'How long have you worked here?'

'Six months next Tuesday.'

So she knew nothing of Kelvin Shoemaker or Frank Wallace or any of the history of the company.

I said, 'Perhaps you're on probation. See how you do before they give you any more responsibility.'

She looked glum. 'I don't think she'll ever do that. She likes her secrets. She doesn't share anything.'

'It's what the company does, I suppose. Hides things.'

A thought occurred to me. 'Has she asked you to get me the number of Kelvin's son in America?'

'No—was she supposed to?'

'She said she would. She's busy, she probably forgot.'

'I'll text it to you.'

'Do you know anything about him?'

Before she could reply we arrived at Jocasta's floor. I let Ann lead the way out.

She said, 'The thing is, you can't see her at the moment. She's interviewing.'

'Which room?'

'Her office.'

'I'll wait five minutes, that's all.'

'Tea?'

'Coffee. One sugar.'

She bustled off and I sat in my usual seat in the foyer, looking out over the view of London that was higher than my own in Apartment 60 and stretched to a further horizon.

I took stock and saw myself sitting in a stranger's building, a little funky from London fumes and the air that crawls into your nostrils and your hair, my leather jacket creaking as I shifted my position, my eyes still gritty from the early-morning call. I hadn't exercised or run in several days and my body missed it. I could have brought my running shoes and found a park to run around in a cold

London dawn but it hadn't been top of my list when I packed to come south again.

Now I felt as though my limbs were stiffening and my chest contracting, the tread of my foot heavy with each step instead of the semi-bounce I liked to feel whenever I walked.

Sitting in the chair waiting for Ann to bring me institutional coffee I felt ten pounds too heavy and five years too old, caught up in a sequence of events that were of no consequence to me, whichever way they fell out, and trying to find someone whose motives I thought I was beginning to understand even while I deplored his methods. I felt as though I'd been three steps behind him all the time, waiting for something to happen and then reacting too slowly when it did.

That's why I was walking the streets on police bail, witness to a murder and close to an explosion that nearly took someone's life. I began to wonder whether this was the kind of role I wanted for myself.

And I didn't know the answer.

Ann returned with the coffee. She handed it over, saw my expression and said, 'I know, it's shit, isn't it?'

'I can stomach the taste—it's the consistency that bothers me.'

She smiled and went away, back to her own desk.

I finished the coffee then stood up and walked to Jocasta Shoemaker's office. Ann watched me approach the door then turned away pointedly. I knocked once and walked inside.

Jocasta was sitting on the comfortable sofa facing a man of about thirty with fair hair combed neatly over a pink face. They both looked up at me with surprise. She stood up and took my arm to lead me away.

'What's this about? Can't you see I'm interviewing?

Where's Ann?'

'Don't blame her, I snuck in. Frank wants a meeting.'

'What? When?'

'I don't know yet. I'm supposed to ring him if you agree.'

'You don't think I should go.'

'How could you tell?'

'It's written all over your face. I could take Simon with me.'

She glanced over her shoulder at the young man sitting on the sofa and now staring straight ahead as if he couldn't hear what we were saying.

I said, 'You're right, I don't think you should go. Certainly not alone, and probably not with Little Lord Fauntleroy there.'

'He's ex-SAS. More experienced than he looks.'

'He could hardly be otherwise.'

She took me further away from him, behind her desk. There was a modern painting of a grey-haired man in a dark suit on the wall behind her chair. I wondered whether it was Kelvin Shoemaker. I also wondered if the painting hid a wall-safe.

She said, 'Look, you've been spending all this time trying to find Wallace and now he's landed in our laps. Give me one good reason why I shouldn't meet him. If he wants our attention, he's got it. If it gets him off our back, I'll play along.'

'Remember John Gale. Frank's dangerous.'

She glanced back at the ex-SAS candidate and then looked up at me.

'Will you come?'

'If Frank will allow it. Don't tell Bennett or anyone else. For all we know this office is bugged and if Wallace thinks we're setting him up to be caught he won't turn up.'

'Okay. Hang on a minute.'

She went back to Simon and stood in front of him.

She said, 'Okay, Simon, the job's yours if you want it. We're a bit pressed so it would be great if you could start as soon as possible.'

Simon stood up. He was as tall as me and was limber and well-made. I thought he could probably handle himself.

He said, 'I can start the day after tomorrow, if you like.'

'Good. See Ann outside and she'll organise the contract through HR. Welcome aboard.'

They shook hands. Simon glanced at me and nodded. I nodded back, one super-fit killing machine to another. He crossed the carpet in three commanding strides and left.

When the door closed I said, 'How much did you tell him?'

'Usual recruitment bullshit—opportunity for rapid advancement, working with an established team, excellent pay and benefits, worldwide travel … although most of the time he'll be propping up a desk on the floor below.'

'Have you told him about this Friday? About the contracts?'

'I'll fill him in Thursday. Now, how should we play this meeting with Frank?'

AFTER LUNCH IN the office—sandwiches brought by Ann—we decided it was time to call Frank Wallace.

I picked up the new phone, which I'd plugged in to charge, and dialled the number he'd given me that morning.

He replied immediately, like an adolescent waiting for a call from a new girlfriend.

'Did she agree?'

'With conditions.'

'Of course. What are they?'

'That I come with her.'

'That's not a condition, Mr Dyke, it's a necessity. Have you got a piece of paper?'

I reached over Jocasta's desk for a writing pad and a Biro with 'Shoemaker' printed on its side. Then I told him to go ahead and he gave me the address and name of a building in St John's Wood.

I said, 'When?'

'Tomorrow night, eight o'clock. Like a vampire, I do all my best work at night.'

'And can we be clear what this meeting's about?'

'I'm not working up an agenda. We'll talk. I'll put forward my case and Mrs Shoemaker will put forward hers. And a reminder—if I so much as sniff someone in the building who shouldn't be there, you won't see me.'

'She's here now. Is there anything you want to say to her?'

'Not really. You can tell her she'll be safe, I'm not going to harm her, or you.'

'I don't know how far I can believe you, Frank, after what happened last Friday.'

'Oh for goodness' sake get over it, Dyke. Be grateful I shot him and not you. It was fifty-fifty for a moment there.'

'You can understand our reticence.'

'Would you believe Gale was the first man I've ever shot? Or killed? I suppose the work I did in IS probably led to some deaths down the line but I never heard of them directly. It's not a nice business. I didn't feel good about it afterwards. Not for Gale, who was a waste of space, but for the action of taking a life.'

I said nothing for a moment. I wasn't sure why Wallace was telling me this. Throughout our relationship he'd wanted to persuade me of his righteousness. Perhaps he was still at it, trying to convince me that killing Gale was essential, although he did at least have the grace to feel guilty about pulling the trigger.

'Frank, self-pity won't work on me this time. I've fallen for that too often.'

He perked up. 'Yes, I suppose in your line of work you have to size people up pretty quickly, don't you? People and situations. Of course you'll get it wrong most of the time — we all do. None of us have enough information to begin with. Like your misjudgement of me, for example. Not quite the old country squire now, am I?'

'You fooled me, Frank. But it only happens once.'

'You think so?'

'I'll see you tomorrow. Don't be late.'

'This is my big moment—why on earth would I be late?'

CHAPTER THIRTY-SEVEN

THAT NIGHT I took a cab to Camden and found Emily's house again.

For a while I stood outside, looking up at the windows and trying to remember which one was hers. There were lights on in three of the apartments but I saw no movement. I wasn't sure which direction this relationship was going in. A couple of years previously I'd lived with a woman for a while but we split up because she thought I spent more time focusing on my work than on her. She wasn't wrong. Worse, she'd been threatened by some very bad people on two occasions and she hadn't signed up for that.

So where was it going with Emily Wallace? I'd found myself thinking about her more and more but very quickly reaching a dead-end in the thought process, like somebody wading into the sea only to find that the land drops away beneath him just five yards from shore. I didn't know whether to dive in or retreat to the safety of the land I knew.

My usual tendency was to dive ... but this was an unusual situation. I had no idea what was going to happen with her father and if somehow I were responsible for his imprisonment, or worse, then what basis would that create for us to have a satisfactory relationship?

Obviously, there would be no basis for it whatsoever.

And in the meantime, how would it work? Would she drive up to Crewe every weekend, or would I catch a train down? Would we find somewhere in-between, like the dreaded Milton Keynes? Or Rugby?

Having just rebuilt my house I didn't want to abandon it …

I was getting ahead of myself. The fact I was even thinking along these lines worried me. I had a bad history with women and I shouldn't have been trying to inflict myself on anyone, never mind a vulnerable woman whose father was turning into a domestic terrorist with egomania.

I rang the bell next to Emily's name and the door buzzed. I pushed and it opened and I went upstairs.

SHE OPENED THE door before I arrived, lounging against the jamb in a simple navy dress that was scoop-fronted and showed her shape. She wore long ear-rings and looked as if she were about to dine in an upscale restaurant.

She said, 'Hello, sailor. Wanna come in and inspect my rigging?'

'You know me—any port in a storm.'

'That's so flattering.'

But she grinned and stepped back so that I had to edge past her to enter the room. She smelled of something expensive and it rose upwards towards me as I brushed past.

Once I was inside she closed the door and came close again, touching my hand with her fingers before walking further in.

She said, 'You hungry? I've made pasta.'

'Pasta is my favourite dish.'

'Really?'

'Well, no, actually it's curry. But I thought I'd be diplomatic for once.'

She nodded as though she understood my dilemma and pointed towards an open bottle of red wine on the dining table, which was already set for two.

'Help yourself while I finish up in the kitchen.'

'Can I look at the books?'

'My dad's? Go ahead.'

She walked languorously into the kitchen so that I'd watch her, which I did, and then I turned to the shelves.

I had no idea what I was looking for. The fact that Frank Wallace kept quoting Blues song titles at me had begun to get on my nerves but also made me think. Everyone had told me that he was a Blues fanatic so perhaps I shouldn't have been surprised that he was able to quote titles in almost any situation.

But I also knew he was a game-player and leaving the chemical formula for shellac, a kind of wax product, in the house in Manchester suggested there was more to it. Greg Last had told me that Wallace took time out to hunt down old disks and even wax cylinders, the prime method by which music had been recorded and sold until flat disks became popular and cheap. Shellac had been used to make 78rpm disks until the fifties but not wax cylinders—so what was Wallace trying to say?

I'd already done a little research and found that the wooden box Wallace had brought with him to Belinda's house, with Edison stencilled on the side, was probably a wax cylinder player, which were more common and cheaper than you'd imagine on e-Bay. It was the right size and shape and was evidently very old. The fact that Wallace had avoided my questions about it suggested he didn't want me to know what it was.

The biographies on the shelves were arranged alphabetically by subject and I started by plucking them out one by one and looking inside. I don't know what I expected to find but I didn't find it. There were no hand-written notes in the margins, no folded-down pages, nothing highlighted in bright yellow. The books had obviously been read because of the condition of their spines but Wallace hadn't marked them in any way.

I took another tack. Beneath the biographies were the histories, in alphabetical order according to author: Roy Carr's A *Century of Jazz*; *The Delta Blues* by Ted Gioia; Alan Lomax's *The Land Where the Blues Began*, and others. I concentrated on the early history, when wax cylinders were the medium of recording and listening.

The last book I glanced through was a visual history of the Blues. It was large format and difficult to hold, but the black-and-white photographs from the beginning of the last century were glorious.

And there was a single, solitary, noticeable tick in a left-hand margin next to a name. The name wasn't that of a singer or musician, a producer or lyric writer. It was the name of a sociologist: Howard W. Odum.

It didn't mean anything to me, but it soon would.

EMILY CAME OUT of the kitchen carrying two heaving plates of penne with chicken arrabiata and we sat at the table to eat it. I hadn't touched my wine so I put that right immediately.

She said, 'Anything more from my dad? Do you have any idea where he is?'

'Maybe tomorrow.'

She started eating but her eyes were on me.

'You're being evasive.'

'It's better if you don't ask me questions about him right now.'

'Aren't I still the client?'

'I haven't invoiced you yet.'

'We signed contracts.'

'If you want to be picky … '

She put down her fork. 'Sam, don't do this.'

'Do what?'

'You're playing games with me. I had enough from my dad without you joining in. Whose side are you on, anyway?'

'Let's not talk about sides.'

'Why not? I thought you were on my side, working for me. But I know you're still doing things for that Shoemaker woman. It makes me feel very insecure because I don't know where I am with you.'

She was right. And it was because I didn't know where I was myself. What I'd read ten minutes before had made me think differently about Frank Wallace and what he was up to. I thought I knew the parameters of the game we were all playing but it turned out I was probably wrong. Things were beginning to come together in my slow-moving brain but I didn't want to share my thoughts with her just yet. I had more work to do first.

I put down my own fork and laid my hand on top of hers. I thought I should at least try to be reassuring.

'Your dad's going to be fine. He's messing some people around but nothing's going to happen to him.'

'Even though he's killed someone?'

I stared at her.

'How do you know about that?'

Her eyes fell to the table.

'He called me to confess. He wasn't happy about it but

he said it had to be done. That's why I'm worried for him. I think he's losing touch.'

'You could have told me this earlier.'

'He only called this afternoon. I didn't know how to bring it up. Is it true?'

'Yes. Don't be fooled by him, Emily. He might have wanted to convince you it was necessary, but trust me, it wasn't.'

'How do you know?'

'I was there. He nearly killed me.'

Her eyes were filled with tears and now they spilled over her bottom lids and ran down her cheeks.

'I never thought he'd do that.'

I didn't know what to say so I squeezed her hand.

I said, 'What else did he tell you?'

'Nothing much. He didn't give anything away, if that's what you mean. It was as if he wanted me to know the worst thing about him. He said it completely calmly.'

'Perhaps he wanted you to hear it from him before you read it in the papers.'

She'd reversed the position of our hands so that hers was now on top of mine. She kneaded my fingers, then took my hand and placed it on her breast.

'I don't think I can eat any more, Sam.'

'Okay.'

I stood up and she stood up and came close to me, putting her arms around my back.

She said, 'I think you should have another look at the best room in the house.'

'Fine by me.'

'You're such a sweet-talker, how can I resist you?'

'Thousands others have managed.'

I felt her smiling into my chest.

I WOKE IN the middle of the night to find her sitting up in the bed, staring ahead.

She said, 'You're meeting him tomorrow.'

'If he turns up.'

'I'm scared for him.'

'He'll be all right.'

'Promise?'

'I won't hurt him and no one else will be there except Jocasta. Do you want me to frisk her first?'

'Don't joke, Sam. It's not funny.'

I agreed with her—it wasn't. Jocasta Shoemaker and I were going to come face to face with someone who'd already killed one man and seemed to be spiralling out of control. What was there to joke about?

CHAPTER THIRTY-EIGHT

LOOKING AT ARIES House from the car park, Belinda thought it unlike any hospital facility she'd known—it looked as though an architect had been given his head but had also been made to drink a pint of vodka before starting his plans. The concrete edifice had several storeys, each one stepping back from the one below to create a small balcony beneath. One end of the building was finished in blue brick and a huge mural had been painted over the surface—a collage of children's faces of all races and colours. The name 'Aries House' was written in a modern slanting print at the bottom of the image.

The front entrance was mostly glass while in the gardens that stretched either side of the gravel drive were signs of the building's previous incarnation as a paediatric out-patient ward: jungle-gyms, slides, roundabouts. Nowadays there were no children to be seen in the grounds; in fact there was no one taking the air or sitting, dazed, in wheelchairs pushed along by white-coated angels. The place seemed quiet, almost empty.

She climbed out of the car she'd hired for the day and walked round to the Reception entrance, where a young woman examined her computer and found her appointment with the Director, Dr Susan Hanks, and asked her to take a seat.

When she arrived ten minutes later, Dr Hanks was little older than Belinda, wore a two-piece suit and had blue-black hair that was not so much coiffed as moulded. Belinda felt momentarily unnerved in her jeans and leather jacket combination but got over it when Dr Hanks started talking to her.

'I agreed to this appointment, Miss McFee, but I'm afraid I don't understand what you want to talk about. Come through here, would you?'

She led Belinda into a room which she knew wasn't the Director's—it was more like an interview room, with a single table and two chairs either side of it. Belinda took one of the chairs while Dr Hanks took out her phone, looked quizzically at a text on the screen, then turned it off and laid it on the table. Then she pulled out the facing chair and leaned back in it.

Belinda said, 'Thanks for seeing me on such short notice. You must be busy.'

Dr Hanks' face remained impassive. 'What makes you say that?'

'Well, you run a place that deals with traumatic injuries. Must be a full-time job.'

'Of course. We give our patients the best possible care. Can you remind me again what you wanted to talk about?'

'I'm looking into the death of Kelvin Shoemaker. I'm sure you remember him.'

Dr Hanks could have been attractive, Belinda thought, if her face wasn't permanently set in a disapproving frown. Now the frown got deeper.

'Mr Shoemaker was one of the first patients we had.'

'And of course it wasn't a traumatic injury, was it?'

Now Dr Hanks smiled thinly. 'I'm sorry, you realise I can't discuss patient details. And what did you mean when you said you were looking into his death? As I recall he had a massive heart-attack. There was nothing we could do.'

Belinda looked around the room, then turned back to the Director.

'What's this room for? A waiting room? In a trauma unit?'

'It's a therapy room. The patients can talk to staff away from the other patients. It was held over from the unit's previous purposing.'

'Looking after poorly kiddies. Where do they all go now? Now that their hospital's been taken away from them?'

'I'm sorry, Miss McFee, I just don't know where this conversation is going. If you'll excuse me ... '

'I was just thinking it was odd that Mr Shoemaker was brought here instead of to an ordinary heart unit when he was first diagnosed. What advantages could you offer?'

If Dr Hanks had been on the point of leaving, she now forced herself into selling mode and sat down again.

'You have to understand that he was instrumental in setting up the unit—he and his wife. So of course they felt they should derive some benefit from ... from ... '

'From having their own private hospital. I understand that. But are you set up to deal with long-term heart conditions as opposed to traumatic injuries?'

Dr Hanks drew a breath and placed her hands on the table as if to calm herself. Belinda found she enjoyed needling this pompous bureaucrat.

The Director said, 'Thanks to the funding we received we have all of the necessary equipment to treat the widest range of critical injuries, including heart problems. Long-term or short-term. Now, have I answered your questions?'

'Could I have a walk around the wards?'

'I'm afraid that's out of the question. You've given me no indication of who you are and who you're working for and have asked a lot of inconsequential and impertinent questions about how we run this business. This unit. So I'm going to have to ask you to leave.'

'Was there anything unusual about Kelvin Shoemaker's condition? Could he have been, you know, slipped something to bring on his major attack?'

'That's it. The door's behind you. Please use it and don't come back.'

Belinda had stood up when the Director had. She looked back at the door as if surprised to find it there.

'Okay, I'll go. Could I get your email in case I have any follow-up questions?'

'Absolutely not. And if you come back again I'll call the police.'

'Is that a threat?'

'It's a certainty.'

IT WAS A hospital, not a bank, she told herself later that night. When she'd left the premises she'd driven out of the car park but only travelled a couple of hundred yards, till she was out of sight of the main buildings.

Then she'd settled down and slept till eleven o'clock. She'd woken up thinking about Sam Dyke. He'd told her he was seeing Emily Wallace tonight; she wondered whether he was still there. And then she asked herself why she was bothered.

At midnight she climbed from the car and headed towards the hospital entrance. Before she reached it she stopped and took an inventory of the surroundings. She had a spirit of adventure and was fearless in most situations, and if doing what she was about to do would pay back Frank Wallace for what he'd put her through, she didn't care that it was Breaking and Entering. In her own mind, she had her legal defence already worked out.

All the same, it was wise to be cautious. So she took time to look at the houses and buildings on the far side of the street. Midnight in London wasn't the same as midnight in most suburban towns and there were still lights blazing in houses and still traffic wending its way through Chalk Farm towards Belsize Park and further west towards Hampstead.

Fortunately, there was little pedestrian traffic.

She slipped through the wide entrance to the hospital, past a large black marble sign reading simply 'Aries House', with no indication what its function was, and headed immediately across the grass towards the rear of the main building. Although it was a private hospital it had none of the embellishments she'd expected: CCTV cameras everywhere, private security and electronic gates. It was as though the unit was keeping a low profile by not drawing attention to itself. But then she had little experience of private hospitals so wasn't sure exactly what to expect.

At the rear of the main building were the usual locked doors that led to the utilities and storage. She took out her wallet of lock-picks and set about the first door that looked like it might afford entrance to the rest of the building. Fortunately there was a clear moon that helped illuminate what she was doing, though she realised anyone looking in her direction from the road would see her bent suspiciously over the door like the burglar she was.

Within five minutes she was inside the building. She'd arrived in a laundry room piled high with fresh-smelling towels and sheets. They'd probably been delivered by a laundry service through the door she'd just entered: no one did their own washing any more.

Dan had told her to find any computer with a keyboard, so she opened the door to get her bearings and found herself on a half-lighted corridor. There was one sign at the end of the corridor to her left directing you towards Reception. Which meant that going to her right would take her deeper into the hospital, though she couldn't tell whether it would be into the wards or into the administrative offices.

She closed the door behind her and walked confidently down the tiled corridor. The building wasn't very large and shortly she turned a corner and found herself walking on carpet and the doors on either side had titles: Personnel, Finance, Deputy Director, Director. A small staff for a small unit.

She froze as she heard voices around the corner. It died out as soon as it started and she realised it was the kind of muffled laughter nurses might indulge in during a night shift. So the administration offices were situated close to the wards after all.

She tapped once on the door marked Finance and turned the handle — it opened easily and she went in.

Now she took out her pocket torch and made her way to the Finance director's desk. As was typical, the computer holding the financial dealings of the company wasn't allowed to leave the building. But neither had the director locked it away. A Dell laptop lay on the desk.

Belinda took the USB stick containing the program that Dan had put in her Dropbox account, stuck it in the port in the side of the laptop, and switched it on.

CHAPTER THIRTY-NINE

WEDNESDAY MORNING I waited until Emily woke up before getting out of bed. She smiled when she sensed me looking down at her, then opened her eyes.

'How long have you been doing that?'

'I've got a stiff neck, if that's any indication.'

'Is that all that's stiff?'

'Unfortunately, yes. I've got to go.'

She sat up, holding the bed-clothes to her chest.

'You've got a lead?'

'Nothing so dramatic.'

I told her I'd had a text from Belinda and we'd arranged to meet. She wanted to tell me what she'd learned from her visit to the Trauma Unit the day before.

'Belinda is the woman who helps you, yes?'

'She is. She works in her own right but seems to enjoy bossing me around from time to time.'

'Then I suppose you'd better go.'

She watched me dress and then I bent over to kiss her.

I said, 'No work today?'

'I've got an eleven o'clock meeting at a client's office. I don't have to go in before then.'

'I'll call you later.'

'See you do that.' She added, 'This is nice, isn't it?'

I smiled at her. 'It has its good points.'

She nodded as if I'd answered a question satisfactorily, then hunkered down in the bed again. I let myself out.

BECAUSE I THOUGHT Frank might be able to follow me anywhere, I'd texted Belinda to meet me in the middle of Trafalgar Square, where it was unlikely Frank could get close enough to listen to us. Then we'd find somewhere more private to talk afterwards.

The weather had stayed warm but there was a cold wind whipping across the square, which even this early in the year was thronged with tourists and pedestrians taking a short-cut. I arrived early and surveyed the crowds. No one stood out—but then I wouldn't expect someone with Frank's experience to make himself obvious.

But I had little doubt that he would have followed me from his daughter's flat despite my efforts at vigilance. Perhaps he'd bugged me. Perhaps my new phone contained a tracking device of some kind, or there was something inserted into the sole of my shoe. He always seemed to know where I'd been and what I'd done, and I couldn't put it all down to John Gale passing on my whereabouts. If I thought about it too long I'd go nuts, so I stopped and concentrated on watching the pigeons instead.

I spotted Belinda heading straight for me with her usual bouncy step so I headed her off, taking her by the arm as if we were a couple of lovers on a tryst.

She looked up at me, grinning. 'Why, Sam, I didn't know you cared. Did that gas rewire your brain?'

'Let's go look at some old pictures.'

She turned to see where we were going and saw the steps

of the National Gallery ahead of us.

'Ah, good idea.'

Once inside we found a bench in one of the vaulted rooms and she began to tell me about the Unit and its Director, Dr Hanks.

I said, 'So she threw you out.'

'I'd been pretty obnoxious, to be fair.'

'Was she more defensive than you expected?'

'Not really. They have patient privacy to protect. I was pushing her buttons because she irritated me. Anyway, I haven't got to the important stuff yet.'

'Go on.'

'So last night I installed the software that Dan had sent me yesterday. He's a very clever young boy, if a little criminally-minded. The thing by-passed the logon security and went straight into the network. And it looks like he's been working on it all night. He sent me a ton of stuff by eight o'clock this morning, which I've had a look through.'

'He'd have been up trading Bitcoins. Anything interesting?'

'Well, first, Dr Hanks is more than just an employee of the Sophocles Trust.'

'What do you mean?'

'She was at the London School of Economics the same time as Jocasta Shoemaker. After they graduated they wrote a paper together—it's listed in her academic publications with Jocasta's name as co-author.'

'Subject?'

'The Protection of Privacy in a Free-Market Economy. Case-study: Shoemaker Systems.'

'Well that figures. So presumably Hanks moved on into hospital administration.'

'Not until she took this job she didn't. A varied career,

you might say. Usually doing something for companies associated with Shoemaker Systems—running their foreign subsidiaries, mostly.'

'Okay, so basically she's a lackey to Jocasta. That helps. Anything else? Anything in the patient records for Kelvin?'

'Lots. Especially in relation to inventory.'

BEFORE WE PARTED I set Belinda another task and then went back to Apartment 60 to prepare. While in the cab I received a text from Ann with Tony Shoemaker's home and cell-phone numbers, and when I arrived at the apartment I called his home in the States.

He had an English accent overlaid with a hint of Southern drawl.

I told him who I was and that I was working for Jocasta Shoemaker.

'Let me stop you there, Mr Dyke. I don't wanna hear anything about her or that goddamn company. I left all that behind. She can do what she goddamn pleases with it.'

'It's not about her. It's about your father.'

'Kelvin? He's been dead for a while now. What's going on?'

I told him rapidly that someone was threatening to reveal Shoemaker Systems' secrets and that his father might be implicated in wrong-doing. I laid it on thickly in an attempt to get him onside. But it was wasted effort.

He said, 'I told you before, I'm not interested. Dad's dead so nothing they say can hurt him now. And if Jocasta gets some pain, I can live with that.'

'Didn't you get on with her?'

He laughed. 'For Chrissake, she's only two years older than me. Neither of us could take it, the weirdness. We went our separate ways. And I didn't trust her.'

'Why not?'

'Do you really want me to go into all this? What good will it do?'

'It'll satisfy my curiosity.'

He was quiet for a moment.

'Okay. If it makes you happy.'

Then he told me.

CHAPTER FORTY

I MET JOCASTA Shoemaker at an upscale bar in Knightsbridge and after a quick drink we took a cab out to St John's Wood. We'd given ourselves plenty of time and so were ten minutes early. The building was an abandoned block of offices whose ground-floor windows were boarded up. It looked like it had been built quickly in the sixties and promptly outlived its use. It sat in a row of commercial properties of various ages, from a prim Edwardian house that advertised itself as a Well-being Clinic through to a two-storey art deco building with a curved balcony that now contained a mini-supermarket.

We stood on the corner of the street glancing at our watches and making desultory conversation. I had little doubt that Wallace was watching us but there was nothing I could do about that. I asked Jocasta whether there'd been any further developments in her relationship with Bennett and her prospective clients but she was cagey and gave little away. I couldn't blame her. She was struggling to keep it all together and the business with Frank Wallace was a massive distraction.

At eight o'clock we approached the entrance door and I

tentatively pulled at the handle next to a cracked glass panel. The door swung open and we went in, treading on dried substances whose origin I didn't want to think about.

The foyer contained two lifts, both of which gaped open, and a door titled 'Stairs'. On this, a sheet of A4 paper had been taped bearing the instruction: '5th floor'.

Jocasta said, 'This place stinks.'

She wasn't wrong. Years of accumulated urine, dog mess and cigarette smoke had created an atmosphere like a witch's brew that hit the back of your throat with the strength of molten tar.

I said, 'Frank's trying to put us off. Disorientate us.'

'It's working.'

I led the way up the stairs, checking behind every now and then to see whether Jocasta was still with me. She must have been fit because she wasn't out of breath. It was all those hours riding horses down at the farm, I thought.

Eventually we arrived at a door leading off the stairs with a further sheet of paper stuck to it: 'Ta-Da!'

The door handle was missing but it didn't matter — the door was ajar anyway. I gestured for Jocasta to stay put then pushed the door open.

As in the house where he'd gassed me, the space I entered was large and empty. There were windows high up on two of the four walls and a grey metal filing cabinet had been toppled over and lay face down on the beige industrial carpet. Whatever other furniture had remained was gone except for three red plastic chairs.

Frank Wallace sat in one of them.

He looked different. His hair was dark brown and he was wearing a green blouson over jeans and heavy work shoes. The blouson had the badge of an American university on its breast. He looked like a retired football coach.

He gestured for me to come in.

'For God's sake what are you waiting for? Bring her in.'

I turned but Jocasta had already appeared in the doorway behind me. She stepped forward and I saw her look around the empty room, as out of place as a swan in a pig-sty.

'Done well for yourself, Frank.'

'Got my mojo working.'

'Oh for God's sake don't start that shit with me. Kelvin used to tell me how you'd do that—entire conversations in song titles.'

'But now the thrill is gone?'

She turned. 'I'm leaving. Dyke, talk to the man.'

Wallace laughed. 'Hey, come on! I'm just having a laugh. Don't you ever laugh, Jocasta? Or are you so up your own backside that you never have fun?'

'There's fun and there's being juvenile.'

Wallace's long face became serious.

'You're right. You came here to talk so talk we shall. Sit down, the pair of you.'

Reluctantly Jocasta walked to one of the two empty chairs, tested it and sat down. I took a last look around the room and pulled the remaining chair to one side before sitting in it.

I said, 'No gas cane today, Frank?'

'I said you'd be all right and so you will. Just behave yourselves and everything will go smoothly. Now, Jocasta, Mrs Shoemaker, Mrs Jocasta Shoemaker, what do you have for me?'

She took a deep breath. She was wearing a black scarf around her neck and black boots that stopped below her knees. She was sombre and serious and hard-edged. I suddenly had a bad feeling about what she was going to say to Frank Wallace.

She said, 'I'm afraid I've got bad news.'

Wallace nodded, pursing his lips.

She went on, 'I wanted to call an end to this dispute, Frank. Honestly, I did. I don't like all our—and Kelvin's—dirty washing being aired in public.'

'But?'

'But I've been overruled by the board.'

Frank nodded again.

'Most of the time they'll do what I ask them to do, especially as I have the controlling vote. However, this time they've told me they're prepared to take special measures and tip me out. So neither you nor I win. They've got dollar signs in their eyes, Frank. They want these contracts. I'm sorry.'

There was silence for about a minute. Jocasta didn't look at me but stared at Wallace defiantly. Wallace seemed to be examining her face, then he turned to me.

'What do you think, Mr Dyke? Should I believe her? I'm still your client, aren't I? Or has that agreement been superseded by events?'

'Take a guess. As it happens I don't trust either of you. I had no idea what Jocasta was going to say but I'm not surprised. If it's true.'

Jocasta glared at me. 'What do you mean, if it's true? Do you think I'm lying?'

'Probably. Given everything else you've lied about.'

'So you think I'm happy for this dinosaur to carry on spreading lies about me and my company?' She turned sideways in the chair to face me more directly. 'Let me tell you something, Dyke. I know people have been telling you I'm a latecomer and I know nothing about the world of intelligence and private security. But I've got news for you.

It's not rocket science. It's about being able to think in parallel to other people, to understand their motives and know what decisions they're likely to make. And it means having a business brain, being able to see opportunities and knowing how to take advantage of them. These days it's not cloak-and-dagger and listening devices and poisoned drinks and honey-traps—it's about being smart and efficient and being able to network with people from a wide range of backgrounds and interests. What's more it's about being honest and having credibility. Yes, sometimes you have to conceal the entire truth but that's not the same as an outright lie told to deceive someone of your intentions. So you can take your accusations and stuff them down that smug face of yours.'

I looked at Frank Wallace, who had a small smile on his lips. I couldn't tell whether it was one of admiration or disbelief.

I said, 'So we're back where we started. What are you going to do, Frank?'

He stirred in the chair and crossed his legs as though relaxing.

He said, 'Well it's obvious I can't trust her, isn't it? I make an offer in good faith and it's spurned at the last minute. What do you expect me to do?'

'I'm not sure we've heard any offer from you. But does any good come from trashing the company? The one that you helped set up?'

Jocasta said, 'Not to mention endangering the livings of everyone who works for the company, here and abroad. These contracts will make us, Frank. Do you want to ruin Kelvin's life work?'

'Strikes me I'm not the one doing the trashing and ruining here. You really are witless, aren't you, Jocasta? You have no idea what the bigger picture is. It's not just about Shoemaker or my legacy—or even Kelvin's. It's about how this Intelligence business works. How it should be allowed to work. All you've done is confirmed that I've been absolutely right in what I've been doing. You're not fit to be a partner with this country's security services. You'll join Burgess, McLean and Philby in the annals of treachery. You won't be able to help yourself. Grubbing for the next dollar will make you vulnerable and someone will take advantage of that, sooner or later. They always do. And you're so naive you won't see it coming.'

She said angrily, 'You belong to a school that's so old they've pulled down the building and destroyed the foundations.'

'Nice metaphor.'

'Things have moved on since you sat in a room with my late husband reading transcripts. Computers do all that now. Satellites roam the skies listening to your conversations. Programmers in Washington write code to inspect your bank transactions. And all of that costs money—money that governments spend inefficiently unless they're helped by experts who know what they're doing.'

'And who worked for the same government five minutes before.' He sighed and stood up. 'This conversation is going nowhere. I'm disappointed in you, Jocasta. I thought you understood *realpolitik*.'

'I understand the real world, Frank. The modern world. Unlike you, it seems.'

'Oh, I understand it. I just don't like it. Now, you two stay here for five minutes. If you don't, there'll be consequences. Just because I'm here by myself doesn't mean I'm here by myself, know what I mean? You can leave the chairs where they are.'

He nodded briefly at me, then turned and walked towards the far wall where there was a Fire Door with an iron push-bar. He looked briefly back at us but then shook his head, a manager disappointed by the efforts of his team. He went through the door and it clanged closed behind him.

Jocasta said, 'I wish we could have put a tail on him or something.'

'This isn't a cop show.'

'It doesn't seem fair that he just gets away.'

'Who said he is?'

She glanced at me with interest.

'At last, am I to believe you're earning your money?'

'Hence the look on this smug face of mine.'

She grimaced and looked away. I didn't expect an apology and I didn't get one.

When the five minutes were up we went back down the main staircase and left through the front door. We walked down the road and eventually I was able to hail a cab for her.

Before she climbed in I said, 'Was it true about the board preventing you negotiating with him?'

'What do you think?'

'I think you consult the board as often as I consult the Norse Gods for a weather forecast.'

'Do you have a problem with that?'

'It's your company.'

She made to pull the door shut but I held on to it.

I said, 'Be at your offices tomorrow morning at nine. And have the combination to your safe handy.'

A look of alarm crossed her face but this time I slammed the door shut before she could say anything and the cabbie drove off.

CHAPTER FORTY-ONE

IT WAS STILL early so I called Emily's mobile phone, thinking I could get across to see her. But instead of the phone ringing or going to voice-mail, a woman's voice told me the number was no longer in use.

I thought immediately of Frank Wallace, interfering again with my channels of communication. He didn't want me to talk to her so he was making it impossible — or at least difficult.

I dug out her land-line number and rang it — this time I heard that strange dull tone you get when a line is not connected.

I didn't like the sound of all this silence so I found a cab and gave him the name of Emily's street in Camden.

We were there in ten minutes. I paid him and walked down the road towards her flat, keeping to the pavement on the other side. It was around nine o'clock and dark enough for room lights to be switched on — there were none visible in her apartment.

I rang again, both numbers, with the same results. Then I crossed the road and pressed her doorbell. I couldn't hear it sounding in the large house but there was no reply at the door in any case.

So I did what people in films always do—I pressed the other buttons until I got a reply. A man's voice said, 'Yeah?'

'Hi, I'm a friend of Emily Wallace's in Flat 5. I can't get a reply on her phone and we were supposed to meet tonight. Could you let me in?'

'You're who?'

I repeated what I'd said and added, 'My name's Sam Dyke.'

A pause, then he said, 'Hold on.'

I expected the door to be buzzed open but it wasn't. Instead a man in his early twenties with a light beard pulled it open, then stood looking me up and down.

'Who are you again?'

'My name's Sam Dyke. I've visited Emily a couple of times and we were supposed to meet here tonight, half an hour ago.'

I repeated the line about trying her phones and getting no reply, then I took a step back from the doorway and tried to look unthreatening.

He was uncertain but finally he retreated and widened the door.

'Come in. We'll go up.'

So we went up the two flights of stairs to her room and I let him rap on the door. He put his head to the wood and listened, then shook it and tried again.

I said, 'Does anyone have a key?'

'You're a bit serious, aren't you, mate? She's probably just gone out.'

'Maybe. But both her phones are dead.'

'Have you tried her work?'

I hadn't but I lied fluently: 'It's gone nine o'clock. There's no one in.'

'All right, wait here. Maisie's the house rep. She's got keys to all the rooms. In case of stuff like this.' He'd started down the stairs but turned back to me to explain. 'We had someone take pills six months ago. Now we're supposed to be more vigilant.'

He trotted downstairs. As soon as he'd cleared the first flight I reached into my pocket and took out my lock picks.

It was a standard Yale and was open in no time. I turned the handle and pushed the door open. I think I was holding my breath.

At first I didn't think anything had changed. The furniture was all there, the side lamps on the tables, the curtains, the cushions on the sofa.

Then I realised that the bookshelves were empty: all the books about the Blues had gone. And when I walked further inside I saw all of the small items were gone, too—a blue vase on the mantelpiece; half a dozen CDs that had been piled next to her sound system, though the system was still there; her laptop from the table; a small bronze Buddha.

I walked into the bedroom—where I'd slept only last night—and slid open the wardrobe doors: nothing inside. I drew back the two top drawers of her dressing table: no make-up, no mirrors, no underwear. She'd stripped out everything personal and left only the bare bones.

I heard voices outside, coming up the stairs, and went to meet them. The young man had arrived with an older woman in a kaftan who looked like a holdover from the seventies: Maisie. She had a small collection of keys in her hand.

'How'd you get in?'

'The door was unlocked.'

She looked at the man. 'Didn't you try the door?'

'Didn't think of it.'

She turned back to me. 'Who are you again?'

'My name's Sam Dyke.'

I explained myself once more and told them I'd started seeing Emily a short while ago. I'd stayed with her in the flat last night but now it was empty. There was an Asian nurse in the building who could tell them she'd seen me leaving one morning.

Maisie said, 'We'd better call the police if you think something's wrong.'

'They won't do anything yet. She's not been missing long enough. Besides, there's no sign of a struggle or anything like that.'

I stepped back so they could come inside and check for themselves, which they did, looking in the kitchen and the bedroom, craning their necks, perhaps expecting to find a body on the floor.

I said, 'She's taken her clothes and her books so I suppose she's all right. It's just that she didn't say anything.'

Maisie gave me a thoughtful look.

'When did you see her last?'

'She was in bed when I left this morning. She said she had a client meeting so didn't have to go to work first thing. Perhaps she moved out as soon as I went. She had a car, I think.'

The young man said, 'An old Rover. She parked it up the road.'

I said, 'Look, I'll stick around in case she comes back tonight.'

I took two of my business cards from my wallet and gave them to Maisie and the young man.

'That's me. I'm a private investigator, based in Crewe.'

Maisie was reading the card. 'And you think that makes you trustworthy?'

I shrugged. 'You've got my address and numbers. Do you want to see my driving licence as well? There's nothing here to steal. I'll just hang around for a couple of hours. I'll be quiet as a church mouse.'

The young man looked at Maisie and she shrugged. She waved the card in my face. 'I'm going to ring this land-line and see what I get.'

'Me and my humorous message on the answer-phone.'

'I'd better, or I'll call the cops. Andrew, hang around at the bottom of the stairs for a couple of minutes, will you?'

The pair of them turned and went down the stairs. I closed the door and went back inside.

The rooms still smelled of Emily, especially when I plumped the cushions to sit on the sofa—they exhaled the scent of her perfume where she'd rested on them.

I looked in each of the rooms again as though I might find something important I'd missed before. It didn't take long: sitting room, bedroom, kitchen, bathroom. As impersonal now as an airport hotel room after cleaning. Where had she gone? Had she gone of her own volition, or had she been taken by someone—perhaps kidnapped by her own father the same way he'd kidnapped Belinda?

I couldn't believe it. I knew he'd been on my case about seeing his daughter, but would he go so far as this to prevent me having contact with her? If not, it meant she'd gone of her own free will. No forwarding address. No phone call or text message with an explanation and a new number to call. First thing tomorrow I'd call the work number she gave me and ask if they knew anything.

I didn't want to believe she'd vanished from my life entirely.

THERE WERE NO further disruptions from Maisie and the

young man from downstairs and in the end I went into the bedroom and laid on the mattress. Emily had left a single sheet covering it and taken the pillow-cases but not the pillows. I turned off the light and laid on the bed, staring up at the ceiling.

Outside, the Camden traffic bustled away, interrupted occasionally by the blare of a police or ambulance siren. London is the only city in the UK that can sound like New York at night.

The rest of the house was quiet except for a low thump of music that sounded as if it was coming from the bottom of a barrel buried ten feet beneath the basement.

I thought about what Belinda had told me earlier. Dan had broken into the patient records at the Trauma Unit and focused, naturally, on the records for Kelvin Shoemaker. It seemed that his death had been exactly as described—he'd gone in initially for a check-up because he wasn't feeling well and it transpired he'd had a minor heart attack without knowing it. They'd kept him under observation for a week but eventually he'd suffered a massive coronary and they couldn't save him.

Then Belinda had looked at the information surrounding Kelvin's admission and, afterwards, his final release to Jocasta for burial. As a modern facility, everything was computerised, including the list of his clothing and other possessions when he'd been admitted. It was a hedge against insurance claims later and although it was doubtful that staff members would steal anything from the new owner of the Unit, the procedure had been followed nonetheless. The initial list contained nothing unusual—underclothes, trousers, shirts, shaving kit, books, iPad, mobile phone, etc.

Four days after he'd been admitted there'd been an increment to the inventory: a package had been delivered to the hospital—a cardboard box, eighteen inches by twelve by nine, heavily wrapped and protected, delivered by UPS from America. It had been recorded into his details at the reception desk and then it had been given to Shoemaker in his room. After he'd opened and presumably inspected it, the box was placed in the cupboard allotted to his private use.

Two days later Shoemaker had died and as part of the release procedure another inventory was taken.

Looking at this second list, Belinda saw the box wasn't on Kelvin's inventory of belongings.

Belinda checked the visitor records and saw that Jocasta Shoemaker had not visited Kelvin every day. But she *had* been to the Unit the day after the package was delivered, which was the day before he'd suffered his final heart attack.

So what had happened to the package on the day Jocasta visited? A tempting conclusion was that she'd taken it without telling anyone, even the Unit's administrators.

I thought about that a bit longer and shifted my position on the bed.

Then I thought about what Tony Shoemaker had told me. He said that when his father married Jocasta, nearly all contact with his father had ceased. They'd never been particularly close but Kelvin had phoned him from time to time and they'd exchanged birthday and Christmas cards. The younger Shoemaker was very philosophical about it.

'You have to understand, Mr Dyke, that Kelvin was never particularly family-oriented. He never expressed much interest in his grandkids or my career. He never came to see us over here. He was always too busy, right from the beginning. In fact, I'd had more interest shown in me by my godfather.'

'Let me guess.'

'Frank Wallace. Do you know him?'

'Yes, I know him. So you were in contact with him?'

'He called me often, kept me up to speed with what Dad was doing. But when he retired I lost touch with him, too.'

'I understand he found it difficult not having anything important to do.'

'Probably. I was a bit hurt, though, when he didn't acknowledge my present.'

'What was that?'

'Maybe it went missing when my dad died. He was in hospital when I sent it, though I didn't know otherwise I wouldn't have bothered him. Nobody had told me he was ill. I came over as soon as I heard but by the time I got there he was dead and Jocasta had buried him.'

'What was the present?'

'I don't know whether you heard, but Frank was wild about the Blues, especially the original stuff, dating right back to nineteen-five, nineteen-ten. I couldn't understand it myself but the music really spoke to him. So when he learned I was living and working over here, in the South, he got me looking out for old discs and cylinders, you know, the old wax things.'

'And did you?'

'Not a lot, to be honest. I was too busy. I found stuff now and then, which I'd post to him hoping they'd survive the trip. Then one day I was working on a house outside Atlanta and I came across these really old cylinders in the loft. They were under a ton of dust and kept inside cardboard canisters, but I knew what they were straight away. I'm not proud of what I did, but the owner of the house had gone to Europe for three months to give me space to convert the loft and re-model the kitchen. I didn't think he'd notice, seeing as they were obviously abandoned and covered with mouse-shit and dust. So I just took the cylinders and sent them to my dad.'

'Why him? Why not Frank?'

'I asked Dad to give them to Frank on his birthday, as a present. I sent them to his office, to his personal secretary, because I didn't want Jocasta coming across them and interfering—she didn't like Frank much, you know. And I gather the office just re-routed them to the hospital. Like I said, I didn't know when I sent them that Dad had been admitted. If I'd known I'd have found another way to get them to Frank.'

'Do you know what happened to them?'

'I assumed for a while that Dad had asked someone to send them on to Frank, even though he was in hospital. But when Frank didn't say anything after a couple of months I began to wonder whether he'd got them. So I phoned him and asked whether he'd received the cylinders. He was surprised and said he never saw them, so we didn't know what had happened.'

'What were they recordings of?'

Tony Shoemaker laughed. 'Jeez, I don't know. I hadn't got anything that could play them. Inside each canister there was a piece of paper with a title and someone's name on it, but I can't remember now who they were. And on the box there was a line hand-written in pen saying "Property of Howard W. Odum," but I had no idea who he was. I'm amazed I even remember the name. I assumed he was a previous owner of the house.' He paused. 'Is all this any use?'

'You bet.'

I stared at the ceiling in Emily's apartment and put it all together. Tonight was Wednesday and the signing was Friday. I had tomorrow to make arrangements, starting with my meeting at nine o'clock with Jocasta in her office.

I turned over to get some sleep. I had to be at the office earlier than that if I was to prevent her getting away with it.

CHAPTER FORTY-TWO

FRIDAY MORNING, THE day of the signing, was another bright day. Spring had caught everyone by surprise but as usual people were getting used to warm weather and travelling everywhere in tee-shirts and light-coloured clothing.

Before I left Apartment 60 I phoned Dan. There was something I wanted to say to him. To my surprise, he answered immediately. Then I realised he probably hadn't gone to bed yet.

I said, 'Hi, just touching base.'

He was suspicious. 'Are you okay? I thought this was the big day for the signing and everything. Did Belinda tell you what I found?'

'I wanted to say thanks. That was good work.'

'Pleasure. Is there something else? You sound weird.'

I'd done some research into Craig, his boyfriend, and I wasn't wild about what I'd discovered. He'd told Dan he ran a restaurant in Wilmslow but when I looked into it I became curious. It wasn't a restaurant, it was a greasy-spoon café— or as close to greasy-spoon as Wilmslow would ever get. And the name on the lease of the property wasn't Craig's but his father's, who happened to run a Porsche dealership down the road. I wondered what other lies Craig might be telling Dan, and I'd been debating with myself for a couple of days how I was going to broach the subject—or even whether I should. I thought if I phoned him the topic might come up.

I said, 'It's a big day. I'm under immense stress and pressure.'

He laughed. 'Yeah, right. Hey, I need to talk to you about something.'

'What's that?'

'It's about Craig.'

I felt a flutter in my chest. I didn't want to lie to him about Craig but neither did I want him to continue being deceived.

I said, 'What about him?'

'Turns out he's a bit of a con-man. You know he said he owned a restaurant? In fact it's a café. Mainly for pensioners who've been to the charity shops and can't afford Starbucks' flat whites. I'd been badgering him for ages to take me and in the end I just Googled it. Should have done it in the first place but I thought it would be sneaky.'

'I thought he was fishy. No one should love his car that much.'

'His dad owns a Porsche dealership, too. He borrows the car on pain of death if he scratches it. No wonder he's so careful of it.'

'So what are you going to do?'

'Done it. Ditched him. I've had too many people lying to me in my life. I'm not going to stand for it now.'

I couldn't believe how good I felt at that moment. It was all I could do to get through the end of the conversation and tell him I'd see him in a few days. I hung up with a big grin on my face. The temptation to tell him what I'd learned had been overpowering. Perhaps the fact I didn't need to would teach me a lesson about letting other people lead their own lives.

But I doubted it.

IT WAS SO warm even my taxi driver taking me from the apartment to the Hilton Docklands was wearing short sleeves and was breaking a sweat at nine o'clock in the morning.

He looked at me in the rear-view mirror of the cab.

'You involved in all the hoo-ha?'

'Not me. Casual observer.'

'Press?'

I shook my head. 'General public. I'm going to make sure they're not wasting our money.'

He nodded sagely.

'Not sure I like it myself. MI5's Government, innit? I don't want some fat-cat company director making money out of national security. Don't seem right.'

I gave him a reassuring smile and looked at the passing traffic. I wondered how many people felt the same way.

The taxi eventually wound its way through the outskirts of a retail park, then a red-brick housing estate, and finally turned up the incline to the entrance of the Hilton. Sited in Rotherhithe, where the Thames takes a lurch south around the Isle of Dogs, many of its rooms looked directly across the river towards the Canary Wharf cluster of skyscrapers. In the hotel itself you walked up the entrance steps and past Reception and then glass doors led outside to a walkway that proceeded along a short undercover jetty called Nelson Dock Pier. Here guests could board the ferry that would take them across the river to the restaurants and bars that huddled around the Wharf, then bring them back at the end of the evening.

And it was from this pier that a specially-contracted vessel was to head into mid-stream and drop virtual anchor while the contracts between Shoemaker Systems and the two Intelligence Services of the UK and the US were to be signed. All other river traffic would be delayed by an hour to accommodate this floating obstruction. There would be a helicopter presence overhead and a couple of boats from the Met's river service would come from the boat yard further upstream. I had no doubt that MI5 also had some frogmen out in the river, too, in case any tricky foreigners attempted to blow up a handful of important civil servants.

When I walked into the reception area it was a flurry of activity. Lots of men and women in smart suits were standing around looking important and focused, or were conferring in power couples, iPads in hand. No one seemed to use an ordinary clipboard any more. I saw the new recruit, Simon, standing in a corner in deep debate with the member of Gale's team I'd challenged in the Shoemaker canteen. They both looked impossibly young and out of their depth, though there were a couple of grey heads amongst the other 'agents', or whatever they called themselves.

I noticed that there were no guests in sight—nobody rolling up to Reception to check out or register. I supposed that Shoemakers had booked all the rooms for the days before and after so that they didn't have any loose cannons to deal with.

For all the activity, I didn't see any men or women who bore the stamp of government office. Everyone, including me, was wearing a Shoemaker pass on a ribbon around their neck, the logo visible from twenty feet away.

I walked across to the pier entrance and looked out. The charter vessel, a weathered craft called The Lancashire Rose, stood massively at attention next to the pier. A stairway had been jerry-rigged to allow dignitaries to climb on board without losing too much face. The gangway looked as though it were made of matchsticks compared to the solid bulk of the ship itself, dark and riding high on a slight swell. I couldn't help feeling this wasn't the right place for such a high class craft.

Beyond it, on the far side of the Thames, I could make out the ferry that would eventually chug its way across, bringing passengers who would probably be wondering what all the fuss had been about. Behind the ferry the featureless windows of the headquarters of shamed foreign banks and other self-important institutions winked in the morning light. I'd been looking at this group of buildings every day I'd been in Apartment 60 and this was the closest I'd been to them, separated by half a mile of gently churning green river.

Jocasta Shoemaker was standing on the wooden slats on the side of the pier facing away from the ship, squinting into the wind with her dark her hair flowing behind her. There was something indefinably Greek and tragic about her pose. She seemed to be communing with herself, perhaps contemplating what the near future was going to bring to her and her company.

She glanced at me as though she'd known I was there all the time, then broke her pose and walked towards me.

She came through the door.

'They're late. Have you seen Bennett?'

'No. Have you seen Frank?'

'No. Do you think he's mined the boat?'

'Was it guarded all night?'

'Of course.'

'Then it won't be mined.'

'I don't trust him.'

'I don't trust you, but I'm here.'

'Bennett should be here by now.'

'You should relax.'

'They were supposed to cancel the river tours.' She pointed back towards the Thames where a glass-sided ferry was bisecting the line between ourselves and Canary Wharf. 'See? They're taking no notice.'

'It's early yet. Perhaps they'll stop later.'

'Something's wrong. I know it. Frank's spooked them.'

'I've got to go.'

She looked panicked. 'Where?'

'Where do you think? I'll see you later. There's an hour to go before it starts.'

'Fuck, I can't stand this.'

She turned and went back through the doors, leaning into the wind as though it might blow away all of her problems. I stood for a moment and watched the vessel rock gently against the wooden pier. Beside it, Jocasta's face was a pale and haunted oval against the sludge-green swell of the Thames.

I hoped my hunch was right.

CHAPTER FORTY-THREE

I COULD TAKE my time so I caught the hotel's own shuttle bus back to Canada Water Underground station, then climbed in a taxi to take me to Shoemaker Systems' office. I had him drop me off a little way short of the office and found somewhere to have a coffee while I waited. I had to get the timing right and not rush it.

Eventually I left the small café and walked the two hundred yards to the Shoemaker building.

The three Robo-Receptionists were on duty but I could tell at once that the building was all but deserted—all hands were on deck down at Nelson Pier to help Jocasta sign the contracts. Or rather, to prevent anyone getting in the way of the contracts being signed.

I ignored the receptionists and went straight to the bank of lifts, heading for Jocasta's floor. I had a pass in my pocket if I needed to get through any electronically-guarded barriers.

On the twentieth floor the lift doors opened and still no one was in sight. I walked down the corridor and found Ann at her station. She glanced up with surprise when she saw me.

'Mr Dyke—I thought you'd be at the signing.'

'I was. It was boring, so I thought I'd visit you. Anything going on here?'

'Here? No. Everyone's on call down at the pier if they're not on other client work. Big day for us.'

'Indeed. So no one's around?'

'Just the guy from the Ministry.'

'Okay—who's he?'

'I didn't catch his name. He had a pass, said he's meeting with Jocasta after the signing.'

'Was he in the calendar?'

She went pink. 'No, but then it's been all over the place …'

'That's okay. Where is he?'

'I left him in the foyer with a coffee.'

'He wasn't there when I came through.'

She half rose from her seat. 'Oh …'

'Don't worry. I'll find him.'

I retraced my steps and went down the short corridor to Jocasta's office.

I went in and saw Frank Wallace on his knees next to a hole in the floor beside Jocasta's desk.

'Frank, I thought I'd find you here.'

He ignored me. He was reaching into the floor-safe and taking out small brown canisters one by one and laying them inside a wide briefcase. The canisters were of the size and shape to hold the black wax cylinders on which music had been recorded in the early part of the twentieth century.

He placed the last one in the briefcase, lowered the safe's thick door and slowly stood up, dusting his knees. He was wearing a smart navy suit and red tie, gold cuff-links glittering at his wrists. His black shoes gleamed. He was every inch the Man from the Ministry, another perfect disguise. No one currently in the building had been there long enough to recognise him.

'I don't expect you to know what these are, Mr Dyke.'

'Tell me.'

He dusted his hands and placed them casually in his trouser pockets.

'In 1905 a young American sociologist called Howard Odum went on a number of field trips in the Carolinas, the Mississippi Delta and Georgia, recording black singers and musicians. He was interested in what he called their workaday songs and wanted to catalogue as many as he could. I don't think he was so much interested in the music itself as what it said about the conditions in which they lived. He was a sociologist, not a music historian.'

'The early Blues.'

'Yes, for the most part. Over a three year period he recorded their music on a primitive recording device which he and his companion carted around with them. Of course the medium on which they recorded this music was the wax cylinder. I don't know how many there were and I don't think anyone else does, either. But what happened to those cylinders was a mystery. Apart from Odum, it's likely no one else ever heard them. They vanished into history and actually he didn't seem too upset about it, though I daresay he was. When he wrote about the experience later he suggested they were either broken or lost, but he didn't seem too clear, or even interested.'

'And if you found them they'd be worth a fortune.'

'To a collector they could be worth millions. At least several hundred thousands of pounds. They would be the earliest known recordings of original Blues songs, many of which resurfaced in popular form later.'

'So your plan was to steal the cylinders and sell them on

the open market.'

'I hardly class it as stealing when they were intended for me in the first place. Did you speak to Tony Shoemaker?' I nodded. 'Then you'll know Jocasta was supposed to give them to me. But she didn't. Kelvin had them in his possession temporarily and Jocasta took them as a way of punishing me.'

'Did you burgle her house?'

He raised his eyebrows. 'Very good. Yes, when Tony asked me about them I realised what had happened and made a little foray into the farm. I couldn't find them so thought she probably kept them here. She could have put them in a safe-deposit box, I suppose, so that would have been my next port of call.'

'And you fitted that safe so you had the combination.'

'Yes, handy, that, wasn't it? When Kelvin asked me to fit it I had an idea that he wanted me to have access to it anyway. He trusted me and he knew if anything happened to him I'd be able to get into it and look after any documents that needed looking after. As it happened, he married Jocasta and she kept me at arm's length until I retired. So I didn't have a chance to look in the safe until now.'

'So all of this was a charade, a distraction, to make sure the office was empty.'

He was delighted—whether it was with me or with his plan, I couldn't tell. 'Exactly! Of course Jocasta would be gone from the office for the signing. Gale had given me the intel on the how and the when, alongside the other stuff I released to the press. But I had to up the ante, as our American friends say, to make sure she was stressed enough to increase security, to strip her people from this building in case anyone recognised me when I came in. So I got you involved, pushed you forward as a knight, you might say, to show her the danger and surround herself with pawns. You did very well—I think Jocasta is thoroughly spooked. Pardon the pun.'

He reached down for the briefcase, then stopped.

'So tell me, why are you here? Is this pure chance or were you playing a hunch?'

'You pushed too hard, Frank. You pointed us towards the Trauma Unit. I think you wanted us to believe that Jocasta persuaded Dr Hanks, her old friend, to have him killed. Perhaps you thought it would muddy the water and make me suspicious of Jocasta.'

'It crossed my mind.'

'But instead we found out about the cylinders.'

He paused briefly, the first time I'd seen him discomfited.

'Ah, really? So my little lecture was wasted on you, then? You already knew? How interesting.'

A gun had appeared in his hand. It was a small gun, perhaps a Walther, but I was sure it would be effective. With his other hand he bent and picked up the briefcase.

He said, 'Well, Mr Dyke, you've earned your money. I made the right choice in you. Thank you for your help. I have a getaway to make now and then some sales to negotiate. You won't find me, so don't bother looking. When I leave, the door behind me will lock and whatever pass you have will be useless. By the time you've called the secretary and found someone to release you, I'll be long gone. Thanks for your help.'

He waved the gun for me to back away from his path to the door. I took a couple of steps sideways and let him pass.

When he arrived at the door he turned to me and raised the briefcase and waggled it slightly at me, as though showing off his trophies.

I said, 'Take them. They were bought with your money.'

He frowned and lowered the bag.

'What do you mean?'

'After speaking to Tony Shoemaker I knew what was in the package and what you were looking for. I did have a hunch, then, and spoke to Jocasta. She huffed and puffed and denied all knowledge—at first. Then she said Kelvin had asked her to look after the cylinders and she had no idea how much they were worth. I doubted that very much and threatened her with telling Tony Shoemaker, with the possibility of a subsequent law suit and more bad publicity, which of course she can't afford now ... eventually she backed down and opened the safe. I spent most of yesterday on eBay hunting down some old cylinders and replacing the originals from the safe with the ones I bought. They're good, but fairly common. I think they're mostly Caruso. I gave cash to a man in Ealing yesterday afternoon so in actual fact it was your money that bought them.'

'And the originals are where?'

'Somewhere safe. I'll make sure the proceeds go to a good home.'

For a split second his face darkened and his lips became thin, his nostrils flaring.

Then he closed his eyes and his expression lifted and he laughed quietly.

He said, 'Mean old world,' opened the door behind him and slipped out. I heard a heavy electronic click as it locked.

CHAPTER FORTY-FOUR

IT WAS HALF an hour before Ann could find anyone from the building's owner—it was rented, after all—to come and spring the lock.

I went downstairs in the lift with her. When I told her the Man from the Ministry had been an impostor she went quiet and stared into space as though considering her future. I told her she shouldn't worry—he'd fooled professional people with much more experience than she had. And no harm had been done. I'd deal with Jocasta.

In the foyer she grabbed my arm.

'Jocasta's called, asking what's going on, has anyone arrived. I told her you were here with a man and she hung up. Did I do wrong?'

'No, of course not. We've all been playing chess with a grandmaster.'

Outside I hailed a cab to the Hilton Docklands and twenty minutes later I was striding through the lobby again, my Shoemaker pass once more around my neck on its cloth necklace. The foyer looked exactly as it did two hours before—the same tribe of Shoemaker clones standing around with serious faces and fixed poses, legs apart, hands folded in front of their groins.

Jocasta was standing by the doors that led to the Pier. She saw me and came over.

'What happened? Did he come?'

'Yes. Like I told you yesterday, he was bluffing. He wanted the cylinders. Everything else was a distraction, making you focus on the signing to the exclusion of everything else.'

'As if I wasn't already doing that. You should have let Simon grab him as soon as he walked in the office. We could have set a trap.'

'He would have known something was up and not come.'

'You give him too much credit.'

'I don't think so. When he started—when he hired me— he didn't know exactly what was going to happen with you and the contracts. The signing might have been in your office, so he would have had to improvise. You helped him out with this extravaganza by the river but it strikes me he's very flexible. He's a good chess player in that way.'

'What have you done with the cylinders? The real ones?'

'I've put them somewhere safe. They'll go back to Tony Shoemaker and he can do what he wants with them.'

'I have a right to them. They were my husband's.'

'I think that's a dubious assertion. They were in his possession but they were intended for Frank.'

'So why didn't you let him have them?'

I shook my head.

'Ethics aren't your strong point, are they?'

'Meaning?'

'Meaning that he killed Gale and almost blinded Darren Givens while plotting to rob your safe. I think he gave up any moral claim to the cylinders after that.'

She glanced at her watch.

'Eleven-fifteen. We're due to sign at midday but no-one's here. I can't get in touch with Bennett. I expected some sort of police presence. Some advance party of spooks to walk through it. We had a rehearsal last week but I still thought they'd be here early.' She looked up at me, her eyes clear and hard. 'That's the inefficiency of public agencies for you.'

Then she saw something over my shoulder and I turned to look through the hotel's entrance. Two large black cars had pulled up in front of the steps.

She said, 'Thank God, at last,' and headed outside. I thought I'd better be with her.

As we reached the bottom of the steps, squinting in the sunshine, the doors of the two vehicles opened and from each one a distinguished-looking man climbed out. They each had grey hair and wore dark overcoats though it was warm enough to do without.

One of them saw Jocasta and stepped towards her, holding out his hand. She shook it.

She said, 'Are you from Bennett? Where is he?'

The man said, 'Jocasta Shoemaker?'

'Yes, of course.'

'My name's Gordon Phillips. My colleague and I represent the Charities Commission, and we'd like to talk to you about The Sophocles Trust and its status. We were told you'd be here. Do you have a moment?'

She looked up at me with venom in her eyes.

I shrugged.

CHAPTER FORTY-FIVE

THE NEXT MORNING, Saturday, I packed my bags in Apartment 60, took one last look at the view, and left.

I navigated my way through the underground system until I found a seat on the Docklands Light Railway heading south over the river again, getting out at Cutty Sark station. I came up out of the darkness and turned left, past Waterstones bookshop and hitting the busy centre of Greenwich, in full swing at lunchtime. I headed uphill towards the Observatory but before I came to Greenwich Park I turned right, along a street of tall town houses.

I looked at the address Belinda had written down and counted off the houses, then opened a gate and climbed a couple of steps before ringing the bell next to an unmarked label.

The high door was opened by a woman of average height with short black hair. She was slim and her eyes widened slightly when she saw me, then her shoulders slumped.

I said, 'Hi, Emily. Is he in?'

She said nothing but stepped back and took the door with her. I walked inside.

It was probably Georgian, on three floors, with a wide

hallway at the end of which I could see a good deal of light: there was doubtless a large garden behind. The floors were oak and the staircase that led upstairs was beautifully turned and swept gracefully around itself before reaching the next floor. There were cardboard boxes labelled 'books' in the hallway—probably the ones she'd taken from her flat a couple of days ago.

Emily saw me taking it all in.

'It was my mother's. She left it to me when she died. How did you find us?'

I tapped the side of my nose. 'Trade secret.'

'I'm sorry I left like that. It was part of the plan.'

'I guessed as much.'

'You shouldn't have trusted me. You were too quick.'

'Is that an apology? If it is, it's not accepted.'

She grimaced. 'He's upstairs. Are you going to arrest him?'

'I can't arrest him. But I can give him a jolly good ticking off.'

She led me upstairs, to the top floor. It may once have been servants' quarters but it was now a spacious living room with tall sash windows and views across to Greenwich Park and the Naval College.

Frank was sitting in a large chair reading a newspaper. When I entered the room he folded it in two and laid it down.

He looked at me with amusement on his face and was quiet for a moment, thinking. Then he said, 'You had Belinda follow me that night we met with Jocasta in St John's Wood. How did you know?'

'I phoned Greg Last. I realised you'd been using places you knew intimately because you'd bugged them or used them as safe houses. He told me that address was one you'd bugged when it was used by the Israelis in the eighties.

There was an exit in the basement that led directly into next door's store room, when the complex of buildings had belonged to one business. I guessed you'd leave through there rather than risk being followed from the back door. I set Belinda to watch the exit from the neighbouring building.'

'So why haven't the stormtroopers battered down the door? I'm a very bad man, responsible for all sorts of naughty things.'

'It'll happen sooner or later. A man called Bennett has the details.'

He nodded calmly. 'I knew him. He'll work hard at it.' He crossed his legs. 'So, I see from the paper that Mrs Shoemaker is in trouble after all. The signings didn't happen yesterday and the Charities Commission are all over her and The Sophocles Trust. And the PM is performing rapid back-peddling on the idea of private security firms bidding for government work—no doubt another Parliamentary working party will report in a couple of years. Meanwhile, egg on face all round, it seems. I wonder how the Charities Commission got involved.'

'I wonder.'

He laughed and I was reminded again of his apparent innocence, his delight in the game.

I said, 'What do you do now?'

He shrugged. 'No music, no money.'

'You killed a man, injured another.'

'Be fair, Mr Dyke, one was an accident. I set the gizmo off when Gale gave me the signal. I didn't know he'd pushed poor Givens through the door. He was going for verisimilitude, I suppose. Though he couldn't have spelled it.'

'Is that why you killed him?'

'Oh, we've been through all that. In the end it came down to you or him and, to be honest, you were more fun to have around.'

Emily and I had been standing just inside the doorway. Now she bustled past me and picked up the handle of a wheeled suitcase that had been lying in the middle of the carpet. She walked past me to go downstairs.

I said to her, 'You were telling Frank every time I called you.'

She stopped to look at me. Her face was clear. I could read no emotion there at all. She said, 'You didn't give much away. But I told him a couple of things, yes. Did you work it out, the great detective?'

'I tried not to listen to my instincts. Big mistake. Didn't it bother you that he killed a man? You seemed upset when you found out he shot Gale. Or were you play-acting all the time?'

She hesitated. 'Not all the time.'

In retrospect I like to think her face softened as she said this, but I'm probably fooling myself.

Anyway, she said nothing more. After a beat she turned and continued downstairs. I watched her go and when I turned around Frank was pointing a gun at me again. It was getting to be a familiar sight.

I said, 'Is that the gun you had before? Is it a Walther?'

He glanced at it. 'Yes. Do you like guns?'

'I know too much about them to like them.'

'Did I ask you whether you'd killed a man?'

'No, you didn't.'

'So, have you?'

'Yes.'

'Feels odd, doesn't it? Like one minute they're there, breathing. The next they're on the floor and it's just a piece of meat. And you've done that, you've made the difference. Can't say I liked it. But I'm prepared to do it again, if necessary.'

Emily came back into the room wearing a light cotton jacket. She went to her father and bent to kiss him on the cheek, then stood up and looked at me.

She said, 'He's not been a great dad but he's the only one I've got. When Mum left he made sure I was looked after. What choice did I have but to help him when he needed me?'

'You were doing what he told you from the beginning.'

'Yes.'

I looked at Frank and I'm sure he couldn't miss the contempt in my face.

'You pimped out your own daughter so you could cheat. Not playing the game according to the rules, were you, Frank?'

He shrugged casually. 'It was her idea. She's a grown woman. If it's any consolation, I think she likes you. At any rate, she fancied you.'

Now Emily was blushing. 'I'm still in the room, you know.'

'Sorry, darling. Go catch your plane. I'll see you later.'

She walked past me again but paused to lay a hand on my arm.

She said, 'I'm sorry,' then turned back to her father. 'Don't kill him.'

I heard her tripping down the stairs and then the slam of the front door.

I said, 'Just you and me, Frank.'

He ignored me. 'When Helen, my wife, left me I didn't know what I was supposed to do. Emily was a baby and I was a professional man living a life in the underworld, so to speak. I barely spoke to her for five years. I know she couldn't talk back but I didn't *address* her—know what I mean? I didn't do that thing you're supposed to do to build bridges or rapport or whatever the hell it is. I don't suppose you can understand that, as an upstanding father yourself.'

'You're wrong. I didn't know Dan was even alive for his first eighteen years. His mother told me she'd had a miscarriage and she'd left me by then, so I wasn't even aware of the fact she'd given birth.'

He was interested. 'But now you get on well?'

'He has his good points and his bad points.'

'Don't tell me—he doesn't trust anyone. Won't let anyone get near.'

'The opposite. Too trusting.'

He laughed. 'Well he certainly doesn't get that from his dad!'

I wasn't so sure. This whole thing had come about because I'd first trusted him and then trusted his daughter.

I said, 'Why was Emily involved? You've made her an accessory to all sorts of criminal acts.'

He shrugged. 'I couldn't stop her. This house was Helen's, her mother's—she died five years ago and left it to Emily. I was staying here before I took the place in Buxton and she came across a notebook I was using—my playbook, so to speak. Stupid of me to leave it lying around. I forgot she liked code and she worked out, in general terms, what I was up to. And she wanted in. She liked the idea of ripping off Jocasta Shoemaker, who she didn't know but thought represented a set of ideas and beliefs she didn't like. When you came into the picture she got all dewy-eyed and romantic about the white-knight private detective. You've seen her—she's a grown woman, she's had a sexual history so I could hardly object on the grounds of prudery. And of course she helped. Tracking bugs in your clothing and so on.'

'Where's she going now?'

'The wild blue yonder. I got her a new identity and a passport and I had money stashed away. She'll be happy enough with a new life. I doubt she'll make Interpol's list.'

He drew a sigh and stood up, still pointing the gun at me. He walked to one of the tall sash windows and undid a catch, raising the bottom half of the window easily with one hand. The sounds of Greenwich floated into the room immediately.

He sat on the window-ledge and looked out.

He said, 'London's such a great city, isn't it? All human life is there, as they say.'

'Crewe has its strengths.'

He threw back his head and laughed. Then became instantly serious.

'We make choices, Mr Dyke, don't we? I chose to be a spy, then I chose to be a thief and a murderer. They don't always feel like choices—sometimes it feels as though someone or something is forcing your hand. And I suppose if you're of that cast of mind you could go through life blaming other people for the direction your life is going.'

I didn't like the direction this conversation was going, either.

I said, 'There are always choices, Frank.'

'Are there? In the end we all aspire to the condition of death. It's where we're always headed.'

Afterwards I wondered whether I could have saved him. As soon as he'd stood up and approached the window I'd been alert. When he'd finished speaking he lowered the pistol and I could have taken two steps and held on to him.

But something stopped me, and it wasn't fear of the weapon. By that time I didn't feel he was going to kill me. I think it was because we both knew it was all played out. He'd shared all his secrets and had nothing left to say.

But he had one more song title. He grinned at me and said, 'See that my grave is kept clean.'

Then he pushed his head out of the window and allowed his centre of balance to shift. His feet rose from the floor and before I could cross the carpet his whole weight tilted and he fell silently out of the room.

The noises of the city, joyful and impersonal, masked the sound of his body hitting the pavement.

EPILOGUE

WAS I IN love with Emily Wallace? I doubted it. Was I *falling* in love with her? Probably. For some reason I was grateful I didn't have to find out one way or the other.

When she'd opened the door in Greenwich there was an inevitability about her presence in the house. Belinda had watched Frank arrive there but hadn't stayed longer than to check the lights went out and write down the address. But if you'd asked me to describe my feelings when I recognised the girl with the short black hair, I would have mumbled something about 'not being surprised' or 'trust Frank to have roped in his daughter'.

So when she left I hadn't watched her go, hadn't worried about her destination, had no intention of trying to find her. When Frank leaned out of the window, almost as though he were diving into a longed-for and tranquil peace, the Wallace family removed themselves from my life leaving me with no qualms. Or so I thought.

A MONTH LATER I had a letter that was posted in France but originated elsewhere.

Emily was writing to express her regret at the way she'd

treated me. That Saturday morning in Greenwich she'd half-expected her father to do something stupid—whether it was to kill me or to kill himself to cover her escape, she didn't know. But she'd thought she owed it to him to have no regrets, to just go away and live her life.

It was a long and rambling letter that I'm not going to reproduce here. Mostly it was a glorified excuse for using me as a distraction, a way of forcing Jocasta to focus on her father and get the troops out of the office. I was a means of applying pressure to make Jocasta insecure. Emily's father didn't give a hoot about the direction Shoemaker had taken—he was retired and had nothing to do with the company. But he considered the cylinder recordings to be his by right and he was damned if he was going to let Jocasta Shoemaker hold on to them.

I folded the letter and threw it in my waste bin. I had a sour taste in my mouth and an acid burn in my gut. The Wallaces, father and daughter, had used me in their game before making their separate ways out. I don't have much time for regret in life—it takes energy I'd rather use elsewhere. And in a way I didn't really regret meeting either of them.

But next time, I thought, I'm going to be a damn sight more careful where I put my trust. It hurts too much when you get it wrong.

A NOTE

Howard W. Odum was a real person and the story of the cylinder recordings is largely true. It seems, however, that the original recordings he made between 1905-1908 were indeed lost to posterity. I've rediscovered them for my own nefarious purposes.

Thanks to Mike Evans' magisterial work: *The Blues - A Visual History* (Unicorn Press, 2014) for inspiration and song titles.

BONUS

FIRST CHAPTER OF *THE INNOCENT DEAD*, CHANTICLEER 'CLUE' AWARD WINNER, PRIVATE EYE/NOIR, 2016.

PROLOGUE

WHEN THE CAR stopped suddenly he looked up from his iPad and glanced through the front windscreen.

He knew they were close to home because he recognised the hedges and the twist of the road ahead. But the car didn't usually stop here. There was never any traffic to obstruct them. And it was the wrong time of day for cows to be herded along the road from one field to the next, the red-faced farmer twitching a long cane against their waggling backsides. That didn't take place till an hour later.

There were no cows but there was a black car angled across the narrow lane. He saw that its doors were open as though the driver had just stepped out to go somewhere and would be back in a moment.

He switched off his iPad and folded down its cover.

Harris, the chauffeur, pressed a button and there was a heavy clunk as all the doors in the vehicle locked.

Their eyes met in the rear-view mirror and then Harris' eyes flicked past him to look through the rear window. He said, 'Shit.'

Now he noticed a man had appeared at his door. He couldn't see much of him but he saw the man was wearing black gloves. Another man was standing in front of the car. He wore something over his face, a woollen mask. The man at the front was pointing a gun at Harris, through the windscreen. Then he lowered it and shot one of the front tyres. The car sagged.

The man raised the gun again and waved it twice, sideways.

The doors unlocked and Harris got out. He walked towards the man with the gun.

Then suddenly his own door was yanked open and a hand fell on his shoulder, pulling him from the back seat.

This man smelled like a dirty clothes basket and was tall.

But then everyone was tall to him.

He was ten years old.

CHAPTER ONE

A FULL FIVE minutes after passing through the entrance gates, the house came into view.

Although to call it a house was like calling Buckingham Palace a beach-hut. The driveway I was travelling along curved in a great arc between wide, scissor-cut lawns, leading towards a circular, gravel-encrusted courtyard. The obligatory stone fountain—two cupids entwined—sat in the middle of the circle, as dead as Ancient Greece. The mansion itself was faux-Victorian, but a very high-class faux. A phalanx of windows on three stories reflected the sky and its scudding clouds while to one side a large orangery, its roof white and domed, seemed to be clinging on to the main building by means of an intricate network of Virginia creeper and ivy. The place was well-tended but didn't look particularly well-loved.

As I drove closer I began to see more of the near side of the house, angling towards the rear aspect in another series of square regimented windows, some of them open to combat the effects of the stifling heat. In others I could see reflected the tops of working buildings clustered around the rear of the house—perhaps accommodation for staff, or garages, or stables or, for all I knew, camps of itinerant labourers milling about aimlessly, waiting to be let loose to tend the gardens or perform other mundane tasks.

I'd seen the estate from above, from Google Earth, and the mansion showed up as a massive brick of a place surrounded by open lawns to the front and rambling forest to the rear. I'd also found it listed in a local estate agent, where the asking price was £5.5 million. Even for Prestbury, apple of the North West's eye, that was steep. I wondered why the owner, Mark Ware, was selling. Had the cash run out? Or was he bored with all the greenery? It was a question I might not ask him — it didn't pay to be rude to clients.

I stopped my car and climbed out, then stood for a moment, stretching, turning to look over the roof of the vehicle beyond a low wall, letting my gaze fall away over the half-mile of flower beds and lawn towards the distant road. There was no traffic out here: less than two miles from Prestbury, it was isolated, cut off, a planet to itself. I rather liked the idea of being separated from people. Lately I'd been getting too close to them. It hadn't been good for me.

I crossed the gravel to the massive front door and after two minutes' searching found a cord that when pulled seemed to ring a bell somewhere deep inside. The sun beat down on the back of my neck and I felt myself heating up like a lobster in boiling water: nowhere to go but still hoping for the best.

The door was opened silently by an Asian woman in a smart pale blue jacket and skirt, her hair tied in a bun on the top of her head. She looked to be about forty though I'm notoriously bad at guessing women's ages. I think her lips were pulled in a tight scowl before she even opened the door, and my actual appearance did nothing to soften her assessment.

She lifted her chin once. 'Yes?'

'I'm Sam Dyke. Here to see Mark Ware.'

'You have appointment?'

'It's a long way to come up that drive without one.'

The scowl was unremitting. 'You wait here.'

The door closed and I continued to boil. I had little time for rich people with staff, though naturally that wasn't the staff's fault. Sometimes, however, the staff seemed to think bad manners were necessary to maintain the rich person's high opinion of themselves.

The door opened again and the woman stepped back.

'You come in, please.'

I did so and after a couple of paces came to a dead halt. My mouth had probably opened when confronted with the sheer size and scale of the hallway in front of me. Black-and-white check tiles stretched away towards a panelled wall in which there were four doors, two of them closed. A massive oak cupboard with half a dozen doors and what seemed like a couple of hundred shelves stood to my right. To my left an elaborate curved staircase ascended first to a mezzanine or balcony—I don't know the technical term—before taking a break and carrying on upwards to another floor hidden from view above. Several large oil paintings hung on the walls of the mezzanine. These weren't depictions of faded ancestors but appeared to be modern landscapes full of swirl and dash. There were more rooms up there and I could see high ceilings and large glass chandeliers.

The Asian woman had been watching me, seeing my response, perhaps basking a little in the reflected glory.

She said, 'Follow, please,' and headed towards the staircase. Our footsteps rang crisply on the tiles until we reached the carpeted stairs, where they were muffled by the warp and weft of deep Axminster. At the top of the first flight of stairs she led me past the manic landscapes and along the mezzanine, turning left to push open a panelled door nearly twice her height.

We entered a large room painted mostly in white and furnished with expensive cream leather chairs and sofas. A grand piano stood in the far corner, its lid open and with the traditional set of photographs arranged on its shiny top, and there was a fifty inch television set hanging on the wall. From where I stood it looked as big as a stamp.

More pictures were grouped on the wall between two open french doors that gave on to a wide balcony—but these were enlarged photographs, the kind you pay a specialist studio to take of you and your children against a white background, playful, fun, capturing a moment in your lives you'll perhaps never know again.

I didn't have any of those photographs. When I was growing up that kind of ostentatious 'fun' was considered indulgent and middle-class. Looking at the photos of the young couple—the man handsome but already grey at the temples, the woman a blonde beauty with large blue eyes, the child, seven or eight years old, staring frankly at the camera—I felt a surge of envy together with a growing kernel of dislike that was perfectly unfair. These were my clients, and that was their son. I had no need for any feelings whatsoever towards them.

I should have kept telling myself that.

About the Author

Keith Dixon was born in Yorkshire and grew up in the Midlands. He's been writing since he was thirteen years old in a number of different genres: thriller, espionage, science fiction, literary. He's the author of seven novels in the Sam Dyke Investigations series and two other non-crime works, as well as two collections of blog posts on the craft of writing.

When he's not writing he enjoys reading, learning the guitar, watching movies and binge-inhaling great TV series. He's currently spending more time in France than is probably good for him.